Dirty Work

Recent Titles by Betty Rowlands from Severn House

COPYCAT
DEATH AT DEARLY MANOR
A HIVE OF BEES
AN INCONSIDERATE DEATH
TOUCH ME NOT

Dirty Work

Betty Rowlands

This first world edition published in Great Britain 2003 by
SEVERN HOUSE PUBLISHERS LTD of
9–15 High Street, Sutton, Surrey SM1 1DF.
This first world edition published in the USA 2003 by
SEVERN HOUSE PUBLISHERS INC of
595 Madison Avenue, New York, N.Y. 10022.

British Library Cataloguing in Publication Data

Rowlands, Betty
    Dirty work
    1.   Women detectives - Fiction
    2.   Detective and mystery stories
    I.   Title
    823.9'14 [F]

    ISBN 0-7278-5974-9

Typeset by Palimpsest Book Production Ltd.,
Polmont, Stirlingshire, Scotland.
Printed and bound in Great Britain by
MPG Books Ltd., Bodmin, Cornwall.

Prologue

'Scud' Dalsey poured two generous measures of single malt from a heavy ship's decanter engraved with a dedication commemorating his five years as president of the Millworth Green Golf Club. He handed one to Josh Dowding with a muttered, 'Cheers!' and they settled into leather-upholstered armchairs, lit cigars with gold lighters and sat back with legs extended, two well-heeled businessmen taking their ease at the end of the day's work.

For a few minutes they drank in silence. Then Scud – the nickname had been acquired at his public school because his unimaginative parents had saddled him with the forenames Samuel Cuthbert – said, 'We've got to do something about Blackton.' A scowl flitted across his smooth features, momentarily wiping away the bland, genial expression he normally presented to the outside world. 'He's not only muscling in on our territory, he's taking some of the best-quality stuff from under our noses.'

'Tell me about it,' said Josh sourly. 'I'd like to know how he does it.'

'He obviously knows something – or someone – that we don't.'

Scud's remark had come as no surprise to Josh. They'd been monitoring their rival's activities for some time. At first it had been pretty small beer, toe-in-the-water stuff, nothing to merit action but worth keeping an eye on just the same. Lately, no doubt emboldened by success, Blackton had pulled off several lucrative deals at Dalsey's expense. Josh had made sure his chief was kept informed but, knowing his uncertain temper and his tendency to see any initiative from his underlings as a threat to his position as head of the organization, he'd deemed it unwise to make any positive suggestion. Scud ran a pretty

1

tight ship; he might ask for suggestions when he was good and ready, but usually ended up doing things his way. So Josh sat back, sipped his whisky from the cut-glass tumbler, contemplated the shine on his hand-made shoes, and waited.

'Yes, we've got to do something,' Scud repeated. 'Any ideas?'

'Do you want him warned off, or airbrushed out of the picture altogether?'

'I want him off our backs.'

'Shouldn't be difficult. We could arrange for a couple of the lads to pay him a visit.' Josh's eyes, narrow slits at the best of times, almost disappeared under the weight of flesh pushed upwards by his smile of sadistic anticipation.

'Sorry to spoil your fun, but in this case direct action's not an option. There's always a chance of it boomeranging on us. You never know who might grass – there's more than enough in Trev Blackton's back pocket to loosen a few tongues.'

'Good thinking. What do you suggest?'

Scud tossed down the last of his drink and said, 'Evita.'

Josh looked puzzled. 'The musical? What's that got to do with it?'

'Don't be a prat. I'm talking about Trev's latest bird.'

'You mean that tom Evie Stanton? Is that what she's calling herself now?'

'Ex-tom – at least, she's not working the docks area any more. She's poshed herself up since Trev took up with her and installed her in a place he owns in the Brunswick Road area. Reckons herself no end, does Lady Evita.'

'Quite a looker, as I remember. And no, I was never a client,' Josh hastened to add in response to Scud's raised eyebrow.

'She's even more of a looker with all the rocks and stuff Trev hangs on her,' commented Scud. 'She gets through a fortune in beauty parlours and dress shops. Turns heads at his club these days, so I'm told. Not that she'll ever look anything but a tart, no matter what he spends on her.'

'Hard to imagine Evie settled down with one man. Next we hear, she'll be starting a family.' The notion appeared to amuse Josh and he broke into a wheezy chuckle before taking another pull from his glass.

'What makes you think she's settled down?' said Scud.

'Don't tell me she's got her eye elsewhere.'

'Once a tom, always a tom. Little Evie used to enjoy the work, so I'm told, and rumour has it that Trev's no great performer between the sheets.'

'Bit of a nympho, is she?'

'By repute.' Despite the implied disclaimer of personal knowledge, the hint of a smirk that flitted across Scud's bland features was open to more than one interpretation.

'Trev likes to keep his birds to himself,' Josh remarked. 'He'd kill her if he thought she'd been straying.'

'Wouldn't he just?'

This time, there was a quality in Scud's slow smile that reminded Josh of a cat with a particularly fat and juicy mouse between its claws. He leaned forward in his chair, cradling his empty glass in his hand. 'You got something in mind, boss?'

A deep, purring rumble emerged from somewhere deep in Scud's well-padded anatomy. He got to his feet, replenished their drinks and returned to his chair. 'How about this, then?' he said softly, and outlined his plan.

When he had finished, Josh thought for a minute or two before saying, 'It's brilliant in theory, boss, but can we find the right sucker to carry it off?'

'I've thought of that – I know just the man. Blackton will be out of our way for a nice long time. In fact, with luck, his outfit might go out of business altogether and we'll be smelling of roses.' Scud raised his newly charged glass. 'Cheers!'

'Cheers!' Josh dutifully lifted his own glass and drank. He still had some reservations, but it was more than his job was worth to voice them.

One

Sukey Reynolds, second-longest-serving member of the Scenes of Crime team based at Gloucester Police Station, parked her elderly Astra behind the building and checked her watch. It was ten past one and her shift began at two; she had left home early to allow herself time for a little early Christmas shopping. She locked the car, transferred her kit to her van and then made her way on foot towards the city centre. As she turned into Bull Lane her spirits rose at the sight of a familiar figure striding towards her.

'Hi, Sukey! Where are you off to?' Detective Inspector Jim Castle's tone carried no hint of anything more than a friendly interest.

Her reply was equally noncommittal. 'Just a spot of shopping before reporting for duty.' The familiar surge of pleasure at seeing him was tempered with amusement at the way he shot a quick glance over his shoulder as they drew level, as if to make certain none of their colleagues was around before pausing to add in a low voice, 'I'm hoping to have some free time at the weekend. Maybe we could do something on Saturday. I'll be in touch, OK?'

'Fine.' She smiled and nodded before hurrying on her way. A passing stranger would have put the pair down as mere acquaintances exchanging the briefest of greetings rather than two lovers agreeing on a date. It was tricky at times, keeping their relationship a secret. In fact, she privately admitted that it was almost certainly known to, or at least suspected by, several people. DS Andy Radcliffe, for example; the two men had joined the force at the same time and done their initial training together. The friendship had endured over the years, unaffected by their difference in rank; they often met for a drink when they were off duty and although Andy was the soul of discretion he could hardly fail to be aware that there was more than a friendly working relationship between DI Castle and one of the most successful SOCOs in the team. Sukey would not have been surprised either to learn that they were the subject of canteen gossip from time to time.

Just the same, she reflected as she turned into Westgate, it was doubtful whether any of their colleagues realized just how far back the association went. Long ago, when she was a young probationer and Jim a constable pounding the beat, and before either of them embarked on what turned out to be disastrous marriages, they had been on the verge of starting an affair. Sukey often wondered how things would have turned out had she not met Paul, married him on a wave of passion that had blinded her to his weaknesses, had his baby, and ten years later found herself abandoned for the wealthy, glamorous Myrna. A lot had happened between then and the day she rejoined the force, this time as a civilian because as the single mother of teenage Fergus she was unable to undertake the commitment demanded of a full-time police officer. She had been considerably taken aback to find herself once more working with Jim Castle, now a detective inspector and divorced without children. The attraction between them had been strong and immediate, although for her son's sake she had insisted that they allow the friendship to develop gradually. Happily, a good rapport had grown between man and boy and this time there had been no doubt how things would eventually turn out.

Sukey walked on with a spring in her step. Her first destination was the Cross, where she bought a copy of the current week's *Big Issue*. To her surprise, instead of the regular vendor, a thin girl wearing a grubby hooded anorak against the chill November wind was huddled against the stone wall of the ancient bell tower that housed the city tourist office. Her pale, rather sullen face was pierced in several places by an assortment of rings and studs.

'I haven't seen you before,' Sukey remarked as she handed over the money. The girl made no reply; she pocketed the coins and took a copy of the magazine from the plastic carrier between her feet. 'What's your name?'

'Lucy.'

'And what do you call this chap?' Sukey bent down to pat a small brown dog curled up on a blanket beside a shabby holdall. It lifted its head in response to her caress and thumped the ground with its tail.

'Scruffy. Kinda suits him, doesn't it?' A smile of unexpected charm transformed the bejewelled features. Lucy gazed down at the little mongrel with the loving expression of a young mother acknowledging interest in her baby.

'He's a friendly little fellow, isn't he?' Sukey remarked. 'I'll bet he's good company.'

'Sure is. Keeps me warm at night, too. Got no heating in the van.'

Sukey found herself unexpectedly moved. The magazine this girl and others like her were peddling was one of the few avenues open to the homeless to earn an honest penny and she had often wondered what kind of shelter they found at night. At least Lucy had somewhere to lay her head.

'What happened to Matt, by the way? The chap who used to have this pitch,' Sukey added as Lucy looked blank.

'Oh, him,' she said after a moment's thought. 'Got mugged, so I heard.'

'Mugged? How awful! Was he hurt?'

'Don't think so. Ask Jack. He saw it happen.' She pointed to a bearded man in a dark coat reaching almost to his ankles who was standing a short distance away on the other side of the street. He too had a dog, which was currently exchanging canine greetings with a poodle whose owner, a well-dressed middle-aged woman, was buying a magazine. She put it into her shopping bag, from which she then proceeded to bring out what looked like tins of dog food, which Jack stuffed into his coat pockets. Their conversation looked like lasting for some minutes, and the time was passing. Sukey still had errands to do. She said goodbye to Lucy, wished her luck and made for the first shop on her list.

Half an hour later, as she headed back to the police station with her purchases, she heard in the distance the familiar wail of a siren and wondered idly if it signified a fire, an accident or a burglary. It turned out to be a particularly brutal murder.

*   *   *

6

'Nasty,' commented DS Andy Radcliffe as he surveyed the elaborate bed on which lay the remains of what might once have been a beautiful woman, although the features were so badly damaged that identification was likely to prove difficult. 'She took a real hammering, poor cow. Any idea how long she's been dead, Doc?'

'Doc' Hillbourne, the forensic pathologist, completed his examination, straightened up and began stowing away his equipment. 'Still warm, rigor not set in yet.' He crossed the room, put a hand on an electric radiator standing against the wall and then hastily withdrew it. 'Practically red hot,' he commented. 'It must be at least seventy degrees in here. That would slow things down, but no more than three hours, maybe not even that.'

Radcliffe checked his watch and nodded. 'That ties in with the time we received the call. A Mrs Pewsey, who lives next door, says she heard sounds of a fight earlier – a man shouting threats, a woman screaming and a series of bumps. Then it went quiet and she heard a car start up and drive away. When she went out later on she noticed the door of this house was open and got concerned so she called us. Two of our chaps went in and found this.' He grimaced and turned away. He was no sensitive rookie, but the punishment the woman had taken must have been savage and it would have been hard to remain unmoved.

'Not a pretty sight,' agreed Hillbourne. He sniffed the close atmosphere in the room; above the cloying perfume was another distinctive smell. 'Recent sexual activity,' he commented. 'We'll know more when we get her back to the morgue. Tell your SOCOs I'll want more photos there.'

'Will do. You finished here, Doc?'

'Yep, she's all yours now.' At the door Hillbourne said with a whimsical smile, 'Try not to find any more bodies today, Andy. I'm hoping to play a round of golf before it gets dark.'

'I'll do my best,' the sergeant replied without returning the smile. He nodded to the officer standing by the door. 'OK, Tony, you call in the SOCOs. I'll go next door and have a word with Mrs Pewsey. She hasn't seen the body, but she's a bit shaken just the same.'

*   *   *

7

'Hi, Sarge. What have you got for us today?'

Sergeant George Barnes, officer in charge of the Scenes of Crime section, reached across his desk and picked up a few sheets of computer paper. 'Afternoon, Sukey,' he grunted. 'Nothing to get excited over. A couple of stolen cars found abandoned – one torched, the other rolled over in a ditch – and a break-in at a cottage in Upton. Owners away, incident reported by a neighbour.'

'Much taken?' Sukey scanned the printout.

'The informant isn't sure – he's trying to contact the owner.'

'Not very exciting, as you say,' she commented with a grimace.

He gave an ironic chuckle. 'You want a nice juicy murder, I suppose?'

'It would liven things up a bit, don't you think?' she replied flippantly.

'Not for the victim, it wouldn't,' said Barnes drily.

'No, I suppose not.' She put the printouts on her desk. 'I'll grab a quick coffee before I set off. Can I get you one, Sarge?'

'Too late, I've beaten you to it.' Mandy Parfitt, another member of the team, entered with a tray bearing three mugs of muddy brown liquid. 'I got one for you, Sukey,' she added as she put the tray on her desk and handed one mug to George Barnes. 'Here you are, Sarge – I put in a double ration of sugar.'

'Thanks,' he said gratefully. 'Maybe this'll keep me awake for the next hour or two.'

'Bad night?' said Sukey sympathetically. Having, somewhat to his surprise, become a father in middle age, the sergeant found it difficult to adapt to broken nights.

'Could have been better,' he sighed between swigs of coffee. 'Young Philip's teething and the wife's got a chesty cough, so one way and the other . . .' He gave a resigned shrug. At that moment the telephone on his desk jangled. Still holding his mug in his left hand he jammed the receiver against his ear with his shoulder and reached for a pen with his right. 'Barnes here, SOCOs' office.' He listened, muttered the odd 'Right,' 'OK', 'Will do,' scribbled on a pad and put the instrument down. 'Looks like you're going to have your bit of excitement, Sukey,' he commented drily. 'A woman's been battered to death in a house near the park. A bit messy by the sound of it.' He tore the sheet off the pad and handed it over. 'You'd better both go, so drink up and get on your way.'

Two

The house in which the as yet unidentified body had been discovered was number 18 in a terrace of twenty Victorian cottages on one side of a narrow lane that the city fathers of the day, no doubt with a sentimental desire to pay homage to Gloucester's Roman origins, had named Glevum Passage.

Mrs Pewsey, the woman who had raised the alarm, lived next door at number 17. She was a small, plump woman in her fifties with short, straight dark hair and bright intelligent eyes. She was outwardly composed as she ushered DS Radcliffe into her neatly furnished front room, but a slight tremor in her voice, as she introduced him to a second woman who sat in a chintz-covered armchair nursing a cup of tea, betrayed a hint of unease.

'My neighbour, Mrs Owen,' she explained. 'This gentleman's a detective,' she went on. 'He wants to ask a few questions.'

'Well, we can tell him a thing or two, can't we?' said Mrs Owen. Her pale eyes, set in a thin, lined face surmounted by sparse grey hair, gleamed with a kind of spiteful satisfaction. 'Didn't I say the day that woman moved in that she spelt trouble? You could tell just by looking at her what sort she was. I said so, didn't I, Mrs Pewsey?' she repeated. 'Didn't I say so the minute we set eyes on her? Remember when she turned up with her fancy man in his fancy car? "She's trouble," I said, "you mark my words, she's trouble." '

Mrs Owen drank noisily from her cup of tea, giving Radcliffe a chance to say, 'Mrs Pewsey, I understand you reported some kind of disturbance going on at number eighteen? Can you remember—?'

'Disturbance! More a stand-up fight!' Mrs Owen broke in, holding out her empty cup for a refill in response to Mrs

Pewsey's outstretched hand. 'Swearing and shouting, things being thrown around and—'

'Excuse me, do I understand that you also heard the altercation?' Radcliffe interposed.

Mrs Owen appeared momentarily floored by the word 'altercation', but she quickly recovered and said, 'I heard all about it from her' – she gestured towards her neighbour – 'when I came home from shopping. Quite upset, she was, and worried as to what she should do. I said, "If you take my advice you'll keep out of it. If that tart took a hiding from her boyfriend it was probably no more than she deserved." What's happened, anyway? I suppose she's been hurt, being as how there was an ambulance outside. I see it's gone now.' Her eyes searched his for further information, but he ignored the challenge.

'All I can say at the moment is that a woman has been violently attacked at number eighteen,' he replied. There was no reason why he should not reveal that the woman was dead; it would become evident as soon as the undertaker's hearse arrived to collect the body, and once the press got wind of it the story would be in the late edition of the local paper anyway. Just the same, something about Mrs Owen's manner filled him with a perverse desire to avoid satisfying her morbid curiosity for the time being.

He turned back to Mrs. Pewsey, who was looking distinctly embarrassed at the way her voluble neighbour was hijacking the conversation. 'But you decided later that it was better to report your suspicions to the police?' he said patiently. She gave a hesitant nod and he was quick to reassure her by saying, 'As we now know, you made the right decision. I don't suppose there's another cup of tea in that pot?' he added, more to put her at her ease than from any need of refreshment.

Mrs Pewsey gave a nervous start. 'Of course, do forgive me,' she stammered. 'I should have offered, I'll top up the pot and fetch another cup.' She bustled out of the room.

The moment she was gone, Mrs Owen said eagerly, 'There's plenty I could tell you about that creature if you care to listen.'

Sensing that she was about to enlarge on her character assassination of their late neighbour, and not wishing to be

11

diverted from his immediate need to establish a few facts, Radcliffe said quickly, 'I'm sure you have some extremely valuable information, Mrs Owen, and I'd welcome an opportunity of talking to you later. Do I understand you live next door?'

'Number twenty-four, opposite.'

'Will you be going out once you leave here? I mean, do you have shopping to do, or anything like that?'

'I've already done my shopping.'

'Then perhaps I could call on you for a word in private when I've finished talking to Mrs Pewsey? It's clear that she's a little shaken by what's happened and it's very important to establish what time certain events took place. I think she'd probably be more comfortable if I could speak to her alone.'

'Oh!' Mrs Owen looked less than enchanted at the suggestion. 'You still haven't told us exactly what happened.'

'That's something I hope you may be able to help us find out.'

To his relief, she took the hint and stood up. 'Right, well, I've got a few things to do before my husband comes home so I'll see you presently,' she said. 'I'll leave you now,' she went on as Mrs Pewsey returned with the teapot in one hand and a fresh cup and saucer in the other. 'The detective wants to speak to me later in private. He thinks I may have important information,' she added grandly. 'Don't worry, I'll see myself out.'

Mrs Pewsey made no attempt to hide her relief at her neighbour's departure. 'She was over here like a shot the moment the first police car arrived, wanting to know what was going on,' she said as she poured out the tea, handed Radcliffe a cup patterned with pink roses and sank, a little wearily, into a chair. 'I thought I was never going to get rid of her. Do sit down, Sergeant.' She indicated the chair vacated by Mrs Owen.

'Thank you.' He took a sip or two of tea and commented, 'What pretty china.'

For the first time since his arrival, Mrs Pewsey smiled. 'Oh, how kind of you to say so. It belonged to my mother.'

'I thought it didn't look modern. It looks as if it might be quite valuable.'

'Do you really think so?' She studied her cup as if seeing it with new eyes. 'I never thought . . . I just use it every day. I'm very careful with it, of course.' Visibly more relaxed by now, she sat back and sipped contentedly.

Having achieved his objective, Radcliffe said gently, 'I'm sure this has been very upsetting for you. Would you like me to arrange for a woman officer to come and sit with you while we talk?'

Mrs Pewsey shook her head. 'There's no need, I'm quite all right, really,' she said in a firm voice.

'Good.' He put his cup and saucer carefully on a small occasional table and took out his notebook. 'How well did you know your next-door neighbour?'

'Hardly at all, really. She moved in several months ago, but I don't see her very often. Just now and again, if we happen to go out or come in at the same time.' She gave Radcliffe a penetrating glance. 'Why did you say, how well *did* I know her?' When he did not immediately reply she said shrewdly, 'She's dead, isn't she?'

'We found the body of a woman, yes,' he admitted, 'but she has not yet been identified so we can't be sure if it's the woman who lives in the house.'

'Well, I don't know who else it could be,' said Mrs. Pewsey. Suddenly, she put down her cup and covered her face with her hands. 'Oh dear,' she whispered, 'I should have called the police earlier. If they'd come and stopped him, she might still be alive.'

'Who do you mean by "him"?' Radcliffe asked.

'I don't know his name, I just heard a man's voice shouting.'

'Can you remember what he was saying?'

Mrs Pewsey coloured. 'He was using a lot of language I wouldn't like to repeat,' she said a little primly, 'but I did hear words like "whore" and "faithless bitch", that sort of thing.'

'Did you hear the woman say anything?'

'She just kept on screaming, "Stop, please stop!" over and over again.'

'Did you hear her call out a name?'

'No.'

'How long did this go on?'

13

'I don't know. A few minutes, perhaps, then it all went quiet and I thought, perhaps they've made it up. And then I heard the car start up and drive away so I thought no more about it for a while.'

'Did you recognize either of the voices?'

'No. She was screaming, like I said, and I've never spoken to him.'

'But you've seen him, I imagine?'

'Once or twice I've seen a man go in there, but I don't know if it's the same one.'

'Can you describe the man you've seen?'

Mrs Pewsey thought for a moment. 'About thirty, I suppose, with a gold ring in one of his ears. And his head was shaved.' She sighed. 'I don't suppose that's much help, is it? I mean, you see so many young men who look like that nowadays.'

'It's a start,' said Radcliffe encouragingly. 'Can you remember anything else about him? His clothes, for example.'

'I think he wore a leather jacket,' she said after another pause. 'Black, as I remember.'

'Did he come by car?'

'Yes. A big red one. Don't ask me what make,' she added with a rueful smile. 'I don't know anything about cars. One thing I did notice, though. He had a key to the house.'

'Ah. Now that is interesting. I'll make a note of that.' Radcliffe closed his notebook, drank his tea and stood up. 'Thank you very much, Mrs Pewsey. You've been a great help.' He was rewarded by a tremulous smile.

'I hope you catch him,' she said as she opened the front door for him. 'A man shouldn't treat a woman like that, no matter what she's done.'

Sukey and Mandy arrived on the murder scene at the same moment that DS Radcliffe emerged from Mrs Pewsey's house. He put up a hand to detain them as they were on the point of entering number 18.

'I wanted a word before you started work,' he said. 'It's just to warn you that if you're buttonholed by a nosey parker called Mrs Owen, don't tell her anything. It's pretty grim in there, by the way,' he added, 'so hang on to your stomachs. We' – he nodded towards DC Hill and a uniformed woman constable

14

who were standing guard outside the front door – 'did our best to avoid contamination or disturbance to the scene, but as you'll see it's a small house and there's not a lot of room to move. Oh-oh,' he added resignedly, glancing beyond them towards a small group of people approaching from the far end of the lane. 'Here comes the fourth estate.'

'Personally, I prefer to deal with the corpse than face that lot,' said Mandy flippantly. 'Where's the body, Sarge?'

'In the room on the right at the top of the stairs; you'll find the door open and that's how we found it. The police surgeon's been and certified the victim dead – not that there was ever much doubt about that – and Doc Hillbourne's done his stuff as well, so it's all yours.'

'Right-ho!'

Having marked out a common approach path along the hall and up the narrow staircase, they made a detailed examination for evidence, logging every find and observation as they worked. They then went up to the room where the killing had taken place. They both had experience of violent death, but this one caused both of them to swallow hard and exchange horrified glances.

'My God, whoever did that must have hated her,' Mandy breathed. She put a hand to her mouth. 'It's stifling in here. And that sickly perfume . . . makes you want to throw up, even without that.' She gestured towards the bloody, naked corpse lying sprawled across the bed. 'D'you reckon it would be all right to open the window?'

Sukey shook her head. 'Better not – it might affect the body temperature. We must check the ambient, though.' She took a thermometer from her bag and took the reading while Mandy logged it. 'Let's not hang about. You make a start on checking for prints while I take some pics.' She took out her camera and began making a systematic record of the scene. As she worked, her professional training took over and she concentrated on making an accurate record of the murder scene: the position of the corpse; the nature of its injuries; the patterns formed by the splashes of blood on the walls, the carpet and the crumpled bed linen. For many nights to come her dreams would probably be haunted by the memory of the crushed features and battered body, but for the moment they had lost their power to shock.

15

At last the corpse, encased in a body bag, was transferred to the waiting hearse and driven off to the mortuary, closely followed by a police car driven by DC Hill. The light was beginning to fade; the sharp November wind blew dust and dead leaves along the narrow pavement and made them shiver, but they both gratefully inhaled the cold air.

'Like a hothouse up there, isn't it?' commented one of the uniformed officers left behind to guard the scene.

'You can say that again.' Sukey glanced round, scanning the little knots of curious onlookers on the opposite side of the street. 'Where's Sergeant Radcliffe, by the way?'

'Talking to a witness at number twenty-four, over the road.'

'We'll need to go back in and collect more samples now they've moved her, but it's beginning to get dark so it'll have to be tomorrow.'

'I'll pass the message on.'

The two SOCOs were taking off their protective clothing and putting their gear back in their vans when a familiar red Mondeo turned into Glevum Passage. DI Jim Castle gave a nod of recognition as he drove slowly past in search of a place to park.

'Looks as if Eagle-Eyes is taking charge of this one,' Mandy commented. 'We'd better make sure our reports are up to snuff,' she added with a grin.

Three

'You two look a bit green,' commented Sergeant George Barnes as Sukey and Mandy entered the SOCOs' office and dumped their bags on their respective desks. 'Are you OK? I'm told it was rather gruesome.'

'It was pretty horrid,' said Mandy. 'Having to work in hothouse conditions didn't help either.'

Sukey took some money from her purse and went back to the door. 'I need a bucket of tea to wash away the taste of that ghastly room. How about you, Mandy.'

'Please.'

'Sarge?'

'Since you're going.' Barnes fished some coins from his pocket and handed them over. When Sukey returned a few minutes later with three large mugs of tea and an assortment of biscuits, he said, 'There's been an interesting development while you've been at work. Apparently the victim was heard to greet a man seen calling on her fairly regularly as "Trev".'

'That's significant?' said Mandy between mouthfuls of tea. 'It's not an uncommon name.'

'IC1 male, thirtyish, shaven head, earring. Drives a flashy red car,' he went on. 'Does that ring any bells?'

'Are we talking about Trevor Blackton, by any chance?' asked Sukey, adding, with a sudden flash of inspiration, 'Would this have anything to do with the fact that DI Castle turned up at the scene just as we were leaving?'

'Clever girl!' Barnes flourished his mug of tea in salute. Blackton owned several clubs and several properties in the city. He appeared to enjoy a fairly lavish lifestyle, giving rise to suspicion of involvement in other lucrative but less lawful activities, possibly drug dealing, but the police had so far been unable to pin anything on either him or on any of his known associates.

'I take it he's been seen at the house, then?' said Mandy.

'Or someone answering to his description. It seems one of the neighbours spends a lot of time observing the comings and goings of the other residents in Glevum Passage. Very useful people, nosey neighbours.' Barnes drank deeply from his mug, drained it, set it down and wiped his mouth with the back of his hand before going on. 'What this lady had to say, added to the evidence of the one who called us in the first place, led Andy Radcliffe to believe that our friend Trev might be involved. So I suggest when you get your samples off to fingerprints you ask them to check them against Blackton's before they look any further. It could save a hell of a lot of time.'

'Will they be on file?' said Mandy doubtfully. 'We've never been able to get anything on him, have we?'

'Not on anything serious, no, but I'm told he has form for assault. Nasty temper, so they say, and a womanizer who likes to keep his birds to himself. From what our informant overheard, the assailant was accusing the victim of having it off with someone else, which wouldn't have made her flavour of the month with Trev. Doc Hillbourne told Andy he reckoned whoever did it went on slugging her after she was dead.'

'Sounds a nasty piece of work,' said Mandy, pulling a face.

'You could say that. Anyway, see what you can turn up.'

'Will do, Sarge, thanks for the tip.'

The two SOCOs settled down to write their reports, label and bag their samples and put them in the out tray for despatch to the various departments. It was with a feeling of revulsion that Sukey checked her notes of the location of every shot she had taken at the crime scene. Each wound on the bloodstained corpse seemed burned indelibly on her retinas. It was a long time since anything had moved her so much. She recalled Mandy's comment: 'Whoever did that must have hated her.' She took the plastic envelope in which she had placed her ruler to avoid soiling other items in her bag and went along to the cloakroom to wash the blood from it, almost gagging as she held it under the tap.

When she returned, Mandy was sitting back in her chair,

her fingers locked behind her head and her eyes closed. She had pushed back her mane of reddish hair, but a few stray tendrils lay over her forehead and her normally rosy cheeks were still pallid. 'I feel as if I've already worked a full shift and it's only five o'clock,' she complained.

Sukey sat down beside her with a weary sigh. 'Me too,' she agreed. 'Let's hope things will be a bit quieter from now on. What have you got for us next, Sarge?'

'Nothing at the moment, but give it time. We might manage a nice juicy RTA for afters.'

'Not funny,' Sukey muttered. She leaned back in her chair and stretched out her legs, then hastily sat upright again as DI Castle put his head round the door and spoke to Sergeant Barnes. 'Tell fingerprints I want the samples from the Glevum Passage murder given priority, George.'

'Right, Guv.'

Castle glanced across at the two women. 'You're both looking a bit peaky,' he commented, his tone softening slightly. 'Hardly surprising, I suppose – the poor woman was in a bit of a mess. I'm afraid you'll have to go back tomorrow and do a more thorough check of the murder scene. Think you can cope?'

Mandy replied, 'Of course we can, sir.' She got up and went to the out tray to retrieve her samples. 'I'll pop across to fingerprints right away.'

'I'll come with you,' said Sukey. 'I could do with another breath of air.'

As the two woman walked across the open space separating the main building from the laboratories, Mandy said slyly, 'You know what, I reckon Eagle-Eyes fancies you.'

Sukey was grateful for the sodium lamps that concealed the colour rising in her cheeks. 'What makes you think that?' she asked, trying to sound casual.

'All that soft stuff about whether we can cope or not.'

'I thought it was very considerate of him. Anyway, it was directed at both of us.'

'Maybe, but it was you he was looking at.'

Scud gazed thoughtfully into his glass of single malt and said, 'Stage one accomplished, then?'

'That's right, boss,' said Josh, his eyes all but extinguished by his smile of satisfaction. 'Lambs to the slaughter, all three of them.'

'Three?'

'The sucker who acted as bait.'

'Oh, him.' Scud's tone was dismissive. Anyone who had served his purpose and was of no further use was likewise of no further interest.

'I had to pay him off.'

'Not too generously, I hope.'

'He wanted enough to stay on at the hotel where I put him and buy a few more clothes. I gave him another hundred and said we'd pay his rent till he found a job.'

Scud scowled. 'Then he'd better get off his arse and find one. We don't want to retain any links that might be traced. What can he do, anyway?'

'How should I know? He'll find something, he's a person-able chap – that's why you picked him, isn't it?'

'Needed to be, didn't he? Let's hope for his sake Blackton's men don't track him down. "Personable" wouldn't be the word to describe him after they've done with him.' A glint of sardonic humour appeared briefly in Scud's hard blue-grey eyes, as if he found the idea amusing. He finished his drink and got up to help himself to another, ignoring Josh's almost empty glass. 'Yes, it's all gone very satisfactorily so far.' Instead of returning to his chair he made for a massive walnut desk in the far corner of the opulently furnished room. 'I've got work to do. You can see yourself out, can't you? Let me know as soon as the police pick up Blackton,' he added over his shoulder.

'Sure,' muttered Josh. He tossed off the dregs of his whisky, put down the glass and went to the door. Scud did not observe the resentful scowl his second in command directed at his back as he passed. It would not have disturbed him if he had. He liked his underlings to know their place.

'Thanks for coming round; I needed company.' Sitting next to Jim on the couch in the cosy sitting room of her little semi-detached house in Brockworth, Sukey began to feel herself unwinding for the first time since entering the house where a fellow woman had been so savagely beaten to death.

'Where's Fergus, then?'

'In Nürnberg, as far as I know.'

'What's he doing there? He's not doing A-level German, is he?'

Sukey chuckled. It was good to have something to laugh at. 'Of course not, he's no linguist. Margaret wanted to go to the Christmas market and Paul agreed to take her and asked Gus if he'd like to join them.'

'I guess Santa will be putting a cuckoo clock in your stocking, then.'

Sukey pretended to shudder. 'Golly, I hope not. Still,' she added, snuggling a little closer to Jim and resting her head on his shoulder, 'it would be a small price to pay for the improved relations since Paul remarried. When we were first divorced, I had a hard time getting him to cough up for essentials, let alone school journeys. He's much more open-handed these days, thanks I suspect to Margaret's benign influence.'

'That's really good news.' Jim glanced at the clock on the mantelpiece and put down his empty teacup. 'I should be getting home; I've got some paperwork to do and I'm on at eight tomorrow. Are you sure you'll be all right on your own?'

'I'll be fine. By the way,' she added slyly, 'I was warned against you today.'

'Who by?'

'Mandy. She reckons you fancy me.'

'Whatever gave her that idea?'

'Something in the way you looked at me. Full of concern because I was looking so pale.'

'I was concerned for both of you.'

'That's what I told her.' She raised her head and kissed him on the cheek. 'You're a very nice man.'

'Thank you.'

'Anyway, does it matter so much if people guess about us?'

'I still think it's better that they don't. Well, if you're sure you're OK . . .' He stood up, drew her to her feet and held her close for a few moments. 'Would you like to go on a trip somewhere? A weekend city break, for example? Not necessarily for Christmas shopping.'

'Mm, that would be nice. Let's talk about it after we've

got this case sorted. Do you really think Blackton is our man?'

'Almost certainly. It's completely in character – someone's been shagging his bird and he lost his rag and killed her.'

'D'you reckon he'll go after the other man – the one he was accusing her of cheating on him with?'

'If he knows who he is, sure to. That's why I'd like to see him behind bars before he gets the chance. We're relying on you and Mandy to come up with some hard evidence.'

'We'll do our best.'

It wasn't going to be easy, going back to that room tomorrow, but it was all part of the job. After the comfort of an hour with Jim, the prospect seemed less daunting. And as he had implied, it seemed a pretty straightforward case.

Four

'I see the paparazzi are out in force,' Sukey remarked to the constable on duty at the end of Glevum Passage, which had been sealed off from the general public by lengths of blue and white tape. She nodded in the direction of a small knot of people with cameras clustered on the opposite pavement. 'What do you suppose they're expecting to see?'

'Search me,' he replied as he unhitched the tape to let her drive through. 'Maybe they're hoping for another body. See if you can oblige 'em – make sure you look under the bed!'

She responded with a wry smile to the touch of gallows humour, not uncommon among officers called on to deal with a particularly unpleasant crime. It was their way of relieving the tension and no disrespect to the victim was intended.

'We looked yesterday, as it happens,' she told him, 'but all we found was a load of fluff and a couple of soiled tissues. We couldn't move the bed to make a proper search while the body was still there, though. It weighs a ton – I'll need some help with shifting it presently.'

'You on your own, then?'

'Mandy should have been with me, but she's having to deal with an RTA.'

'No problem, one of the boys'll give you a hand.' He nodded in the direction of two uniformed officers who were methodically checking every square inch of the pavements and gutters on either side of the narrow street. 'If you find any diamond rings, spare a thought for me!'

'Are you kidding? Don't you know it's finders keepers in this game!'

She rolled up the window and drove on. Her spirits lifted a little after the exchange of banter, but just the same she was aware of the familiar queasy twinge in her stomach as

23

she parked outside the house. It would have been easier if Mandy or one of the other SOCOs had been with her. Then she told herself not to be a wimp. This sort of stress went with the job and you had to get on with it. Just the same, she was relieved to see the familiar face of her old friend WPC Trudy Marshall, who was stationed at the door of number 18 to fend off any resident of Glevum Passage hoping to gain access to the murder scene.

'Hi, Trudy,' she said as she lifted her bag of equipment from the back of the van. She glanced up and down the little street, empty except for the two officers and a couple of police cars. 'Where are the resident ghouls? I expected to see them all keeping an eye on what's going on.'

Trudy shrugged. 'I've no doubt they are, but they're staying well out of sight behind their curtains. Except for the ghastly Mrs Owen at number twenty-four,' she added, pulling a face. 'She's been popping over every few minutes on a pretext of having remembered something that might be important and wanting to know if those two have found any clues. Driving us potty, she is, insisting we make sure to pass it all on to the officer in charge of the investigation.'

'George Barnes says she's supplied some quite useful infor-mation,' said Sukey. 'It seems she practically keeps a dossier on the comings and goings of her neighbours.'

'You'd think she could find something better to do,' said Trudy with a sniff. She gave a sudden sneeze and shivered. 'If she'd come up with something to relieve me from having to hang around in this wind I'd forgive her.' She sneezed again and blew her nose. 'I think I'm starting a cold,' she grumbled.

'Bad luck!' Sukey sympathized. 'By the way, I take it DI Castle isn't here?' She had already registered the absence of Jim's Mondeo.

'He dropped by a while ago to check on developments, but I understand he's gone back to the station to direct the hunt for Trevor Blackton. Seems he's done a runner.'

'That's hardly surprising.' Sukey took a deep breath, steeling herself for the task ahead. 'Well, I'd better start work, I suppose.'

As if sensing her reluctance to enter the house, Trudy gave

her a comforting pat on the shoulder. 'It can't be as bad as yesterday,' she said.

'I know. I'm not usually so squeamish, but there's something about this case that gives me the shudders, like someone walking over my grave.'

Trudy unlocked the front door and stood aside to let Sukey pass. When it closed behind her, it made a dull thud that seemed to echo through the house. Like a death-knell, she thought, then gave herself a mental shake and said aloud, 'Oh, pull yourself together, woman – it's just another job!'

The air in the hallway felt surprisingly chilly. Someone – presumably in accordance with an instruction from DI Castle – must have turned off the central heating. Perhaps, she thought as she climbed the narrow staircase, it would mean that the smell in the bedroom where the woman had been murdered would be less pungent. She took another deep breath to steady her stomach and pushed open the door. Inside it was decidedly cooler than she remembered, but it had a dank staleness that she found even more repugnant than the sickly hothouse atmosphere of the previous day. She cracked the window open a few inches before starting work.

When she had finished photographing and bagging up the bloodstained bed linen she called for help to shift the heavy iron bedstead. The two constables were only too happy to take a break from poking through the contents of dustbins, although their task was hampered by the restricted space that necessitated a great deal of pushing and shoving first one way and then another before she was able to complete her examination of the entire area. Their combined efforts brought results in the shape of a pair of huge gold earrings shaped like the shields carried by medieval knights, heavily bloodstained and encrusted with dust from the unswept carpet.

DS Radcliffe was in the SOCOs' office when Sukey returned to the station. He fairly pounced on the plastic envelope that she placed in front of him.

'Just what we hoped you'd find!' he exclaimed. 'Doc Hillbourne said her earlobes were torn as if someone had used considerable force to yank out some earrings. A very handy shape and size, too,' he added with satisfaction as he held the exhibit up to the light. 'Nice flat surface on the back. With luck, we'll find our friend Trev's dabs on at least one of them. Wonder what he had against them, though? They look expensive to me.'

George Barnes craned to take a closer look. 'Maybe he thought they were too flashy,' he suggested. 'I wouldn't want to see my missus wearing them. Still, there's no accounting for taste, is there?'

'I'd have thought they're just the sort of thing Trev would choose,' said Radcliffe. 'He's a flashy type himself and he always goes for flashy birds.'

'Maybe he didn't choose them,' remarked Sukey.

Radcliffe gave her a sharp look. 'Meaning?'

'We already know the woman's assailant was accusing her of being unfaithful while he was beating her up. Maybe he wasn't the one who gave them to her. Maybe that was what gave him the idea that he had a rival and that's why he dragged them off her. In which case,' she went on thoughtfully, 'we might, with a bit of luck, find an extra print or two on them.'

'Good thinking. Will you take them over to the lab and ask them to be extra-careful cleaning them up, and then see what prints they can pick up.'

'Will do, Sarge.'

'What else did you find?'

'I dusted pretty well everything dustable and lifted quite a few more prints, and I've brought all the bedding for DNA testing. These,' she held up another plastic envelope, 'are coloured fibres from an upholstered chair by the bed that could have come from a woollen jumper, but I couldn't find anything in her clothing drawers or cupboards that matches them. She didn't seem the type to go in for woollies.'

'As far as I know, Trev prefers leather gear,' Radcliffe remarked. 'It's beginning to look as if he had a point. I wonder who the other boyfriend was? Perhaps we should start looking for him. There won't be much left of him if Trev finds him first.'

'Do we have an ID for the victim yet?'

'Not yet. We're hoping to get a match with dental records, but it's not going to be easy because her jaw was busted in two places. According to the barman at one of Trev's clubs, his current bird calls herself Evita. She didn't show last night and neither did Trev, although that's not unusual.'

'I take it the neighbours haven't been able to help?'

'Not directly – not even the all-seeing Mrs Owen,' said Radcliffe with a rueful grin. 'We found some carrier bags in the kitchen and we're making enquiries at the local shops.'

'What about any other visitors?'

'No luck there so far. We do have a technician working on an E-FIT of the driver of the red car. He's been spotted there quite a few times and the descriptions all fit Trev. It's a pity we can't just stick up a "Wanted, Dead or Alive" poster like they did in the Wild West.'

George sighed. 'Life was so much easier in the good old days, wasn't it? Now we get smart-arse lawyers claiming their clients won't get a fair trial because of media publicity.'

By Thursday the victim of the Glevum Passage murder had been identified as Evie Stanton, a former prostitute who had renounced her profession to become the full-time mistress of club owner Trevor Blackton. Enquiries at the local Council offices revealed that the house where her body was found was one of a number of properties owned by the said Blackton. According to some of Evie's former associates he had been one of her regular clients when she was still 'in the business' and become so besotted with her that he had installed her for his exclusive enjoyment at number 18 Glevum Passage.

'Spent a small fortune on jewellery and stuff, even before he set her up in a place of her own,' confided a pasty-faced girl called Julie who claimed to have been Evie's best friend before she became, as she put it, 'too toffee-nosed to speak to me no more. I warned her against him,' she added, becoming increasingly loquacious under the effects of the double vodka and tonic that DC Tony Hill had put in front of her. 'I told her he had a reputation for being jealous and handy with his fists, but she wouldn't listen. Said she was tired of being on the game and fancied the life of luxury he was offering. "It don't make sense to me," I tells her, "you enjoy the job, it's not just the money with you." '

'Bit of a nympho, was she?' said Hill.

'I'll say. Into the kinky stuff an' all. Loved prancing around

27

in a frilly apron and not much else.' Julie swallowed the rest of her drink and fingered the empty glass. 'Any chance of another?'

'Have you any more to tell me?'

She thought for a moment, screwing up her thin features. Even in the warmth of the pub, she had a cold, pinched look about her and her coat was thin and shabby. 'Maybe another vodka'd help jog me memory,' she said hopefully.

Hill took the glass to the bar to be refilled. She received it with a grateful smile and downed a large mouthful before saying, 'I do remember something she said that might mean something to you.'

'And what was that?'

'Once, when the pair of us was waiting for punters and this guy Trev turned up, she said, "Oh, sod it, not him again. He's bloody useless at it," and I said, "He pays, don't he? You have to take what's on offer, so don't be so bloody fussy." And when she told me she'd accepted his offer of a fancy house and all the trimmings, I thought to myself, If he's no good in the sack she'll soon get bored and be looking around elsewhere for a bit of fun. I reckon that's what happened, don't you?'

'Haven't they picked up Blackton yet?' said Scud impatiently. He threw aside the evening edition of the *Gloucester Gazette* and got up to pour himself another drink. 'You said the police would be on to him straight away and he'd be banged up within twenty-four hours.'

'They've got to find him first,' Josh pointed out. 'He must have any number of bolt holes where he can hide. He may even have plans to leave the country.'

'Well, I suppose that would be better than nothing,' Scud admitted grudgingly. 'Just the same, I'd be happier if he was behind bars. That was the idea of this scheme of yours, remember?'

Josh forbore to remind his boss that so far from it being his idea he had merely been carrying out orders. Had things gone entirely according to plan, Scud would of course have claimed the credit. Keeping his thoughts to himself, he said, 'It occurs to me that he might be trying to track down his rival.'

'You mean our agent provocateur who played his part so

magnificently? Why don't we get him to do us another favour?'
The almost benevolent smile that played briefly round Scud's
features was belied by the hardness of his eyes. 'We'll give
things a nudge in the right direction, shall we? I take it our
young friend is still living at the same address?'

'So far as I know.'

'Right, then. Let the dog see the rabbit.'

Five

At about eight o'clock on Friday morning Jim Castle rang Sukey and said, 'I thought you'd like to know we're making progress in our hunt for Evie's mystery lover.'

'Oh, great,' she said drowsily.

'You don't sound very interested.'

'I was still asleep. I've been on late turn all the week, remember?'

'Sorry. D'you want to hear more? I may not be able to call later.'

Stifling a yawn, she sat up and pulled the duvet round her shoulders. 'OK, I'm listening.'

'There's a narrow alley running behind the houses in Glevum Passage with gates into the gardens – well, they're not much more than back yards, really. Some of them have got sheds that used to be privies before the houses were modernized. It appears the gates are hardly ever used by the occupants, in fact most of them are kept locked and festooned with barbed wire to discourage the local yobs, but it seems that for reasons of her own Evie left hers open from time to time. A friend of Mrs Pewsey who was staying with her a few days before the murder happened to be looking out of her bedroom window one morning and saw a man leaving that way.'

'Which suggests Evie was doing a bit of moonlighting and Trev must have found out about it. I suppose she thought she could get away with it by letting her clients in through the back door.'

'That's what it looks like. I sent Tony Hill to chat to some of her old associates. One of them said Evie liked variety and would never be content with one bloke. Seems her idea was to have her cake and eat it – her own house, Trev's money and a bit of fun on the side when he wasn't looking.'

Sukey was wide-awake now. 'It would be interesting to know how Trev found out,' she said thoughtfully.

'Does it matter? She just got careless, I suppose.'

'Or someone shopped her.'

'Why would anyone bother to do that?'

'I don't know – it was just a thought.'

'Still fancying your chances as a detective?' he teased.

She couldn't deny it. She had been a uniformed officer with ambitions to join the CID before marriage and motherhood had put an end to her career in the police. Money had been tight after Paul had ditched her for Myrna; once Fergus reached the age of fourteen she had started to look for a job and a former colleague suggested she train as a Scenes of Crime Officer. For the most part she thoroughly enjoyed the work, but she still dreamed of one day being able to take up full-time detective work. It was an inclination that sometimes led her to overstep the accepted boundaries of a SOCO's function and had on more than one occasion put her on a collision course with Jim.

'I have had the odd success,' she reminded him.

'And the odd narrow squeak,' he countered. 'Seriously, Sook, I don't want you sticking your neck out over this case. There could be some pretty ugly customers involved.'

'OK, I promise to be good,' she assured him. 'Anyway, how come we didn't know about the rear entrance?'

'A bit of an oversight on our part, I'm afraid. None of the neighbours mentioned it during the initial house-to-house, and with so many sightings of a man answering Blackton's description coming and going at the front and no sign of a forced entry, no one thought about spreading the net a bit wider. It wasn't until after Mrs Pewsey phoned her friend and told her about the murder that she came and told us.'

'That accounts for the fact that Trev was the only man the neighbours saw calling on Evie.'

'Trev, or someone very like him,' corrected Jim, always a stickler for accuracy.

'Was Mrs Pewsey's friend able to give a description of the other chap?'

'She didn't think she'd be able to recognize him again, but she said he looked youngish, quite clean and what she described as "respectable looking". We're doing another house-to-house to see if anyone else noticed him – or any other of Evie's fancy men, there may have been more than one – and we'll issue a statement asking him to come forward as he might have valuable evidence.'

'You'll be lucky! Respectable young men aren't normally keen to admit they've been visiting a prostitute, especially one who's been murdered.'

'You're probably right, but it's worth a try. In the meantime we'll want the back yard searched and the latch on the gate and the handle on her back door checked for prints. Incidentally, we've had some interesting results from the samples you took from the murder room. Blackton's prints were found all over the place, which comes as no surprise, and there were plenty of Evie's, of course, plus some more they haven't got on record.'

'Well, that sounds promising.' As the week progressed she had found the initial horror of the Glevum Passage murder gradually receding from her thoughts, and her first reaction to Jim's call had been resentment at being woken from sleep to be reminded of it. In the light of this new development she found herself able to take a more detached view. 'You'll keep me posted, won't you?' she said with genuine interest.

'Of course. By the way, there's a good concert in Cheltenham Town Hall tomorrow evening. Shall I try for tickets or is there something else you'd rather do? We could have supper first at—'

'Oh, Jim, I'm sorry, I've already agreed to have dinner with Paul and Margaret.'

'You what?' He sounded incredulous. 'Why on earth—?'

'You know they took Gus to Germany with them during half term? They got back last night and—'

'So?'

'Paul took his camcorder and he's running through the video tomorrow evening. They've invited me along as well.'

'How very hospitable.'

'Jim, don't be like that. I've said I'll go . . . and besides, I'm keen to see the video. Gus phoned during the week and said they'd been to some wonderful places and the scenery was out of this world.'

'I'm sure it's unmissable.' His tone was flat and she sensed irritation as well as disappointment. 'You obviously forgot you had a date with me.'

'It wasn't definite, you said you'd be in touch, but—'

'Which is what I'm doing now. You obviously forgot all about it.'

'I'm really sorry.' It was true; their brief exchange on Monday morning had completely slipped her memory. So much had happened since then.

'It can't be helped.'

She could tell that he was hurt and in an attempt to mollify him said, 'Why don't you come round for Sunday lunch? Gus would love to see you and tell you about his trip.' She sensed even as she spoke that it was hardly the most tactful way of wording the invitation.

'Tell Gus I'm sorry to disappoint him, but I'm tied up on Sunday,' he said frostily. 'I have to go now.' There was a click as the connection ended.

'Damn!' she said aloud as she slammed down the receiver and reached for her dressing gown. It wasn't like Jim to be so touchy; he had known all along that she had to keep a balance between her relationship with him and doing what she felt was best for Gus. Normally, he would have been all right about it. After all, he knew how disturbed she had been by the Glevum Passage killing; he should have made allowances. Maybe the fact that she would be seeing Paul had something to do with it. There had been moments in the past when he had shown a touch of jealousy towards her ex-husband, but now Paul had remarried he must surely know there was nothing between them other than a mutual responsibility towards their son.

She went downstairs and filled the kettle. After a cup of tea followed by a shower she felt better. She ate some breakfast before spending the rest of the morning on household chores and checking her fridge and store cupboard. With Fergus away, she had allowed stocks to run low; it would be good to have him home again. The message telling her that the return flight from Germany on Thursday had been delayed, and that he would be returning home some time on Friday, had included the invitation for Saturday. She had accepted without thinking, but it crossed her mind that if she were to call Margaret or Paul to explain the situation with Jim they would have been happy to suggest an alternative date. Had Jim been more reasonable she might have done just that; as it was, she dismissed the idea on principle. The misunderstanding would soon blow over and things would return to normal. Next week she was back on the eight-to-four shift, which made life a lot easier. By the time she reached the station and signed in she was feeling more optimistic.

For a change, the local criminals appeared to have been taking things quietly during the night and her only assignment to begin with was to return to number 18 Glevum Passage to check the rear entrance. On reaching the house she went along the hallway to the small but surprisingly well-equipped and tidy kitchen. Like the rest of the house it had been freshly decorated; it still smelt of paint and showed little sign of use, suggesting that cooking had not been one of Evie's preferred occupations. She checked the cupboards, most of which were empty except for one containing several bottles of gin, whisky and vodka, a supply of mixers, packets of crisps and a few odd glasses. There was also a small can of oil tucked away in a corner with a scrap of rag. On impulse she dusted them all for fingerprints before turning her attention to the door leading out into the yard, a solid wooden affair with a Yale lock and a bolt top and bottom, neither of which had been fastened. She carefully dusted the bolts, the lock and the door itself before opening it and stepping outside.

It took her a moment or two to locate the door into the alley as it was partially concealed by a straggly, stunted holly bush that had probably grown from a seed dropped by a bird and been allowed to grow unchecked. Anyone using the entrance would have had to push past it and might even have sustained scratches to face or hands. She spent some time examining it and was intrigued to find some fibres that just might, she thought with a twinge of excitement, match the ones she had taken from Evie's bedroom. She checked the door, which was fastened with a simple latch; it too had bolts top and bottom and again, both were unfastened. In contrast with the rusty barbed wire protecting the adjoining properties, the top of the frame and the newly repointed brick wall were crowned with loops of shiny new razor wire. After checking the latch for prints she released it; the door swung smoothly and noiselessly open and she ducked under the bush and stepped into the narrow alley.

The first thing that struck her was an unpleasant smell; evidently the local cats and dogs found it a convenient place to relieve themselves. It was choked with weeds and littered with debris, most of which appeared to have been blown in from the street. To the right it ended in a blank wall and there was no sign that anyone had walked that way recently. To the left she could see the street that ran at right angles to Glevum Passage, with traffic passing to and fro. From the gate to that end the undergrowth had been trampled down in the middle, forming a narrow path.

Carefully picking her way through the mess, Sukey spent several minutes taking photographs and hunting for possible clues before returning to the house. She put her samples away and called the office.

'I've finished here,' she told George Barnes when he came on the line.

'Find anything interesting?'

'Maybe. It's obvious someone's been accessing the house from the rear and I've picked up fibres that might match the ones I found earlier. Have CID reported any developments?'

'Not that I'm aware of.'

'Have you got anything else for me?'

'There's been a break-in at a private hotel in Barnwood,' he said. 'Uniformed have attended and asked the usual questions. Trot round and see what you can pick up, OK?'

The hotel was situated in a quiet street off the main road. A car was parked outside; as Sukey drew up behind it, DC Tony Hill came out of the house and walked over to her.

'Anything exciting?' she asked.

He shrugged. 'Funny business, actually. Someone called round yesterday and enquired after one of the residents, a chap called David Somers. The owner, a Mrs Milroy, directed him to Somers' room but there was no one there. The visitor didn't leave his name or a message, just said he'd call back. When Somers came in later on and Mrs Milroy mentioned he'd had a visitor he got rather agitated, packed up his things and left. This morning, when the cleaner went to do up the room, she found the door had been forced and the place turned over.'

'Anything missing?'

'Like I said, Somers had checked out and taken his stuff. Mrs Milroy didn't seem to think anything else had gone. Not that there'd have been much to nick, by the looks of things – it's not exactly a four-star establishment.'

'Why did they send you, I wonder?' said Sukey. 'It doesn't sound like a case for CID.'

'That's what I thought, but apparently DS Radcliffe happened to pick up the message and thought there might be an outside chance of a link with the Evie Stanton murder. Could the young man checking out in a hurry after someone enquired after him be Evie's mystery lover on the run from Blackton? It seems a bit of a long shot, but—'

'I'll see what I can pick up,' said Sukey. 'Did Mrs Milroy give a description of the visitor?'

'Yes, quite a good one. She's going to call at the station and have a look at a few mugshots. 'By the way, did you find anything interesting at Evie's place?'

'Possibly.' She told him briefly of her observations. 'I gather you've been involved in the enquiry, using your charm on one of Evie's old mates.'

He grinned. Back at the station, he was considered something of a ladies' man, a quality his superiors found useful from time to time in extracting information from impressionable females. 'You mean Julie? Yes, she was quite helpful. I left her my number in case—' At that moment his mobile phone rang and he broke off to answer. Assuming their conversation had ended, Sukey took a step towards Belstone House, but he caught her arm to detain her. 'Hang on a minute,' he said into the phone, 'let me jot this down.' He got into the car and rested his notebook on the steering wheel to write. 'Thanks, Julie, that's great. See you this evening around six, usual place, OK?' He put away the phone and leaned out of the car.

'Something interesting?' she asked.

'Could be. Julie's been talking to a close friend of Evie's. It sounds as if she might be able to help us track down the mystery boyfriend. Watch this space.' He gave a jaunty wave, started the engine and drove away.

Six

B elstone House Hotel was a substantial detached building of grey stone, its ground-floor windows screened from the road by a laurel hedge. A notice hanging from a wrought-iron lamp standard advertised bed and breakfast accommodation with evening meals by arrangement, rooms with en suite facilities and colour TV, and proudly announced that the accommodation had been inspected and approved by the local tourist board. Sukey noticed as she pressed the bell that a sign reading 'Vacancies' had been propped inside an adjacent window.

The door was opened by a slim, elegant woman whom Sukey judged to be about fifty. She was carefully but discreetly made up and wore a burgundy jacket and skirt over a white shirt, with a pearl choker and earrings. Her platinum blonde hair, inconspicuously streaked with grey, was tied back – a little incongruously for a woman of her age and style, Sukey thought – in a ponytail.

'Mrs Milroy?' said Sukey.

'That's right. May I help you?' The words were accompanied by a gracious, professional smile; the voice was carefully modulated with a hint of slightly dated refinement that seemed to go with the surroundings.

'I'm a Scenes of Crime Examiner.' Sukey held out her ID. 'I understand you've had a break-in.'

'Oh, yes, do come in.' Mrs Milroy stood aside for her to enter, then closed the door and turned the key. 'I never had to keep the place locked before this unfortunate business,' she said with a sigh and a shake of her head that set the ponytail swinging. 'It's most inconvenient for our guests to have to ring the bell every time.'

'I believe my colleague mentioned that I'd be along,' said Sukey.

'Oh, yes, that nice young detective who was here a few minutes ago.' Mrs Milroy's face lit up and her smile acquired a warmth that had been absent in the formal greeting. Evidently Tony Hill's ingratiating manner had worked its usual magic.

'I'd like to see the room where the break-in took place, if that's all right with you.'

'Yes, of course.'

Mrs Milroy led the way upstairs to the second floor. On the way, Sukey said, 'Is there much missing?'

'Well, actually, nothing so far as we can make out. It's difficult to understand what he was looking for.'

'You're sure it was a man?'

'Well, it was obviously that suspicious character who was enquiring after Mr Somers.'

'You were suspicious of him at the time?'

'Well, no, I suppose not, but with hindsight—' Mrs Milroy appeared slightly nonplussed, as if recognizing that there had been a breach of security.

To save her further embarrassment, Sukey said quickly, 'I'll see if I can spot anything that might give us a clue.'

'That would be very reassuring. Here we are.' She stopped in front of a cream-painted door bearing a brass figure eight on the centre panel. A length of blue and white police tape had been stretched across the frame; Sukey carefully detached one end and examined the woodwork, which was badly splintered for several inches above and below the lock.

'He made a mess of that, didn't he?' she commented. 'It wasn't a professional job, by the looks of it.'

'What do you suppose that means?' asked Mrs Milroy. She was standing with her hands clasped in front of her, showing no inclination to return downstairs and leave Sukey to her task.

'Simply that whoever did it hasn't had much practice in breaking and entering.' The hint of flippancy in the casual remark failed to draw a smile from Mrs Milroy. Evidently she considered the matter far too serious for levity.

Sukey put down her bag and pulled on a pair of latex gloves before setting to work. She took a cast of the damage to both door and frame, explaining in response to Mrs Milroy's question that every tool left its own individual mark, before dusting the brass handle and the door itself for prints.

'Right, let's see what we can find inside,' she said. With Mrs Milroy at her heels, she pushed open the door and glanced round. The room was simply furnished with a pine chest of drawers, a bedside cabinet and wardrobe, a few rugs scattered over the wooden floor and a single divan bed. The en suite facility consisted of a partitioned-off cubicle concealing a shower, toilet and washbasin; the only other concession to luxury was a small television.

It was evident that someone had carried out a thorough search. The bed had been stripped, the rugs flung aside, every drawer pulled out and thrown on the floor and the doors of the empty wardrobe left wide open. 'Well, as you say, it doesn't look as if robbery was the motive,' Sukey observed. 'If he was looking for something he could flog to pay for a fix, he'd have gone for the telly.'

'A fix? You mean, drugs?' The carefully pencilled eyebrows lifted in horror at the thought of anything so squalid affecting Belstone House. 'Well, whatever he was looking for, I simply can't imagine why he found it necessary to leave the place in such a state. Anyone could have seen that the room had been vacated.'

'I think it's more likely he was hoping to find some clue as to where the previous occupant has gone,' said Sukey thoughtfully. 'Did Mr Somers leave a forwarding address, by the way?'

'No. He packed up and went off in such a hurry, I never thought to ask.'

'This man who was enquiring after him? Did he call back later?'

'Yes, he did – at least, he telephoned. My assistant took the call; he said the man sounded annoyed when he was told Mr Somers had left without leaving an address. You know, I'm really rather concerned about him,' Mrs Milroy went on. 'I don't think he's in the best of health; in fact, his uncle said he'd been ill and needed a quiet place to recuperate. He certainly looked rather thin and pale when he arrived a couple of weeks ago, but I thought he was starting to pick up. He was eating better; we don't usually get asked for evening meals at this time of year but once or twice he asked if we could provide one and as it happens I –' Mrs Milroy cleared her throat and gave a slightly coy smile – 'well, as it was just the two of us, I invited him to eat with me in my private apartment. He was a very charming, well-spoken young man, but I had the impression he'd had some recent difficulties in his life. Not that I asked him a lot of questions,' she added hastily. 'My guests' private lives are no concern of mine, of course, although you'd be surprised how many people are only too ready to confide in me.' She gave another, slightly self-deprecatory simper.

'It must be your sympathetic manner,' said Sukey.

This proved to be exactly what Mrs Milroy wanted to hear. 'It's very kind of you to say so,' she beamed, displaying a row of immaculately kept teeth. 'And of course, I always assure them that anything they choose to tell me will be in the strictest confidence.'

'Did Mr Somers tell you anything about his background?'

'Not really, except that he'd been living away from home for some time, working as a salesman.'

'Did he mention what company he worked for?'

'Somewhere based in Bristol, I think he said – but he doesn't work for them any more. His uncle had found him a new job and he was hoping to make a fresh start. Perhaps there had been some trouble between him and this other man – over a woman, perhaps.' A gleam appeared in her slate-blue eyes, as if she sensed an intrigue.

'This uncle,' Sukey paused in the act of dusting one of the drawers, 'did he give his name?'

'No, and I must admit I never thought to ask. I mean, it isn't as if he was asking me to keep an eye on David – Mr Somers, that is – or anything like that. He might have given him the money to pay for the room, I suppose, but that was nothing to do with me.'

'Did he leave an address or telephone number?'

Mrs Milroy shook her head. 'No, nothing. He waited while Mr Somers paid for four weeks' accommodation in advance – he probably wanted to make sure I gave a proper receipt, but I assure you I am *most meticulous* in all business matters. And then he said, "Goodbye for now, and remember what I told you," and left.'

'Did you tell DC Hill about this gentleman?'

'No, it didn't occur to me.' Mrs Milroy frowned. 'Do you

think I should have done?' Her frown changed to a smile as she added, 'perhaps you could ask him to come back if you think it's important.'

'I'll mention it in my report. It will be up to his sergeant to decide whether it's worth following up.'

'I promised to call in at the police station tomorrow morning to look at some photographs, in the hope that I can identify the man who was asking for Mr Somers. Perhaps I could have a word with Tony – Constable Hill – at the same time?' she added hopefully.

My, Tony, you've really scored a hit with Mrs Milroy! Sukey thought. Aloud, she said, 'It would certainly be worth mentioning. There does seem to be something a little odd about all this.' She put away her kit and closed the case. 'I think that's all I can do here. I'm sorry about the grey powder – it does make a bit of a mess.'

'Have you finished? Can I have the room cleaned now?'

'Yes, no problem.'

'What about the damage to the door? It doesn't make a very good impression, especially with that.' She indicated the blue and white tape.

'I'll get rid of that for you, and you can arrange for someone to come and repair the damage.'

'Oh, that will be a relief.'

'You're not the only one feeling relieved,' Sukey muttered to herself as she returned to the van. She had found the affected manner of the proprietor of Belstone House increasingly irritating.

The rest of the day brought the usual crop of thefts from cars, garden sheds and garages, most of which had been left unlocked by careless citizens who were nevertheless aggrieved at their misfortune. 'There was a time when you could go out and leave your house unlocked and no one would dream of coming in and stealing anything,' was a frequently heard complaint, particularly from the elderly.

'They just don't seem to be able to accept that times have changed,' Sukey remarked to George Barnes as she sat down to write her reports at the end of her shift. 'If they'd only get real they'd save themselves a lot of grief – and us a lot of time.'

George shrugged. 'So what else is new?' he said resignedly.

41

'What did you find at Belstone House, by the way? Tony Hill seemed to think there's something odd about it.'

'I didn't notice anything odd about the hotel itself – it's just an ordinary bed and breakfast sort of place – but there's certainly something fishy going on between that chap Somers and whoever was enquiring after him. It must be pretty serious to scare Somers off like that.'

'Did you pick up anything useful?'

'Plenty of prints, but unless we can find a match they won't tell us anything. I'll be making a few notes to pass on to Andy Radcliffe.'

'Maybe the mystery caller's a dealer trying to collect a debt.'

'Could be.' Sukey gave a sudden, gleeful chuckle at the memory of Mrs Milroy's pained reaction to the word 'fix'. 'That'd upset the oh-so-ladylike woman who owns the place. She'd have a fit at the thought of a room in her quiet, respectable establishment being occupied by a junkie!'

Seven

When Sukey reached home soon after ten o'clock on Friday evening, she found to her surprise that Fergus was already in bed. He had sent her a text message earlier in the day to say that he was home and she had been looking forward to hearing about the trip. Seeing the light under his door she tapped on it and called, 'I'm home, Gus. Are you OK?'

'Yes, fine,' he replied, but there was a flat note to his voice that aroused her concern. After a brief pause, he said, still in the same listless tone, 'What sort of day have you had, Mum?'

'Quite interesting. May I come in?'

'Sure.'

He was propped up against a heap of pillows with an open book in his hands and several others strewn over the bedcovers. He pushed them to one side and she sat down on the edge of the bed. 'It's not like you to turn in so early on a Friday,' she remarked. 'Are you very tired, or do you have to get up early in the morning?'

'Not specially.' He looked away from her and began fidgeting with the duvet. 'There's footie practice tomorrow, but not till eleven.' Gus, a keen sportsman, had recently been picked for his college team.

'How was the trip?'

'It was fine.'

'Did you find your letter from Anita? It came this morning and—'

'Yes, I found it.' He was still avoiding her eye and her concern increased.

'Gus,' she began, 'I don't want to pry, but is there something wrong?'

'Oh, Mum!' His mouth buckled the way it used to do when he was a child struggling to hold back tears. His eyes were

43

bright as he met hers. 'That letter from Anita—' His voice grew unsteady and he took a deep breath.

'Is she ill?'

'No, but—' Emotion was plainly close to the surface and there was another pause before he went on, 'Mum, I think she's fallen for some bloody Frog.'

'Oh, surely not!' Anita, who was a year older than Fergus, was spending a gap year in France as au pair to a French family before going to university to study modern languages. The teenage relationship had started when the two were still at the local comprehensive and had, to the surprise of both families, proved surprisingly resilient. Sukey knew that Fergus had been counting the weeks until Christmas when Anita was planning a trip home to spend a few days with her parents. 'Whatever makes you think that?' she asked gently.

'Her letter was full of this chap Marcel and how she went to some party with him and what a great dancer he is and how loads of other girls were chasing him but he spent all his time with her. She's mentioned him before, said how good he's been about helping her with her French and all that and I didn't think too much about it. I mean, she always tells me how much she's missing me.'

'Who's Marcel?'

'He's the elder brother of the kid she's supposed to be looking after.' His downcast expression went straight to her heart as she recalled her own teenage years. To be rejected by a boy she imagined herself passionately in love with and to know he was dating someone else had seemed like the end of the world.

'Gus, I know how easy it is to imagine the worst, but I'm sure Anita wouldn't cheat on you,' she began, but he made a despairing little gesture and then put his hands over his eyes.

'I know she wouldn't cheat,' he said, his voice unsteady, 'but if she's fallen for him, why can't she say so, not leave me—' He broke off, choked by a sob that he had been desperately trying to control.

Sukey took the hand nearest to her and gave it a squeeze. 'Gus, if that were the case, I'm sure she *would* say so,' she said earnestly. 'You've told me lots of times how open and direct she is and how she always speaks her mind even when it leads to the odd spat between you.'

'I know, but that's when we're together and we can have it out at the time. Maybe she doesn't want to say anything in a letter for fear of hurting me.' Gus took a deep breath and his expression became even gloomier. 'I'm beginning to dread Christmas.'

'Now, stop feeling sorry for yourself,' said Sukey briskly. 'If Anita was seriously interested in this chap Marcel I'm sure she'd come right out and tell you. She's probably feeling flattered at all the attention she's getting from the most popular boy on the block, as the Americans say. She's young and away from home and you can't blame her for having a good time, but I'll bet she'd much rather be with you.'

'You reckon?' There was a mixture of hope and doubt in his voice.

'I reckon,' she said firmly. 'Tell you what, why don't you write back and make a joke of it – say you'll challenge Marcel to a duel if he tries any of his Froggie wiles on your woman, or –' she hunted around for some other equally ridiculous suggestion – 'that you won't fancy her any more if she gets impregnated with his garlicky breath.'

To her relief, the nonsense worked and Fergus smiled, a little shakily. 'Thanks, Mum, you're probably right.'

'Aren't I always?' she replied with assumed smugness.

'I'll get a letter off to her first thing.'

'And don't forget to tell her you love her and how much you're looking forward to seeing her at Christmas.'

'Of course.' He leaned back against the pillows with his hands clasped behind his head, a slightly faraway look in his eyes as if he were already composing the letter. Then, as if remembering that his mother had mentioned that her day had been interesting, he said, 'Tell me what you've been working on today. Something exciting?' He was aware of her long-term ambition to become a full-blown detective and shared her interest in her cases, particularly where murder was involved and where she had – sometimes despite DI Castle's outspoken disapproval – taken a more proactive role than was expected of a mere SOCO. He had even on at least one occasion contributed to the successful conclusion of an investigation.

45

'Well,' she said, glad to pursue the change of subject, 'there was a particularly nasty murder on Monday that's been keeping CID busy.'

His eyes lit up in anticipation. 'No kidding? Is Jim in charge of the case? Do tell.'

'Not now, I'm tired. I'll bring you up to date in the morning and you can tell me all about your trip.' She gave a deep yawn. 'I think I'll make a cup of tea before I turn in. Would you like one?'

'No, thanks, I had a Coke just before you came in. Are you seeing Jim over the weekend?'

'No. I couldn't see him tomorrow because of our date with Paul and Margaret and he's busy on Sunday.' The question was a sharp reminder that she had seen him only once during the day, when he had put his head round the door of the SOCOs' office while she was writing her reports. There had been no one else there at the time, but he had merely said something about looking for one of the other officers and left. Presumably he was still feeling put out over Saturday. *Well, hard luck*, she thought to herself. *I'm not going to be taken for granted by him or anyone else.*

'Hasn't he called you?' Fergus persisted.

'He's been pretty busy.'

He gave her a keen look. 'You two haven't had a run-in, have you?'

'No, of course not.' It was her turn to sound unconvincing. 'At least,' she admitted, 'he did sound a bit miffed because I'm not available tomorrow.'

'Because you're having dinner with Dad and Margaret and me?' Comprehension dawned in her son's eye. 'He just hates you having contact with Dad, doesn't he?'

'I wouldn't go that far, but he certainly wasn't best pleased. He seemed to think I had a date with him, but there was nothing definite.'

'Oh, well, I expect he'll ring tomorrow.' He gave her a searching glance. 'You aren't seriously worried, are you? I mean, things are OK between you otherwise?'

'Of course they are,' she said confidently. She was touched by his concern; he was surprisingly perceptive for an eighteen-year-old. 'I'm sure he'll come round.' Fergus began to gather up the books scattered over the bedcover and she stood up. 'Right, I'll say goodnight, then. Sleep well.'

'You too.' Unexpectedly, he grabbed her arm, pulled her towards him and kissed her cheek. 'Thanks, Mum, you're a pal,' he whispered.

She ruffled his hair and returned the kiss. 'That's what mums are for,' she said softly. As she spoke, her eye fell on a heap of discarded clothing on the floor. 'And to clear up after untidy offspring,' she added as she scooped them into a bundle. 'I take it this lot's for the wash?'

'Oh, er, yes please,' he replied with a sheepish grin. 'I meant to put them in the machine, but I forgot.'

'That's my boy!'

Over breakfast the next morning, Fergus listened with rapt attention to Sukey's account of the Glevum Passage killing and then plied her with questions.

'Where d'you reckon this chap Blackton is holed up?' he asked between spoonfuls of muesli. 'D'you think he's fled the country?'

Sukey shook her head. 'He might have done, but what we're worried about is that he's more likely to be trying to track down the man Evie's been having it off with. If he gets his hands on him, he'll quite likely do the same to him as he did to her.'

'And that's why you're so keen to track this other chap down as well – for his own safety?'

'That's the main reason, although I think CID are hoping that he may have picked up some useful information from Evie that could help them get their hands on Trev. And Tony Hill has a contact with one of Evie's old pals that he thinks might lead to something.'

Fergus nodded. 'Another tom, I suppose?' he said, with an air of worldly wisdom that made her smile. His use of the vernacular, gleaned partly from listening to his mother's conversations with DI Jim Castle and partly from watching police series on TV, never failed to amuse her.

'As it happens, yes,' she said.

'What other cases have you had this week?'

'Nothing very special – the usual run of burglaries and stolen cars. And someone broke into a room in a private hotel after the occupant had checked out. We think the intruder was trying to collect money owed for drugs.' She gave him a brief account of the circumstances leading up to the break-in.

He thought for a moment. Then he said, 'Supposing the chap who checked out in a hurry is Evie's mystery lover? He must have guessed that it was Trev who killed her in a fit of jealousy and when he heard some bloke had been after him he thought it was one of Trev's mob and couldn't get out quickly enough.'

'As a matter of fact, Andy Radcliffe has already thought of that.'

'Well, there you are, then – great minds think alike!' Fergus beamed. 'Tell your people I'm available as a consultant,' he said airily. 'For a small fee, of course.'

'I'll suggest they appoint you a supernumerary.'

'What's that?'

'A kind of extra.'

'Like in a movie? Would I get paid if I cracked the case?'

'Oh, sure, big bucks. What about that toast you were making?'

'Coming up.'

The telephone rang just as they were clearing the table. 'That'll probably be Jim. I'll go and post my letter to Anita,' said Fergus, and disappeared.

Sukey picked up the phone and said, 'Hello.'

'Hi, Sook,' said Jim.

Her pulse quickened at the sound of his voice but she tried to keep her tone casual as she replied, 'Hi, Jim, how are you?'

'Fine. A bit tired – it's been a gruelling week. Did Gus enjoy the German trip?'

'Yes, he had a great time.'

'I was just wondering . . . is the invitation to Sunday lunch still open?'

'I thought you had a more pressing engagement.'

'I did, at least, I'd arranged to meet a former colleague who's getting married and asked me to be his best man. The idea was to discuss arrangements for the wedding, but he called me last night to say the engagement's off.'

'So you're at a loose end and have to fall back on your own significant other for nourishment?'

'You wouldn't want to think of me having a pub lunch all by myself, would you?'

'It would break my heart. Well, I suppose we can stretch the leg of lamb to feed one more.'

'That's great. About midday, then?'

'Come earlier if you like. I'm sure Gus would love to quiz you about the Glevum Passage killing.'

'You shouldn't encourage him. I have enough trouble with you playing detective without him developing a morbid interest in the business.'

'We can't help it, it's in the genes.'

'Well, see you tomorrow. There was a barely perceptible pause before he added, 'Have a good time this evening.' He rang off. Sukey switched on the radio and sang along with an old Beatles number as she began clearing away the dishes.

Eight

W hen Jim Castle arrived at Sukey's house on Sunday morning, she greeted him with a hug and said, 'I'm sorry about your friend's engagement, but it's lovely to see you. What happened?'

He returned the hug before taking off his coat and handing it to her. 'It seems they had a big row when she told him he'd have to cut down on his drinking and trade in his sports car for a family model because she wanted to start a baby as soon as they were married,' he explained.

'Silly woman. She should have waited till after the wedding.'

'That's what you'd do, is it?'

'Of course.' In the act of hanging up the coat, she glanced over her shoulder and treated him to a provocative grin. 'Never try to alter your man until you've got him well and truly hooked.'

'Watch it, you!' He put on an expression of mock ferocity, took her by the elbow and brushed her chin with a bunched fist.

She cringed in mock terror. 'Just kidding, honest. Is your friend very upset?'

'He makes out he is, but between you and me, I think he's a bit relieved. I've had a feeling for some time that he was beginning to get cold feet about the whole idea of marriage. Anyway, he's gone off to drown his sorrows with a crowd of his mates. He wanted me to join the party, but I said there was something else I'd much rather do.' He put his arms round her and pressed his cheek against hers. 'It's been one hell of a week.'

She leaned against him for a moment and whispered, 'I've missed you.'

'Likewise.'

She pulled away and said, 'Let's go into the kitchen. I have to see to the roast.'

'It smells gorgeous.'

Fergus had put glasses and packets of crisps on the table and was taking cans from the refrigerator. 'Hi, Jim,' he said. 'Fancy a beer?'

'Thanks.'

'I'll join you.' Fergus handed Jim one of the cans, pulled the ring from the other and began pouring the contents with a practised hand.

'He acquired a taste for it in Germany,' said Sukey, seeing Jim's eyebrows lift.

'Well, why not? He's old enough to marry and vote. What are you having, Sook?'

'A gin and tonic. Will you fix it for me, please? You know where everything is.'

'No problem. So how was the trip, Gus?'

'Oh, I had a great time.'

'That's good. How did your dad's video turn out?'

'It was super, wasn't it, Mum?'

Sukey finished basting the leg of lamb and roast potatoes, pushed the dish back into the oven, closed the door and straightened up. 'It was very interesting,' she agreed, deliberately keeping her tone matter of fact. 'Nürnberg's a beautiful city, very historic with lots of lovely old buildings. Paul's film could do with a bit of editing, though,' she went on, aware of Jim's eyes on her with what looked almost like a challenging expression. 'When you've seen one gabled roof you've seen 'em all. I'm afraid I found myself dropping off once or twice.'

'Home movies do have a tendency to go on too long,' Jim remarked, with a trace of condescension.

'I thought Dad's camerawork was brilliant,' said Fergus, pride in his father's achievement making him forget for once the need for diplomacy.

'Especially the shots with you in them,' retorted his mother. 'Jim, you wouldn't believe the size of the beer stein he was tackling!'

'It was empty, I was just putting on an act for the camera,'

Fergus protested.'Oh, sure, we believe you,' she said and they all laughed. The moment of edginess had passed. Jim handed Sukey her gin and tonic and poured out his own beer. They saluted one another with their glasses and drank in a companionable silence for a few moments.

'Mum's been telling me about the Glevum Passage murder,' said Fergus, helping himself to crisps.

'Oh, yes?'

'It sounds pretty horrid.'

'Knowing what a bloodthirsty chap you are, I suppose that's why you're interested in it,' Jim remarked with a sly wink at Sukey.

'No, that's not the reason. It's because of the other case – the break-in at Belstone House.'

Jim shot an enquiring glance at Sukey. 'It was only a minor incident. Nothing was taken and there was only minimum damage, but Andy Radcliffe thought there might be a link with the Glevum Passage killing.'

'And you told me there was something fishy about the chap who did a runner,' Fergus reminded her.

'I only said he left in a hurry when he heard another man had been asking for him.' She gave Jim a brief outline of the incident. 'We've no idea who the man was.'

'I'll have a word with Andy tomorrow,' he said, 'but it was probably someone trying to collect a debt for drugs. It's an interesting idea, Gus,' he added, seeing the lad's face fall, 'but it would be stretching coincidence a bit too far. We're constantly getting reports of people trying to settle private disputes by taking the law into their own hands. It's mostly over something quite trivial.'

'Murder isn't trivial,' Fergus persisted. 'If you get good descriptions of both men and they look the same—'

'All right, I'll bear it in mind,' Jim promised. 'Sukey, isn't that leg of lamb cooked yet? I'm starving.'

After lunch, well wrapped up against the chill wind, they went for a walk on Cooper's Hill before returning for tea and buttered crumpets in Sukey's cosy sitting room, followed by an evening spent watching a video. There was no further reference to crime, but later, as Jim was leaving, Sukey said quietly, 'Don't you think there's any mileage at all in a possible connection between the Glevum Passage killing and that break-in?'

'To be honest, no. If we assumed that every private spat was linked to a major crime we'd be snowed under. We're overstretched as it is.'

'You must have mug shots of some of Blackton's mob. If Mrs Milroy picks one of them out—'

'I've already told you,' Jim cut in sharply, 'our Trev is highly skilled at keeping his nose clean, and that applies to the people who work for him as well. Sook, don't spoil a lovely day with any more ideas for wild-goose chases. And don't get any fancy ideas about following up this one on your own either,' he added with mock severity. He took her face between his hands and gave her a lingering kiss on the mouth, then put his arms round her and held her close. She responded eagerly, pressing her body against his. 'I wish I could stay with you tonight,' he whispered in her ear.

'Me too.'

'When will Gus be going away again?'

'Not till Anita comes home for the Christmas holidays,' she sighed. Although Fergus knew of their relationship, it had become an unwritten rule never to spend the night together while he was at home.

'It's been a frustrating week, knowing you were here on your own and being so tied up with work. Still, maybe you'll come to my place one evening? You're on early turn next week, aren't you?'

'That's right. We'll fix something then.' The prospect sent a surge of electricity coursing through her system. 'Love you,' she whispered.

'Likewise.'

As she closed the door behind him and began locking up for the night, it struck her that until Jim put the idea into her head it hadn't occurred to her to do any private nosing around over the Belstone House incident. It was, perhaps, something worth considering.

When Sukey returned to the station at lunchtime the following day she almost bumped into Mrs Milroy, dressed in an eye-catching scarlet woollen coat, Cossack-style boots and a fur hat.

'Good morning, Ms Reynolds!' The hotel proprietor flashed a radiant smile at Sukey. 'I've just been looking at some photographs – mug shots, I believe you call them – and I'm so thrilled, I've identified the man who was asking about Dave Somers.'

'Well, that *is* good news,' said Sukey warmly.

'I hope they manage to catch him. I'm rather anxious about Dave, I do hope he's all right.'

'I take it you haven't heard from him?'

'Not a word, or from his uncle either. I mentioned the uncle to the young officer who showed me the photos and asked her to tell Tony – I mean, DC Hill – as you suggested. I hope I've been of some help.'

'I'm sure you have.'

In reception, WPC Pam Andrews was talking to the desk sergeant. Sukey indicated the sheaf of photographs that she carried and said, 'Hi, Pam. I've just been talking to Mrs Milroy and she tells me she's made a positive ID of the dodgy character in the Belstone House incident.'

Pam gave a rueful grin. 'I didn't have the heart to tell her, but she fingered a villain who's been banged up in a young offenders' institution for the past six months.'

'Bad luck.'

'And she was very insistent that I tell Tony Hill about some bloke claiming to be the uncle of the chap who scarpered. Says she never thought to mention him when Tony called round about the break-in and suggests he drop by again so that she can give a detailed description.' Pam gave a knowing grin. 'I think she took a shine to our Tone.'

'Wouldn't be the first, would she?' said the desk sergeant dourly. 'He sure knows how to charm women. He's welcome to that one, though.'

'Too sophisticated for an innocent young chap like you, Sarge?' said Pam cheekily, and scuttled away with her photographs without giving him time to reply.

The SOCOs' office was temporarily deserted. Sukey fetched a cup of coffee and settled down to eat her sandwiches. It had been a busy morning and she had had no time to think about her parting conversation with Jim the previous evening, nor about the glimmering of an idea for a little detective work of her own that she had been mulling over in her head before falling asleep. Seeing Mrs Milroy had set her mind working again. So far, they had been concentrating on the man suspected of carrying out the break-in at Belstone House and – apart from Mrs Milroy's concern for his welfare – scant attention had been paid to the one who had made such a hasty departure. He was not suspected of any wrongdoing and had not been reported as a missing person, so why should they? Jim could be right, of course, but if CID were too busy to follow up such an unsubstantiated suggestion, there could surely be no harm in a curious SOCO doing a little nosing around. If she turned up anything that looked promising, she would risk Jim's disapproval and report it immediately.

Before setting off on her afternoon assignments, she made a quick visit to one or two shops in the city centre, stopping on her way back to buy the new edition of the *Big Issue* from Lucy. As she took the money and handed over the magazine, Lucy remarked, 'That feller Matt you was asking about – the one what got mugged.'

'What about him?'

'There was this posh guy asking after him the other day.'

'Was he one of Matt's regular customers?'

'I dunno, I'd never seen him before. I told him Matt had gone before I came an' that's how I got this pitch. I told him to ask Jack.' Lucy nodded across the street to where her fellow vendor was squatting down feeding biscuits to his dog.

Sukey crossed over to him and said, 'Lucy tells me someone was asking after Matt. Do you know who it was?'

Jack looked up and shot her a suspicious glance from beneath bushy black eyebrows. 'Who wants to know?'

'I was one of Matt's regular customers and I was very concerned when I heard he'd been mugged,' she explained. 'Do you know where he is now?'

'No idea. This chap asked me the same question.'

'Had you seen this man before?'

'Sure. It was him who saw to Matt after the mugging.'

'Saw to him? Was Matt hurt, then?'

Jack stood up and drew the back of his hand across his nose.

'Don't think it was anything serious,' he said. 'I didn't see it happen, I only saw Matt getting up from the ground with blood on his face. He seemed all right, just a bit dazed.' He spoke in a tone of near indifference; such events were doubtless unremarkable in the world of the homeless.

'So you didn't see who hit him?' Sukey persisted.

'No.'

'And this other man – the one who's been asking about him – went to help?'

'He took him into that caff over there.'

'That was kind. Have you seen Matt since?' Jack shook his head. 'When was this?'

He shrugged. 'Can't remember exactly.'

'This other man, what does he look like?'

The look of suspicion returned. 'You ask a lot of questions,' he said sharply. 'What's it to you?'

'I'm just concerned about Matt, that's all. I used to chat to him and he told me a bit about himself. I had a feeling he had problems and needed help.'

'We all need help, don't we?' He glanced down at the dog. 'This chap costs a bit to feed for a start.'

'I can imagine.' Sukey fished a two-pound coin from her pocket and gave it to him. He accepted it in a grimy hand and said, almost grudgingly, 'Well-dressed bloke, posh accent, clean-shaven.'

'What age?'

'Fiftyish, I suppose. Didn't take that much notice.' Jack bent down and picked up the pile of magazines that he had placed on the ground while feeding the dog. He moved past Sukey, holding them out in front of him and shouting, '*Big Issue*! Buy the *Big Issue*!' to the passers-by. It was the clearest possible signal that the conversation was at an end.

Nine

S ukey's final assignment that afternoon was at a filling station where a youth brandishing what appeared to be a gun had tried to rob the till. When she arrived on the scene she found blue and white tape across the entrance, a police car on the forecourt and a bright yellow sports car by one of the petrol pumps. A uniformed constable unhitched the tape to admit her; she parked her van, took out her case and went into the shop.

Inside, a burly young man in jeans and a bomber jacket was leaning against the counter with his hands in his pockets, looking relaxed and, she thought, distinctly pleased with himself. By contrast, a grey-haired man whom Sukey took to be the proprietor was sitting with bowed shoulders on a chair, shivering violently in spite of a thick woollen rug draped round him. A second uniformed officer standing beside him said, 'Do you feel able to tell me exactly what happened, Mr Curtis?'

'It all happened so quick,' Curtis said shakily. 'This bloke came in with something black in his hand and shouted, "This is a gun. Open the till or I'll shoot!" I just stood there, I couldn't believe it was happening.' He passed a hand over his eyes. 'I was scared stiff, I can tell you.'

'It must have been very frightening,' said the officer. 'So what happened next?' he asked after a moment, as the victim stared at his hands without speaking.

Curtis gave a slight start, as if aroused from sleep, and said, 'Oh, yes, I remember. He shouted at me again and said, "Open the effing till, you stupid old git!" and waved the gun under my nose.'

'That's the only adjective these punks seem to know,' commented the burly young man, who had remained silent until that point.

The policeman turned to him and said politely, 'And your name is, sir?'

'Sam Wrigley.'

He made a note and turned back to Curtis. 'And then?' he prompted.

'I did as he said – opened the till, I mean – and he reached over the counter and grabbed a handful of notes and ran out. I think I must have sort of frozen for a moment and then I heard a yell and looked out of the window and saw the guy on the ground with this gentleman' – he cast a grateful glance at Sam Wrigley – 'on top of him.'

Sam looked smug. 'Made a citizen's arrest, didn't I?'

'Quite so, sir. And what happened next, Mr Curtis?'

'I pressed the alarm button and shouted to Mr Wrigley that I'd called the police.'

'I see. Thank you, sir. Now, Mr Wrigley, may I have your account of the incident?'

'It was like this,' said Sam. 'I'd just filled the car and was putting the hose away when I saw this kid go barging into the shop with his hand in his pocket. I had a feeling he was up to no good so I ran across the forecourt and reached the door just as he came bursting out with a wad of notes in one hand and what looked like a gun in the other. He pointed it at me and yelled at me to get out of the way so I sidestepped and stuck out a foot. He tripped over and went sprawling, I grabbed him and hung on until you and some more of your lads arrived and took charge. The old gentleman was a bit shaky so I got a rug from my car to put round him.'

'Very nice of you, lad,' said Mr Curtis.

'Yes, indeed, sir. Did the intruder put up a struggle?'

'A bit,' Sam's grin broadened as he added with relish, 'especially when I took the loot away from him.'

'The money from the till, you mean?'

'That's right.'

'What did you do with it?'

'Shoved it in my pocket. I thought you might want to check it for fingerprints. I've watched SOCOs at work on the box so I know the drill.'

'Quite right, sir. And it so happens that this lady is a Scenes of Crime Examiner.' The officer beckoned to Sukey. 'Will you kindly give the money to her?' He turned back to Curtis. 'Naturally, I'll give you a receipt for your money, sir, and it will be returned to you as soon as possible.'

'If you wouldn't mind putting this on first?' Sukey stepped forward and handed Sam a latex glove, which he pulled on to a large, powerful-looking hand before drawing out a wad of notes and dropping them into the plastic bag Sukey held out to him. 'Seems a waste of time when the villain's been caught red-handed, but I suppose you have to do everything by the book.'

'We take this kind of incident very seriously,' the officer said solemnly, 'and we have to make the evidence as watertight as possible before we take the case to court.'

'I know, on account of crap lawyers trying to rubbish you,' agreed Sam knowledgeably.

A smile flickered over the officer's rather wooden features as he said, 'That's one way of putting it, sir.' He studied his notebook for a moment, running a pen down the page. 'Right, I think that's all for now, except if I could just have your address and phone number, Mr Wrigley, in case we want to ask you any more questions?'

'Sure, no problem.'

While Sam supplied the information, Sukey went outside and looked round. She had already spotted what appeared to be a handgun lying on the ground a few feet away. She took a picture of it and then with a piece of chalk drew a rough outline round it before carefully transferring it to a plastic bag and taking it back into the shop. 'Imitation,' she announced, holding up the exhibit for them all to see. 'I'll send it to the lab for a fingerprint check when I get back to the station. I take it no one has handled it since it was dropped in the struggle?'

'Correct,' Sam assured her.

'And before I go I'll need to take prints from you gentlemen for elimination purposes.'

The officers went back to their car and drove away. Sukey took her prints, photographed the area where the fake weapon had fallen, cast a further brief look round and then, concluding that there was nothing more she could do in the way of gathering evidence, went back into the shop.

'Right, you can open up again now if you feel up to it,

Mr Curtis,' she told the proprietor. 'I'll get rid of the tape for you.'

To her surprise, Sam said, 'He's still a bit shaky, so I'll stay with him for a while. By the way,' he added, 'I've just remembered, I've seen that punk before.'

'Oh? Where?'

'At the entrance to the market hall in Eastgate, flogging magazines.'

'You mean the *Big Issue*?'

'That's the one. I'll mention it to the police if they get in touch with me again.'

'Yes, why not?'

Sukey packed away her kit and stowed it in the van. It was half-past three. She checked with the office and was told there were no jobs outstanding. She had half an hour to spare before her shift ended and it so happened that she was only a few minutes' drive from Belstone House. The opportunity was too good to miss.

When she reached the hotel, Mrs Milroy was at the reception desk. On seeing Sukey she said eagerly, 'Have you come to tell me our burglar has been arrested?'

'I'm afraid not,' said Sukey. 'We have to find him first.'

'Oh dear, how disappointing. I hope you'll find him soon.'

Sukey did not have the heart to tell her the truth. 'These things take time,' she said rather lamely. 'It's about the gentleman who came with Dave Somers, the one who claimed to be his uncle.'

'Oh, yes. I asked that young policewoman to mention him to DC Hill. Did he get my message?'

'Well, yes, but as I happened to be working on a job round the corner he asked me to call in and have a word,' said Sukey, mentally crossing her fingers over the blatant untruth. 'If you could tell me what it's about, I'll pass it on to him and then if he wants more information he'll come and see you.'

'Oh, all right.' Mrs Milroy's momentary look of disappointment changed to a smile with Sukey's final words. 'It's just that I never told DC Hill about the uncle, and I thought, if you could find him, he might be able to help us find Dave.'

'You may well be right, and Dave may know where the man who broke into his room hangs out. Can you give me a description of the uncle, and Dave as well, while I'm here?'

'Of course. I only saw the uncle once, you understand.'

'Never mind, just tell me what you can remember.'

Mrs Milroy closed her eyes for a moment. 'He was in his fifties, I'd say, and a little on the heavy side,' she began. 'Not fat, just . . . well built, you know.' Her smile was slightly arch as she went on, 'And he was wearing a smart grey suit, almost certainly made to measure . . . and he was *very* well spoken, a real gentleman.'

'Did he have a beard or a moustache?'

'No, he was clean-shaven.'

'What about his hair?'

'Sort of sandy coloured, I think, or maybe it was grey. I can't be sure, I'm afraid.'

'Never mind, that's something to go on. What about Dave? You saw more of him, obviously, as he was staying here.'

'Yes, of course.' Mrs Milroy gave another coy smile. 'Well now, he was about five foot ten, I suppose, and very good-looking – short brown hair, dark eyes, clean-cut features. He was clean-shaven too,' she went on, 'and nicely groomed, except for his hands. The nails were quite badly bitten. I remember scolding him about that.'

'Anything else? Any distinguishing marks, tattoos, scars—'

'If he had anything like that, I wouldn't know, would I?' Mrs Milroy simpered.

'Well, thank you, that's very helpful,' said Sukey as she put away her notebook and prepared to leave.

'If I think of anything else, I could phone the station and leave a message for DC Hill, couldn't I?'

Sukey hastily took one of her cards from her pocket and said, 'It might be better if you phoned me direct. Messages go astray sometimes.' The last thing she wanted was for it to become known that she had been doing the very thing Jim had forbidden her to do.

As she drove back to the station a new and somewhat disturbing notion began to form in her head. Mrs Milroy's description of Dave Somers' uncle tallied, so far as it went, with Jack's description of the 'posh bloke' who had come to Matt's rescue, but it was difficult to reconcile the 'nicely

61

groomed' young man who had stayed at Belstone House with the long-haired, bearded, scruffily dressed individual with whom she had often chatted as she bought her weekly copy of the *Big Issue*. Still, cleaned and smartened up, he might be quite presentable. She tried to visualize his hands, but was frustrated to find that her memory failed at this point. She had only a vague impression that, like the rest of him, they were rather grubby. But, she reflected as she turned into the police station yard, he did have dark eyes.

'You know something, Josh? I'm rapidly coming to the conclusion that you're a complete waste of space.'

'That's not fair, boss,' protested Josh. 'How was I to know the guy would jump ship like that?'

'You're the one who should have jumped, to stay ahead of that young stud you recruited. That's what I've been paying you for.' Scud strode up and down the Chinese washed-silk carpet, scowling. 'You sold me that crackpot scheme and then made a complete balls-up of it.'

Like a roller approaching the shore from a distant point out at sea, Josh felt the stirrings of a long-suppressed anger rising within him. The whole thing had been Scud's own idea; he had given specific instructions and Josh had followed them to the letter. When all appeared to be going well, Scud had preened himself on the plan's success. As soon as it started to go pear-shaped, it had suddenly become Josh's misbegotten brainchild.

It was just the latest in a long line of back-stabbings and humiliations. Josh knew that he was an object of pitying amusement to his colleagues, but he had laughed off the slights and the subtle bullying without betraying his festering resentment for one simple reason: money was his god and there was plenty of it in this game. But a man could take only so much. He felt the tide of rage within him gathering momentum as he watched Scud pouring himself a drink, pointedly refraining from inviting Josh to do the same. Instead, he held out the heavy decanter and said, as if addressing a servant, 'Put that away, will you?' Josh took it mechanically, but made no move to return it to its place.

Scud resumed his pacing up and down. 'Yes,' he said, taking

first a pull from the whisky tumbler and then a puff from his cigar, 'I think it's time to think about replacing you with someone who can do a job without making a cock-up of it.'

In a hoarse voice that he hardly recognized as his own, Josh said, 'You can't do that to me. Not after all this time, not after all I've done for you.'

'Who says I can't?'

'You're forgetting something, aren't you?'

'What's that?'

'I could drop you in the shit any time with the authorities.' Josh spat out the words; his voice rose to a thin squeak and his grip on the neck of the decanter tightened with the intensity of his fury.

'So it's blackmail now, is it?' The familiar, hateful, almost feline smile crept over Scud's fleshy features. 'You surely don't think you could get away with grassing me up without dropping yourself in the shit as well,' he said contemptuously. 'That's just the sort of half-arsed idea that confirms my belief that you've had your day.'

'You've got nothing on me,' Josh declared. He was on a roll now, throwing caution to the winds. 'I'm on your legitimate payroll and all our other dealings have been on a strictly cash basis with no records kept, remember? One anonymous phone call to Crimestoppers and the police would take you apart.'

Scud laughed, the deep, rumbling sound that always reminded Josh of an angry tomcat. 'Oh, yes, the little safety net you insisted on when we made our deal? I remember.' He drained his glass, looking Josh straight in the eye. 'What sort of a fool do you take me for?' he said softly. 'I've got enough on you to put you away for a long, long time, and it's tucked away where you can't get at it.' He turned his back and nonchalantly tapped the ash from his cigar into a heavy onyx ashtray.

'You treacherous bastard!' Josh hissed through his teeth. 'I've done your dirty work for you, I trusted you, and now you chuck me aside as if I was a piece of garbage.'

'In this game, dear boy, it's a mistake to trust anyone. Let it be a lesson to you.'

Ten

'Gosh, Mum, you really could be on to something!' exclaimed Fergus.

'You reckon?'

'But isn't it obvious? Dave Somers is your *Big Issue* seller Matt, and his so-called uncle is the posh guy who took care of him after he'd been mugged and then cleaned him up and installed him in that hotel . . . and I'll bet he wasn't just playing the Good Samaritan either.'

'You think the uncle's a crook?'

'Don't you?'

'Yes, Gus, I think I do, and I'm seriously worried about Matt. He's quite young and vulnerable, and like all the *Big Issue* sellers he's homeless and short of money. He'd be easy prey for a dealer to exploit.'

'You reckon the uncle's a dealer?'

'It wouldn't surprise me. I said at the time I thought the break-in might have something to do with drugs, and Jim said the same thing when we told him about it. He poured cold water on the suggestion of a connection between Evie Stanton's murder and the Belstone House incident, but just as he was leaving he warned me in no uncertain terms not to do any sleuthing on my own. And I also know the police suspect Trevor Blackton's got some scam going even though they can't pin anything on him.'

'Wow!' The lad's eyes sparkled. 'And Jim thinks there could be something in the idea, but he doesn't want you to risk getting mixed up with any serious villains.'

'In which case –' Sukey stopped in the middle of separating cauliflower florets – 'Matt might well be in serious danger.'

'So you have to find him and warn him.'

'Hang on, let's think this through. All we know for certain

about Dave Somers is that someone claiming to be his uncle installed him at Belstone House and he left in a hurry when he heard someone else was asking for him.'

'And hasn't been heard of since, and "uncle" hasn't enquired after him,' countered Gus. 'Doesn't that strike you as odd?'

'He could have made contact with uncle as soon as he left and been put into accommodation somewhere else.'

'All right, but that doesn't explain what made him do a runner in the first place.'

'No, but it doesn't prove that Dave and his uncle are the same people as Matt and the chap who rescued him from the mugger. The fact that they answer the same description – which is pretty general, when you come to think about it – could be pure coincidence. And there's nothing whatsoever to connect either Dave or Matt with Evie.'

'You're beginning to sound like Jim,' said Fergus accusingly.

'I'm just trying to be rational, but like you I have this nasty feeling about it. The trouble is, there's nothing concrete to go on.'

'Then let's dig around and see if we can turn something up. What about the fingerprints?'

'What fingerprints?'

'The ones you found at the murder scene. You said there were some unidentifiable ones that we presume belong to the boy-friend. Suppose you find a match with the ones in Dave's room?'

'I suppose I could have a check made.' Sukey stirred the beef stew she was reheating on the stove and threw the cauliflower florets into a pan of boiling water. 'I'll think about it. Dinner's nearly ready; get out the cutlery, will you?'

After dinner Fergus went up to his room, saying he had an essay to write. Later, they watched a film. As they said good night before going to bed, Fergus said to his mother, 'Don't forget about getting the prints checked, will you?'

'All right, anything to shut you up,' she said, giving him a gentle punch on the arm. Common sense told her it would probably be a waste of time, yet she could not rid herself of a sense of foreboding on behalf of the softly spoken young man who had sold magazines on a Gloucester street and then suddenly disappeared.

*　　*　　*

'Morning, ladies!' said George Barnes affably as Sukey and Mandy entered the SOCOs' room together on Tuesday morning. 'I hope you're feeling fit and strong. No gippy tummies or anything like that?'

'Why, is there a bug going round?' asked Sukey.

'No, just a rather messy corpse.'

'Oh, Lord, not another!' groaned Mandy. 'I've only just stopped having nightmares about Evie Stanton.'

'Not so much blood, but quite a bit of vomit to make up for it.' Barnes handed over the printout. 'I'm told the victim puked over a rather expensive carpet before he died.'

'Charming!' muttered Mandy as she studied the sheet. 'Where's Bishop's Heights?'

'It's an exclusive new block of flats on the Evesham Road. Good hunting, and try to hang on to your breakfasts.'

'That man's a sadist,' said Sukey as they made their way down to the yard to pick up their vans. 'Were you serious about the nightmares, by the way?'

'Not really,' Mandy admitted. 'I was just fishing for sympathy.'

'You'll be lucky!'

They consulted their maps, agreed on a route and set off.

Meanwhile, in the penthouse in Bishop's Heights, DI Castle and DS Radcliffe watched while Doc Hillbourne examined the inert form lying on the floor in a plainly but expensively furnished sitting room. From somewhere close at hand came the sound of hysterical sobbing.

'The housekeeper,' Radcliffe explained in response to Castle's questioning glance. 'She was the one who found him.'

'Isn't there anyone with her?'

'Trudy Marshall's making her a cup of tea.'

'I'll want to talk to her presently, so tell Trudy to find something a bit stronger than tea.'

'There's enough booze in there to stock a pub.' Radcliffe pointed to the well-equipped bar that occupied half of one wall.

'Better not touch that. There's probably cooking sherry or something in the kitchen.'

'I'll go and have a look.' Radcliffe left the room and Castle

66

went and stood beside Doc Hillbourne, who was squatting beside the body and studying the wound on the victim's forehead.

'Someone hit him a fair old crack,' commented the pathologist. 'That's the weapon, presumably.' He indicated the shattered remains of a heavy glass decanter which, judging from the discoloured patch on the rug and the whisky fumes that went some way towards neutralizing another, less agreeable odour, had been far from empty at the moment of impact.

'You reckon that was what killed him?' asked DI Castle.

Hillbourne pursed his lips and shook his head. 'Probably not. More likely he was only stunned by the blow, fell over backwards and choked on his own vomit while he was lying there unconscious. I can't be a hundred per cent sure till I've done a proper examination.'

'Any idea how long he's been dead?'

The pathologist got to his feet and peeled off his latex gloves. 'He's good and stiff, but it's a warm room and he's on the heavy side, so rigor would tend to be slow to set in. Over twelve hours, not more than thirty-six, is the best estimate I can give at the moment.'

'Let's hope we can get a bit closer when we've spoken to some witnesses,' said Castle.

'When the housekeeper's calmed down, see if she can tell you what time he had dinner yesterday evening. That might help. Right, I'm going to have my breakfast. You'll get my report later.' He picked up his bag and left the room just as Radcliffe returned.

'How he can think about breakfast after dealing with that is beyond me,' the sergeant commented with a grimace.

'Cast-iron stomach,' Castle observed.

There was a tap on the door. A uniformed policeman popped his head in and said, 'The SOCOs are here, Guv.'

'OK, bring them in.'

Even before her eyes focused on the recumbent figure, Sukey felt her gorge rise as she entered the room. Mandy put a handkerchief over her nose. 'George Barnes wasn't kidding, was he?' she muttered.

'Doesn't exactly smell of roses, does he?' commented Jim.

'That should be an incentive not to hang around . . . but not an excuse to cut corners, mind you.' He glanced round the room. 'Nothing seems to have been disturbed and there's no sign of a struggle, so it shouldn't take too long. Sergeant Radcliffe and I are going to talk to a couple of witnesses. Let one of us know when you've finished in here.'

'Yes, Guv.'

Mandy cast an appraising glance round the room. 'No books, no telly, no flowers or ornaments,' she commented. 'Just those leather armchairs, a coffee table, a cupboard and that enormous desk in the corner. All top quality and very pricey by the looks of them, but it's not exactly cosy.'

'Perhaps he used this room as an office,' Sukey suggested. 'He was probably a businessman who liked to talk to clients at home. And give them plenty of booze,' she added as her eyes went to the bar.

Mandy shrugged. 'Maybe. Any idea who he is?'

'Not a clue. Let's get on with it, shall we? This place stinks.'

They set about their gruesome task. Whenever they worked as a team, it was Sukey who photographed the scene while Mandy checked for fingerprints. At the same time they both kept their eyes open for any piece of evidence, however small, which might help the detectives in their hunt for the criminal.

'That's interesting,' said Sukey. She pointed to the glass-topped coffee table on which stood a heavy onyx ashtray, and then to a line of grey ash on the polished marble hearth. 'He must have lit a cigar not long before he was killed. He tapped one lot of ash into the ashtray, but before he'd smoked it down much further someone bashed him over the head and it fell onto the hearth where it burned itself out.'

'Good thing it didn't fall on the carpet or the whole place might have gone up in smoke,' observed Mandy. 'And here's something else. He was having a drink as well. There's a whisky tumbler behind the chair. I almost missed it.'

'So there is. It must have rolled when he fell.' Sukey crouched down and focused her camera. 'Is there another one anywhere?'

'Doesn't seem to be.'

'So he wasn't having a drink with his killer?'

'Doesn't look like it. And from the looks of things,' Mandy squatted down beside Sukey, 'that was empty when he dropped it. There's no sign of any spillage from it.' With a gloved hand she hooked a finger inside the tumbler and carefully transferred it into a plastic bag.

'He was struck from the front, so either he was having a face-to-face argument with the person who attacked him, or he was tapping the ash from his cigar but still facing the door when someone who'd sneaked into the flat without his knowledge burst into the room, grabbed the decanter and lashed out at him,' Sukey mused. 'If this was premeditated and the attacker had lain in wait for him, he'd surely have chosen a better weapon. It looks to me like a spur-of-the-moment attack with whatever came to hand.'

'Here we go again!' said Mandy. 'Try to remember you're a humble SOCO, not an ace detective. Maybe the killer took a swipe at him because he was narked at not being offered a drink,' she added facetiously.

'Ha ha, very funny!' Sukey glanced round the room. 'Have we done?'

'I think so. I'll have these checked in the lab.' Mandy held up some more plastic bags containing the neck of the shattered decanter and other fragments of glass. 'By the way, this thing was engraved. It looks as if it was presented to him by some golf club.'

'That should help CID track down some of his contacts,' Sukey remarked. 'Mandy, will you go and report to DI Castle while I finish packing my stuff away?'

'OK, see you in the car park.'

Mandy bustled off. Sukey put away her camera, closed her bag and went to the door. Something made her pause and turn round; despite her wish to escape from the fetid atmosphere of the room into the fresh air, she felt impelled to take another look at the murder victim. Until now, she had regarded him with a professional detachment, working quickly and methodically, taking her pictures from every angle and in every sickening detail. Now, for some reason she could not have explained, she found herself thinking of him as a human being. A well-built man with thinning grey hair, middle-aged, wearing a Cartier watch, a designer suit and shoes that looked hand made. A wealthy man who enjoyed an expensive lifestyle. Someone whom people like Lucy and Jack would undoubtedly have described as 'posh'.

She stared at the body for several seconds and then, again without stopping to analyse her motive, she did a quick tour of the other rooms in the apartment. There was, she felt, something odd about the set-up, something she could not quite put her finger on.

Eleven

Having left the SOCOs to carry out their examination of the crime scene, DI Castle, guided by the sound of quiet weeping, put his head round an adjacent door and beckoned to WPC Marshall. She came out into the hall, closing the door behind her.

'Is the housekeeper in a fit state to be interviewed, Trudy?'

'Just about. I found some brandy and put a slug of it in her tea; it's calmed her down a bit, but I don't think it would take much to set her off again.'

'Right, I'll treat her gently. What has she told you so far?'

'Her name's Mrs Pomeroy, she's a widow and she's been Mr Dalsey's housekeeper ever since his mother died about five years ago. She's got no children so he's been an important part of her world.'

'Is Dalsey the victim's name?'

'So she says.'

'What else has she told you about him?'

'Not a great deal – just the usual stuff about what a lovely gentleman he was and how could such a thing happen to him, and if only she'd found him earlier he might still be alive.'

'She could well be right,' said Castle thoughtfully. 'Doc Hillbourne was pretty sure the blow on the head only stunned him. I understand the 999 call came at about half-past eight this morning, so presumably she doesn't live in.'

'No, she has a council flat in Cheltenham. She commutes by bus every day Monday to Friday to clean the place, make his bed, do his washing and cook his evening meal. It wouldn't surprise me if she did his mending and cleaned his shoes as well – she seems to have been absolutely devoted to him.'

'You've done well to get all that out of her in such a short time.'

71

'I didn't really have to ask her, it all came pouring out,' the young policewoman admitted modestly.

'It's your sympathetic manner, Trudy,' DS Radcliffe interposed with a grin. 'When you retire from the force you'll make a splendid agony aunt for the *Daily Scream*.'

'Quite,' Castle agreed without a smile. 'You'd better sit in while I'm questioning her, Trudy. Andy, you go and find the caretaker or whoever's in charge here and see what information he can give you about the victim himself. Ask him about visitors, either regular or occasional, and see if you can locate any witnesses who've noticed anyone arriving or leaving or hanging around the premises within the crucial period.'

'Right, Guv.' If Radcliffe felt any irritation at being told to do the obvious, he gave no sign. Jim Castle was like that; he treated every case with the same detached, professional thoroughness, taking nothing for granted and leaving nothing to chance.

'OK, let's get on with this interview,' said Castle. 'Where is the lady?'

'This way, sir.' Trudy led the way into the kitchen. A middle-aged woman was seated at a heavy oak table in the centre of the room with her back to the door. Her shoulders were hunched and her head bowed; she had stopped crying, but she was breathing heavily in short, strangled gasps and gave no sign of being aware of their presence.

The kitchen had evidently been designed and equipped without regard for cost, although he noticed that, as in the room where the body had been found, there was nothing that was not strictly functional. Evidently Mr Dalsey had plain, if expensive tastes. A watery November sun struck highlights from polished marble work surfaces and gleaming stainless-steel utensils and appliances.

Castle touched the woman gently on the arm and said, 'Mrs Pomeroy? I'm Detective Inspector Castle. Do you feel able to answer one or two questions?'

She raised her head slowly, like someone waking from a deep sleep. Her face was blotchy and her features distorted; she made an abortive effort to wipe away the tears still silently welling from reddened eyes so swollen that they appeared half closed. She nodded without speaking, her free hand clutching the handle of an empty mug as if for support.

'Would you like another cup of tea?' She shook her head. 'I understand how distressing this must be for you,' he went on. 'You've had a terrible shock.' She nodded again and scrubbed her eyes with a lump of sodden paper tissue. Trudy took it from her hand and gave her a fresh supply from a box lying on the table.

'Thank you,' she whispered. 'You're very kind.'

Trudy sat down beside her and put an arm round her shoulders. 'I'm sure you are as anxious as we are to find the person who attacked Mr Dalsey,' she said. 'Just do the best you can to answer the Inspector's questions. The more help you can give us, the more chance we have of catching him.'

'I'll try.'

Castle pulled up a chair and sat down on the other side of the table while Trudy pulled out her notebook. 'I understand from WPC Marshall that you have been Mr Dalsey's housekeeper for about five years,' he began. 'Is that right?' Mrs Pomeroy nodded.

'And I believe you found him a very good employer?'

'One of the best. A perfect gentleman and very considerate.' Her eyes began to fill again and Castle hastily moved on to his next question.

'It seems there is someone who doesn't share your high regard for him,' he said. 'Have you any idea at all who that person might be? A business rival, for example?'

Mrs Pomeroy started as if she had been stung. Castle had the impression that up to now the shock of finding her employer's body had so traumatized her that her mind had not fully grasped the fact that there was some individual who bore him such ill will that they attacked him and then left him lying unconscious to choke to death on his own vomit. Grief suddenly gave place to fury.

'No idea at all, but I hope you catch the swine and lock him away for ever!' She spat the words out through her teeth, her features contorted with hatred.

'We'll catch him, you can be sure of that,' Castle assured her. 'Now, as you've worked for Mr Dalsey for so long, perhaps you know some of his friends or business acquaintances.'

Mrs Pomeroy shook her head. 'I never saw any of them,' she said. 'I wasn't here in the evening and Mr Dalsey was out during the day, attending to his business.'

'What business was that?'

'I don't know. He never spoke about it to me.'

'What did you talk about when he was here?'

The question seemed to puzzle her and she ran her fingers through her short, iron-grey hair. 'I didn't really see that much of him,' she said after a moment. 'We'd chat for a few minutes when he came home, but only about ordinary things.'

'So you were alone during the day?'

'That's right. I didn't mind.' She sounded almost defensive, as if the question implied a criticism of her employer. 'I used to do the housework and the shopping and so on, cook and serve his dinner in the evening and then go home.'

'And you come in at what time in the morning?'

'Eight o'clock. Mr Dalsey would usually be up and in the shower and he'd come in here for his breakfast at half-past.'

'So what happened this morning?'

Mrs Pomeroy shuddered and put her hands over her eyes. 'It was terrible,' she whispered. 'When half-past eight came and there was no sign of him I realized his radio wasn't on and I hadn't heard him moving about. I got worried so I went and knocked several times on his bedroom door and he didn't answer, so after a moment I peeped round the door and saw his bed hadn't been slept in. I went into his office and saw him lying there in a dreadful state, his face all blue . . .' Her voice trailed away on the final words.

'Did you touch him?' asked Castle. She shuddered and shook her head. 'Did you touch anything else?'

'No.' Her voice was so faint he could barely hear it. Without warning she collapsed in a further storm of weeping which lasted several minutes while Trudy made soothing noises and stroked her hand.

When she was quiet again Castle said, 'When Mr Dalsey came home yesterday evening, did you notice anything unusual about his manner?'

She shook her head. 'No, he was his normal self.'

'Did he say anything to you?'

'Nothing special, just asked if everything was all right and if there was any post.'

'Did he receive much post?'

'Not much. It was mostly junk anyway. I think most of his letters went to his business address.'

'Do you know where that is?' Again she shook her head. 'Where did you serve his dinner?'

'Here.'

'What time would that be?'

'Seven o'clock, on the dot. Regular as clockwork, Mr Dalsey was. He'd come in about half-past six and go into his office until his dinner was ready. I never had to call him, he'd appear in the kitchen just as the pips were going on the radio for the news.'

'And did you clear away afterwards, before going home?'

'No. He'd leave the dishes on the draining board and I'd clear them away and wash up when I came in the next morning.'

'By his office, I take it you mean the room where you found him?'

'That's right.' The reference to the death scene threatened to trigger a fresh wave of grief, but Mrs Pomeroy made a brave effort to keep her self-control. 'His desk's in there, and a cupboard behind it for his computer.'

'I see.' Castle made a note to have the computer checked. 'Did he ever have a guest for dinner?'

'I never cooked for more than one. Sometimes he'd say he was having a meal out and tell me I could go home early. Maybe he entertained guests at a restaurant, but I wouldn't know. Sometimes I'd find a second whisky glass and cigar end in the office and I just assumed a friend had called during the evening, but I never saw them.'

Castle had a feeling that his next question would cause offence, but it had to be asked just the same. He cleared his throat and said, 'Mrs Pomeroy, did you ever notice anything to suggest that Mr Dalsey entertained a lady in his flat? Did you detect any hint of perfume, or . . .' he hesitated again in an unaccustomed fit of embarrassment on seeing her swollen features turn a dull crimson, 'any suggestion that the bedding had been disturbed . . . or perhaps . . . stained?'

75

'Certainly not!' If breathing fire were a physical possibility, the detective would have been consumed in a sheet of flame on the spot.

'I apologize if I've offended you,' Castle said hastily. 'I'm afraid it's sometimes necessary to ask unpleasant questions.'

'Yes, well, I'll thank you not to blacken the name of a gentleman who can't defend himself.' Mrs Pomeroy rose to her feet, gathered up the empty mugs and put them in the dishwasher. 'If that's all, I've got work to do,' she said. 'There's last night's dishes to see to,' she indicated a small amount of crockery and cutlery stacked on the gleaming, stainless-steel draining board, 'and the office carpet to clean up. Goodness knows how I'm going to get rid of the stain. Mr Dalsey's very particular, he'll be so upset—' She clapped a hand over her mouth and uttered a low moan. 'What am I saying? The poor man's dead and gone. What will I do now?'

Castle and Trudy exchanged glances. 'You'd better stay with her for a while,' he said in a low voice. 'Find out if she has any relatives or a neighbour we can contact. I'll go and see if the SOCOs have finished and then arrange to have the body taken away.'

In the hall he bumped into Sukey as she emerged from the room opposite. 'Find anything interesting?' he asked.

'Not a great deal. A few fingerprints, but not many. It looks as if the room has been spring-cleaned recently – every surface shines like a new pin.'

'That figures. His housekeeper seems to be a housework freak – she must spend most of her time cleaning and polishing. Looking after him seems to have been her main interest in life. She couldn't tell us much about him, though, except that he runs some kind of business, but she doesn't know what.'

'We think he belonged to a golf club.' Sukey reported Mandy's findings. 'We're going to get the boffins to piece the decanter together so we can find out which one.'

'That should be a help. Have you looked in the other rooms?'

'Just a glance, but they don't tell us anything. There's a sitting room with a wonderful view across to the Malverns and a dining room and two bedrooms with en suite bathrooms, but everything has a sort of unused appearance. Except for the toilet things in one of the bathrooms and the robe hanging on the back of the door, you'd be hard put to it to guess which room he slept in. The place is like a hotel suite made ready for the next guest.'

'I wonder why he went to the expense of living in a place like this and only used a couple of rooms,' Castle observed, almost to himself.

'It does seem unusual,' Sukey agreed. 'If that's all for now, sir, I'll be getting back to the station with these films.'

As Castle watched her striding briskly towards the lift he made a mental note to call her at home later on to find out if by chance Fergus had any plans to be away before the Christmas holidays. It seemed a long time since they had spent a night together. He went back into the apartment, mentally cursing the lost opportunity when Fergus had been in Germany and he hadn't known about it through sheer pressure of work.

His thoughts were interrupted by Trudy, who emerged from the kitchen and said, 'She lives with her elderly mother but she won't hear of anyone phoning the old lady for fear of upsetting her. There's a sister in Evesham; I've tried to call her but there's no reply. Mrs P. thinks she's probably out shopping so I'll try again in a little while.'

'Fine. Remember to get her prints – and make sure she understands they're only elims. We don't want her to think she's a suspect.'

'Right, sir.'

'I'll go and find Andy Radcliffe now and see if he's come up with anything.'

As he waited for the lift, it struck Castle that throughout the interview Mrs Pomeroy had used the past tense when speaking of her late employer. In his experience, more often than not when witnesses were in a similar state of shock, they would speak of the deceased as if he were still alive, as if they had not yet fully grasped the finality of death. In spite of the fact that barely two hours had passed since she raised the alarm, it was only at the end that she had referred to him in the present. It might mean nothing at all, of course, but it was something to bear in mind.

Twelve

W hen Sukey stepped out of the private lift from the penthouse she found DS Radcliffe at the entrance to the foyer talking to a thickset, ruddy-faced man of about fifty clad in jeans and an anorak. As she approached, the man was saying, in a loud, emphatic voice with a distinctive Gloucestershire burr, 'There's no way anyone can get into this building without either knowing the security code or by pressing this buzzer for whatever apartment they want and being let in by one of the residents.'

'That seems pretty foolproof,' said the sergeant. 'Well, sir, I'm very grateful to you for your assistance.'

'Delighted to be of service to the boys in blue! If there's anything else I can do to help you clear up this tragic business, just give me a call. You have my number.'

'Yes, sir, thank you very much. I'm sure you have a lot of things to attend to so I won't detain you any longer.'

'Oh, yes, always something to see to in this job.' The man gave an exaggerated salute, strode away along a flagged path separating the building from an immaculately tended garden and vanished round the corner. Moments later he reappeared at the wheel of a blue Vauxhall, drove slowly down the drive and turned into the road.

'Pompous prat,' observed Radcliffe.

'Is he the caretaker?' asked Sukey.

'Sort of. He's the tenants' first line of contact if there's any kind of problem in their apartments, and he also supervises the maintenance of the grounds. He doesn't live on the premises, but there's an extra garage at the back of the building that does double duty as an office and storage for tools, ladders and so on. He holds a master key to the apartments, but he was very quick to assure me that it never leaves his possession.'

'So he could have got into Dalsey's apartment any time he wanted?'

'Of course.' Radcliffe looked amused. 'Another suspect for Sook the Sleuth to investigate? The Great White Chief won't be pleased if you go muscling in on his territory.'

'Have you and Jim been talking about me behind my back?' she demanded, a little resentfully. 'I just keep my eyes open, that's all.'

'There's no need to get on your high horse. We're both concerned that you don't go running into danger.' He was, so far as she and Jim were aware, one of only a handful of officers at the station who knew of their relationship, and he seldom alluded to it. The friendship between the two men went back many years and the difference in rank made no difference during their off-duty hours.

'I know you mean well,' she admitted. 'I also know you've both been quite dismissive on occasions of what have turned out to be flashes of brilliance on my part.'

'Yes, I can't deny that,' he admitted. 'Just the same, it might be an idea in future to let us know what you're up to before you make your next arrest.'

She put up a hand in mock surrender. 'OK, Sarge, point taken. I must get on, so I'll leave you to it.'

She went back to the visitors' car park where she and Mandy had left their vans along with three police vehicles, one of them unmarked, and DI Castle's Mondeo. An undertaker's hearse was parked discreetly in the far corner. Two people in plain clothes whom Sukey recognized as members of the CID were there as well, one chatting to Mandy and the other talking on her mobile phone. As Sukey approached she snapped off the phone, beckoned to the driver of the hearse and called, 'All clear for you guys to take the body,' before turning to her colleague and saying, 'As soon as they've done their stuff, we can go in and get on with the search.'

'Any ideas?' asked Mandy as she and Sukey packed away their equipment.

'What about?'

'Who dunnit, of course!' said Mandy with a twinkle. 'Don't tell me you haven't yet spotted the vital clue that leads to the killer!'

'Don't you start!' said Sukey in mock exasperation. 'I've already had Andy Radcliffe giving me a lecture because I happened to point out that the caretaker had unrestricted access to the apartment.'

'Good thinking, Sherlock. I'm sure none of the CID whiz-kids would have thought of that.'

'I can see I'll have to crack the case on my own to make you all take me seriously,' Sukey sighed. At that moment her mobile rang. Mrs Milroy was on the line.

'Oh, Ms Reynolds, I thought you'd like to know that Dave's uncle has been here looking for him,' she said. 'When I told him he'd left he was very surprised . . . and rather perturbed. He said if Dave should get in touch I was to tell him to call him right away.'

'Did he leave an address or phone number?'

'No. I did suggest it, but all he said was that Dave knew where to find him, and he left.'

'When was this, Mrs Milroy?'

'Yesterday afternoon, about five o'clock. I would have called you before, but I was very busy at the time and I'm afraid it slipped my mind.'

'That's all right. Thank you for letting me know.'

'Something interesting?' asked Mandy, seeing Sukey momentarily lost in thought.

'I'm not sure.' The idea that had begun to form in Sukey's mind as she stood taking a final look at Dalsey's body was still in an embryonic state and she was not yet prepared to share it with anyone else, but it occupied her thoughts on and off during the rest of her shift.

When she arrived home she found a note from Fergus on the kitchen table. *Have had a call from Anita. Everything OK, she thought my letter was a hoot and says Marcel's a creep anyway. She asked me to pass a message to her parents and they've invited me for supper. See you later, Gus.*

'Well, thank goodness for that,' Sukey said aloud as she filled the kettle for a cup of tea. Life in the little semi in Brockworth would be easier without the shadow of teenage angst hanging over it. Having been apparently comforted by her words of wisdom and taken her advice to write a light-hearted response to the letter from his beloved that had blighted his life, Fergus had nevertheless spent the past few days rushing to the phone every time it rang and handing it over to his mother with an expression of deepest gloom when the call was not for him. It was a relief to know that what might have mushroomed into a major crisis between two emotional young people had been amicably settled. It also meant that she had the evening to herself.

She was about to reach for the telephone when it rang and a voice that sent a warm wave of happiness through her body said, 'Any chance of seeing you this evening?'

'Oh, yes, please!'

She read the note aloud and he said, 'Great! I'll be with you around six.'

She was drifting off to sleep when Jim raised himself on one elbow and whispered in her ear, 'When are we going to eat?'

She turned over and nestled against him. 'What's the hurry?' she murmured.

'I didn't have any lunch.'

She put an arm round him and ran her fingers down his spine. 'Poor old thing,' she said, her lips brushing his chest.

'Aren't you hungry?'

She nestled even closer. 'Only for you.'

He gave a groan of mock despair. 'How do you expect a man to cope with an insatiable woman on an empty stomach?'

She silenced him with a lingering kiss. After a few seconds she broke away with a sigh of resignation, 'All right, I suppose I'll have to feed the brute.' She slid out of bed and began putting on her clothes. 'Steak and chips OK?'

'Brilliant. Any idea what time Gus will be home?'

'Probably not before ten, but we'd better be decent in case it's earlier.'

They went downstairs to the kitchen and Sukey began preparing the food while Jim opened the bottle of wine he had brought with him.

'This feels almost like a celebration,' she remarked as they clinked glasses. 'Gus's ruined love life has been miraculously restored and you and I have had a chance to –' she moved

81

round the table and kissed him gently on the cheek – 'make up for lost time.'

He held her close for a long moment. 'That's what police work does to one's love life,' he said.

'But you wouldn't be happy doing any other job.'

'True.'

'So bring me up to date with what you've been doing for the past ten days. Any progress in the Evie Stanton case?'

'Not a lot. Tony Hill's been drip-feeding vodka and tonic to one of her old associates called Julie who claimed to have useful information, hoping he might pick up a lead to Evie's last visitor before she was killed.'

'And was it useful?'

'Not really. She added a bit to her original story; she told Tony that when Evie was on the game she used to offer the kinky stuff, but we knew that already; we found some of the gear in her room. It's gone to forensic, but where it'll lead us, if anywhere, is anybody's guess. Julie also said that she heard from another girl who used to work the same patch as Evie that after Trevor Blackton took her up she boasted that she was having fun and games on the side – with more than one playmate.'

'More than one, eh?' Sukey raised an eyebrow. 'Evie was quite a goer, by the sound of it.'

'Right. What she couldn't tell us was who the playmates were or how many of them there were. We've now had two sightings of young men sneaking through the back gate, but the descriptions were too vague for us to establish whether they were two different blokes, or the same one making a return call.'

'Bit of a waste of vodka,' Sukey observed as she turned the steaks under the grill.

'You never know, it might turn out to be useful, once we can lay our hands on Trevor Blackton.'

Mention of the name sent a chill down Sukey's spine. Her immediate thought was for Matt. 'No sign of him yet?'

'Not a sniff. We think he's still in the country, but we've no leads.'

'I reckon he's keeping out of sight while he tracks down the guy Evie was two-timing him with.'

'That's what worries us. We're asking the Super to authorize us to release a picture of Trev. It would be useful if we could put an E-FIT of Evie's mysterious visitor together, but the descriptions are useless.'

'I've just had an idea,' said Sukey.

'Oh, yes?' Jim cocked an eyebrow as he topped up their glasses. 'Another flash of Sherlockian inspiration?'

'Could be,' she retorted. 'Matt the *Big Issue* seller hasn't reappeared, so why don't you let me have a go at an E-FIT of him? Suppose he's one of the toy boys?'

'Be reasonable. Where would a down-and-out get the money to pay for sex with a tart?'

'From the posh guy who played the Good Samaritan when Matt was mugged, perhaps? No one seems to know who he is, or why he took such an interest.'

'Really, Sukey, aren't people allowed to do good deeds without you suspecting them of an ulterior motive?'

'Suppose he's a dealer who was planning to use Matt in his organization? That would put money in his pocket. Or,' she paused with her glass halfway to her mouth as she remembered the possibility she and Fergus had considered, 'supposing he's part of Blackton's mob?'

'Now you really are letting your imagination run away with you.'

'Why do you brush aside every suggestion I make without even considering it?' she demanded in a sudden wave of irritation. 'You can be so bloody patronizing at times.'

'And you can come up with the most far-fetched ideas.'

They glared at one another, their earlier intimacy for the moment forgotten.

'Well, here's another far-fetched notion for you to sneer at,' she said angrily. 'I had a call from the owner of Belstone House today saying that the uncle had turned up to see Dave. A well-dressed, prosperous looking gentleman.'

'So?'

'She said he had no idea his nephew had left the hotel and he seemed very concerned. He said if she should hear from Dave would she ask him to get in touch, but he wouldn't give her his address or phone number. Doesn't that strike you as odd?'

'Why should it? Presumably Dave would know where to find his uncle if he wanted to.'

'Supposing he can't? What if Trevor Blackton's boys have caught up with him already?'

'What if we dropped the subject and had something to eat?' He took her hand in a conciliatory gesture. 'Come on, love, don't spoil a beautiful evening.'

'Oh all right, have it your way,' she said, a little ungraciously. Experience told her there was no point in pushing him further.

Later, however, when she put out her light and snuggled down in the bed where they had so recently made love, she made a resolution. Neither Mandy's teasing, Andy's lecture nor Jim's dismissive attitude was going to stop her pursuing her hunch that between a series of apparently unconnected incidents lay a connecting thread that a little judicious probing might bring to the surface.

Thirteen

O ver breakfast the following morning, Sukey asked, 'How was your supper with Anita's folks, Gus?'

'Oh, fine.' A beatific smile spread over her son's face. 'Anita's French family took her with them to their country house and she emailed them some photos. Her dad printed off these copies for me on his computer.' Fergus passed his mother half a dozen pictures of Anita with her host family, including several of various members of the party out riding. 'Doesn't she look wonderful on a horse?' he said, gazing rapturously at a shot of his beloved mounted on a handsome chestnut.

'She certainly does,' Sukey agreed. 'Do all those nags belong to the family?'

'Oh, yes, they've got their own stables and a groom to look after them.'

'They must be filthy rich.'

'I guess so. They're going to take her with them to Martinique in the summer,' Fergus went on. His face clouded for a moment and he said wistfully, 'I'd give anything to go with her.' He began feeding slices of bread into the toaster. 'What sort of a day did you have yesterday, Mum?'

'A bit gruesome.' Sukey shuddered at the recollection of the scene in the penthouse apartment. She pushed aside her cereal bowl and picked up her glass of orange juice. 'We've had another messy murder.'

Her son's eyes gleamed in anticipation. 'Do tell!' he said eagerly.

'I'd rather not go into details. It's enough to put both of us off our toast and marmalade.' She finished her juice and filled the kettle for their coffee.

'Who was the victim?'

'A man called Dalsey. We don't know much about him at

the moment except that he was once president of a golf club and his housekeeper thinks the sun shines out of his backside.' She sketched in the circumstances without describing the scene in graphic detail. 'Incidentally,' she added, 'it occurred to me that Dalsey might be Dave Somers' mysterious uncle.'

Fergus looked puzzled. 'What gave you that idea?'

'I just had this weird feeling – it's almost as if there's a sort of equation. Dave Somers plus his mysterious uncle equals Matt and his Good Samaritan. Matt goes missing, Dave goes missing, and Uncle lurks in the shadows. There's been no further sign of the Samaritan, but a man answering his general description has been topped. Is there a connection?'

'Gosh!' The lad's eyes sparkled with excitement. 'So you still reckon this Matt/Dave character could be Evie's toy boy?'

'I think it's a strong possibility, but Jim got quite shirty last time I mentioned it. The police are pretty sure Trevor Blackton's planning a revenge attack, but they're not interested in Matt – he's not even listed as a missing person. No,' Sukey got up and began spooning coffee into the cafetière, 'there's only one thing for it. I'll have to do a spot of sleuthing of my own.'

'Mum, Jim warned you against doing just that,' Fergus said anxiously.

'Don't worry, I'm not planning anything risky, just asking some of the other *Big Issue* sellers. There are at least four of them selling the magazine from various pitches in the city centre and I'm pretty sure they all know each other. One of them might know where Matt used to doss before Uncle took him under his wing. Maybe they know where he is now and are protecting him.'

'You think he knows he's in danger and that's why he did a runner from the hotel?' Fergus frowned. 'I don't like it,' he said. 'You might be putting yourself in the firing line. Supposing one of Blackton's boys got wind of what you're up to?'

'I don't see how they could.' Sukey took two mugs from a cupboard and filled them with coffee. 'One thing puzzles me, though, and that's how Uncle fits into the picture. Assuming he and Dalsey are one and the same, what would Trevor Blackton have against him?'

'Search me. Unless,' Fergus went on with a flash of creativity, 'he introduced Matt to Evie, so Trevor holds him responsible for her faithlessness and is out for further revenge.'

'That would make him a paranoid psychopath. The police have had an eye on him for some time because they think he's into some kind of scam, possibly the drugs scene, but so far as I know they don't think he's a fruitcake.'

'I don't suppose they know everything about him.' Fergus looked at his mother with a slightly uneasy expression. 'Mum, I really think you should keep out of it.'

'Don't worry; I'm not in the business of tracking down psychopaths. All I want is a quiet word with Matt.'

'You mentioned once that he had problems. What were they?'

'He's a well-educated chap, but he had a very disturbed home background so he dropped out of school and ran away. He always seemed very nervous, almost as if he expected his stepfather or some kind of official to turn up unexpectedly and cart him back where he came from.'

'But they couldn't do that, not unless he's under age.'

'That's what I told him, but he had a kind of fixation about it. I think he needs therapy, but of course he'd never get it while living rough and he refused point blank to consider going into a hostel.'

'In that case, would he have agreed to go and live at Belstone House?'

'He might, if there was sufficient inducement. That's where the mysterious uncle comes in. And if he was involved with Evie, he's in very real rather than imaginary danger. If only Jim would listen to me.' Sukey slammed her empty coffee mug on the table in exasperation.

'Mum, I do believe you're turning into a Good Samaritan yourself.' Fergus got up and gave his mother a hug. 'You will be careful, though, won't you . . . and be sure to pass on to Jim right away anything you find out about Matt or Blackton.'

'Of course I will.' She glanced up at the clock on the wall and leapt to her feet. 'Heavens, look at the time! I must go to work and you must get ready for college. See you later.'

At lunchtime, finding herself at an assignment close to the city centre, Sukey went back to the station to eat her sandwiches in the canteen. As she collected a cup of tea at the counter she spotted Trudy at a table on her own, tucking into sausages, egg, bacon and chips.

'Hi!' she said. 'Mind if I join you?'

Temporarily speechless, Trudy gestured to Sukey to sit down. When she was free to speak, she said, 'Any more stiffs this morning?'

'No, thank goodness, just common or garden break-ins and a stolen car recovered with a known villain's prints all over it.' Sukey took a swig of tea and unwrapped her packet of sandwiches. 'How did you get on with Mrs Pomeroy yesterday? Did you manage to contact the sister?'

'Eventually. It began to look as if she was out for the day, but I got hold of her at last and handed Mrs Pom-Pom over to her at about one.'

'So you were stuck with the old dear for a couple of hours. Poor you.'

Trudy shook her head and speared a chip and a piece of sausage. 'As a matter of fact,' she said when she had swallowed them, 'she's not that old. It was quite interesting talking to her after you and everyone else had gone. I gave her another slug of brandy and after a while she came out of her state of shock and let drop one interesting bit of information.'

'Really? Do tell.'

'Well, not exactly information, more of a titbit.'

'What sort of titbit?'

'I think Mrs Pom-Pom's sweet on the caretaker.' Trudy giggled at the recollection. 'She was a bit tight by this time and when I asked what the arrangements were for maintenance of the apartments and the grounds and so on, she went all giggly and pink and said it was someone called Mr Granger who's "ever so nice". It's not as improbable as you might think,' Trudy added, seeing Sukey's look of astonishment. 'She was quite passable-looking once she'd tidied her hair and bathed her eyes.'

'It must be the man I met after I'd finished checking the murder scene,' said Sukey. 'Andy Radcliffe called him a pompous twit, and I must say that's how he struck me.'

'Well, there's no accounting for taste.'

'Tell me, did Mrs P. mention any visitors? A young man somewhere in his twenties, for example?'

Trudy raised her eyebrows. 'You think Dalsey might have been attacked by a gay lover?'

'No, that isn't what I had in mind. Well, did she? Mention visitors,' Sukey repeated impatiently, as Trudy still appeared to be digesting the possible implications of the question.

'No, she didn't. In fact, she repeated what she'd said earlier about never seeing any of Dalsey's visitors. It's amazing really how little she's learned about him in five years. He could have had any number of visitors at various times and she'd have been none the wiser.'

'But never more than one at a time?'

Trudy shrugged. 'Presumably not. I don't see where all this is leading, though.'

Sukey glanced round to make sure no one was within earshot. 'Look, Trudy, will you promise to keep to yourself what I'm going to tell you now?'

Trudy looked dubious. 'If it's something crucial to the investigation, I don't think I can. In any case, if you know something important, why don't you tell DI Castle? I'm sure you have his ear.'

Sukey ignored the implication. 'It isn't anything I know, just a hunch. And as it happens, I've already told him and he brushed it aside.'

'OK, spill it.'

Sukey lowered her voice and rapidly outlined her theory. When she had finished, Trudy gave a soft whistle. 'Bloody hell!' she exclaimed. 'I've heard some conspiracy theories in my time, but that takes the biscuit. I'm not surprised Eagle-Eyes turned it down. Just the same,' she went on after a moment's thought, 'there could just be something in it, I suppose. Nothing's impossible. Why have you told me, anyway?'

'Because I'd like you to keep me up to date with anything you find out about either of the two cases. I can't ask anyone in CID or it'd get back to Jim – DI Castle – in no time and he's warned me off playing at private detectives.'

Trudy grinned. 'Won't you ever learn?'

Sukey grinned back. 'I doubt it.'

'All right, I'll do it – on one condition.'

'What's that?'

'That if you and I manage to crack the case together, we share the medals.'

'Done!'

Sukey finished her tea and sandwiches and checked the time on the canteen clock. She still had fifteen minutes left of her lunch hour; there was just enough time to pop into the city centre and see who was on *Big Issue* duty.

Fourteen

Sukey hurried along Bull Lane and turned right into Westgate. On reaching the Cross, she was disappointed to find that there was no sign of Lucy. However, a short distance along Eastgate, Jack was apparently on the point of leaving.

'Sorry, love, sold out,' he said cheerfully in response to her greeting. 'Been a good day today, the weather's put people in the right mood.'

'Yes, it's great to see the sun, isn't it?' she agreed. 'Actually I wanted a word with you, if you aren't in a hurry.'

'I was just about to pop over the way for a coffee,' Jack said.

'Fine. Have it on me.'

'And a burger,' he added hopefully.

'Be my guest.'

'Cheers!' Jack hoisted a shabby holdall onto his shoulder and gave his dog's lead a tweak. 'Come on, Jordan.'

'That's an interesting name for a dog,' Sukey commented as they headed towards the cafe.

'I called 'im Monty when I first got 'im, but I changed it to Jordan 'cos he likes going in the river.'

'Do you doss near the river, then?'

Jack straightened up from tying Jordan's lead to a convenient cycle rack and looked her straight in the eyes with a wary expression on his bearded, none too clean face. 'What's that to you?' he demanded sharply.

'Don't worry, I'm not asking for an invitation to dinner,' she said lightly, but there was no answering smile. 'Shall we go in and order, then? I haven't got long, I'm due back at work in fifteen minutes.'

They went inside. Sukey bought Jack a coffee and a giant

burger, which he doused liberally with tomato sauce before picking it up and taking a huge bite. He devoured the food hungrily, sinking his teeth into the thick bun and chewing noisily.

'So what d'you want to talk about?' he asked with his mouth full.

'I wondered if you'd seen any sign of Matt since we last spoke?' He shook his head and brushed away with the back of his hand some crumbs that had fallen into his beard. 'And you've no idea where he might be?' she persisted. 'I really would like to have a word with him.'

Jack gave her another direct stare and squirted more tomato sauce onto his burger. 'What about?'

'I told you earlier—' she began, but was interrupted by a ring from her mobile phone. 'Sorry, I'd better take this.' She pressed the answer key and said, 'Yes?'

George Barnes was on the line from the office. 'Sukey? Where are you?'

'It is my lunch hour,' she reminded him. 'I'm in town doing a bit of shopping. Is there something urgent?'

'Aggravated burglary at sixty-three Copenhagen Road. Woman seriously injured, uniformed in attendance, ambulance and dog handler on way. Get along there asap, OK?'

'Right, Sarge.' She snapped off the phone, pulled out her notebook and scribbled down the address. She turned back to her companion. 'I'm afraid I have to go in a moment. You were asking—'

She broke off at the sight of Jack's furious expression. 'You're a fucking copper!' he snarled at her.

'No, I'm not, I'm—'

'*Right, Sarge!*' he mocked in a squeaky falsetto. 'Well, that's it. You can keep your sodding grub!' He threw down the last piece of burger and overturned his coffee mug with a sweep of his hand, sending it crashing to the floor. He jumped to his feet, overturning his chair, and stormed out of the cafe with Sukey in pursuit.

'Jack!' she shouted at he bent down to untie Jordan's leash. 'Please, let me explain.'

He straightened up and rounded on her, jabbing a grimy forefinger still greasy from the food a couple of inches from her face. 'If you think I'm grassing up a mate to the filth for a fucking cheeseburger, you can think again!' he snarled.

'Jack, please listen. I'm not the police . . . that is, I do work for them, but I only want to help Matt, truly.'

'He don't need help from the likes of you.'

'But I believe he's in danger, and so do the police. Real danger, from a very ruthless, violent crook,' Sukey insisted.

Jack appeared to waver. 'Why should you bother, anyway?' he said suspiciously.

'I often used to chat with him when I bought the *Big Issue* and he told me about some of his problems. Then he disappeared and I got worried about him. Yes, all right, I'll pay for the damage,' she added as the indignant cafe proprietor emerged and waved the shattered remains of the mug under her nose. 'Just give me two minutes. Jack, wait!' she called desperately as, taking advantage of the interruption, he made off in the direction of the Cross. She ran to catch up with him and once more grabbed him by the arm, but he wrenched himself free.

'Stop harassing me or I'll call a cop!' he threatened. Sukey burst out laughing at the illogical nature of the threat and it was as if a barrier had suddenly collapsed. He turned slowly to face her. 'OK, tell me what you want with Matt,' he said with a sheepish grin.

'The police think he has some information that could help them solve a particularly nasty murder,' she began. 'No, they don't suspect him, but they think he's in danger and they want to get to him before the killer does. Look, I haven't time to explain it all now. Will you be here tomorrow?'

'Maybe.'

'I'll see you then.'

'Not in my place, you won't,' said the cafe proprietor grimly as Jack shambled away with Jordan at his heels. 'Are you going to pay for the damage?'

'Yes, of course, I'm really sorry about that,' said Sukey. She took a fiver from her wallet and offered it to him. 'Will that cover it?'

'Suppose so,' he muttered ungraciously as he pocketed the note. 'There's all the mess to clear up,' he added pointedly, but she pretended not to hear and hurried off back to the station.

*   *   *

93

Copenhagen Road was a tree-lined avenue in a prosperous neighbourhood a mile from the city centre. The two police cars standing at the kerb were sufficient to identify number 63 without the need for Sukey to crawl along checking house numbers. She drove a short distance further on and parked her van behind a dark green Rover whose driver, a young man in a leather jacket, was talking to a uniformed officer. As she switched off her engine she heard the wail of a siren and an ambulance came into view, its blue light flashing. It drew up behind the police cars and two paramedics jumped out. Directed by another uniformed officer, whom Sukey recognized as PC Gerry Prior, they hurried up the path to the front door of the house and disappeared inside, with Sukey a short distance behind them.

'What happened?' she asked Gerry.

'It appears the tenant of the ground-floor flat, a middle-aged woman, came home from shopping and disturbed an intruder. She challenged him and he hit her over the head with a poker, grabbed her handbag and scarpered. A passing motorist – that gentleman over there – saw a man dash out of the house and leg it down the road carrying a plastic supermarket shopping bag, got suspicious and went to the house to investigate. He saw the front door open, went inside, found the victim unconscious and raised the alarm. We've called up a dog handler and scrambled the chopper; we reckon the villain can't have got far.'

'Is the lady badly hurt?'

'We hope not. She's dazed and shaken, but she came round soon after we arrived and was able to tell us what happened.'

'Do we have a description?'

'Only that the attacker was a young IC1 male in jeans and a hooded top.'

'Which could apply to half the yobbos in Gloucester,' Sukey remarked drily. 'Which flat is it?'

'The one on the right off the entrance hall. It looks as if he broke in through there.' Gerry pointed to a shattered ground-floor window.

'Right. I'll have a look at that while the ambulance crew are dealing with the victim.'

A large brick lay on the ground beneath the broken window among shards of glass and the remains of a window box, which had split and scattered earth among the trampled remains of some lavender bushes. Sukey worked quickly and methodically, taking photographs of the damage, bagging up samples of glass and scrutinizing the stone sill for traces of cloth from the culprit's clothing or blood where he might have cut himself. She peered inside and saw a neat, well-equipped kitchen. Nothing appeared to have been disturbed, but the door stood open. With any luck there would be fingerprints.

The ambulance crew reappeared with a wheelchair in which sat a woman so muffled in blankets that only her heavily bandaged head was visible. They lowered a platform at the rear of the vehicle; one of them carefully pushed the wheelchair onto it and the other pressed a button and raised the platform. The doors were closed, the driver climbed into the cab and the ambulance sped off with its siren wailing and its blue light flashing.

'Can I go in now?' Sukey asked.

Prior nodded and stood aside. 'You'll find Sergeant Moon inside, checking the rest of the building. It doesn't look as if the flat's been ransacked, but we don't know yet what's missing.'

The wide entrance hall was heavily carpeted. An elaborate chandelier hung from the ceiling and a curved staircase with a wrought-iron handrail led to the upper floors. On either side was a heavy mahogany door with a brass number-plate and a knocker in the shape of an animal's head. The one on the right, bearing the figure 1, stood open. As Sukey entered, the tall uniformed figure of Sergeant Moon appeared on the staircase. 'OK for me to start work?' she asked.

'Sure.' He gestured at the open door. 'Go right in. It looks like a quick in-and-out job by a villain on his own looking for whatever he could carry off in his pockets. No sign of a getaway car or accomplice, according to the witness who called us. There's no one else at home in the other five flats so if the poor lady hadn't had the misfortune to come home at the wrong time he'd have got away unnoticed.'

Sukey put down her bag and donned her protective suit. 'Right, I'm ready.'

'The attack took place in here.' He led her to a cosy sitting room, attractively furnished and decorated with flowers and some choice ornaments and bric-a-brac. Apart from an over-turned occasional table beside an armchair by the fireplace and some gaps on the mantelpiece that suggested easily portable items had been removed, the only indications that a struggle had taken place were a patch of blood on the beige carpet and a heavy brass poker lying on the floor. Sukey's anger rose as she pictured the chain of events. An innocent woman returning home from a shopping trip, no doubt looking forward to her lunch, finding doors that she had left closed now standing ajar and uneasily conscious that there was something wrong. Perhaps she had heard a noise from the sitting room and with beating heart pushed the door wide open to find herself face to face with a threatening stranger. She might have screamed, but there was no one in the empty house to hear. Or turned to run and call for help, but had not been quick enough, or simply been momentarily frozen with terror, giving the intruder time to strike her down and make his getaway, leaving her senseless and bleeding. 'Bloody toe-rag!' Sukey muttered under her breath. 'She could have bled to death for all you'd have cared.'

She set about her task quickly and methodically. As she worked she was conscious of the throb of a helicopter not far away. Less than an hour later, as she was packing away her kit, she heard its engine fade into the distance. 'Have they caught him?' she asked Gerry Prior.

He squinted at the sky, shading his eyes against the watery sun as he watched the helicopter disappearing. 'Either that, or they've widened the area of search,' he said. 'We'll know in a moment.' They went out to the front gate and looked along the street. 'Yes, here they come; they've nicked him.'

'He only looks a kid,' said Sukey. A thin youth was being marched along between Sergeant Moon and another officer, followed by a dog handler holding the leash of a German shepherd in one hand and a plastic carrier bag in the other. As they drew level, Gerry exclaimed, 'Well, what do you know? Little Tommy Tucker himself! Thought we'd have a change from robbing filling stations, did we?'

The youth mouthed a string of obscenities as the group

stopped by the nearest police car. On the pavement opposite, a group of schoolgirls who had stopped to watch the fun, jumped up and down, cheering and waving.

'Give your fans a nice smile, then,' goaded Gerry, unleashing a further tirade.

'Does he specialize in filling stations?' asked Sukey, her interest suddenly aroused.

Gerry grinned. 'Did one only a couple of days ago. Nicked on Monday, bailed on Tuesday, GBH on Wednesday. Makes Solomon Grundy's life sound pretty tame, doesn't it?'

Sukey brushed the witticism aside. 'Was it the filling station in Barnwood? A Mr Curtis threatened with a fake gun?'

'That's the one. Did you deal with that?'

'Yes. Keep an eye on that for a tick, will you?' She dumped her bag at Prior's feet and ran to the car where the prisoner was fiercely resisting attempts to get him inside, despite being handcuffed and firmly held by two policemen while a third was inside gripping him by the shoulders,

'Could I have a word with him, please, Sarge?'

Moon, who was supervising the operation, turned and looked at her in astonishment. 'What for?' he demanded.

'I've got a feeling he might know where a . . . a friend of mine has gone. It's quite important,' she added, seeing him frown and shake his head.

'It's very irregular,' he said, 'and not exactly the best time.'

'Oh, please, Sarge. It'll only take a moment. It might calm him down if I were to speak to him,' she added as the youth, showing a surprising degree of strength, wriggled and kicked and cursed, obstinately keeping up the struggle.

'Oy, you, Tucker!' Moon shouted. 'Watch your mouth, a lady wants to speak to you.'

'I don't want to speak to no fucking lady!' Tucker snarled, but the interruption caused him to momentarily slacken his resistance and the next minute he was sprawling face down on the back seat of the car. One of the officers leapt in after him and a second scrambled in the other side. After a further tussle he suddenly stopped struggling and sat quietly between two of them with his head bent while the third officer hurried round to the driver's door. Before he reached it, Sukey seized her opportunity, wrenched it open and leaned inside.

'Tommy,' she said urgently, 'you used sell the *Big Issue*, didn't you?'

'So what?' he muttered without looking up.

'Do you know where Matt is?'

'Matt?' He raised his head just enough to shoot her a suspicious glance. 'What d'you want with that fruitcake?'

'I just want to talk to him.'

'What about?'

'Never mind that. Where is he?'

'How should I know? Ask Jack.'

'All right, that's enough.' Sergeant Moon put a hand on Sukey's arm and she obediently made way for the driver to get into his seat. 'I don't think DI Castle would approve of you mixing with his sort,' he said sternly.

'Please, don't say anything to him,' Sukey pleaded. 'Matt's homeless – all the *Big Issue* sellers are – and I believe he needs help, but he disappeared a few weeks ago and no one seems to know where he is. The man who nabbed Tucker at the filling station said he'd seen him in town selling the magazine, so I thought he might know something.'

'If this fellow Matt's a fruitcake, you'd best stay away from him.'

'He's not a fruitcake, he's an educated chap, a bit out of Tucker's league. Tucker was winding me up, that's all.'

She went back to reclaim her bag and stowed it in her van. It was unfortunate that Sergeant Moon had overheard the exchange between her and Tucker but it had been unavoidable. She would keep her fingers crossed that he wouldn't mention it to Jim Castle. 'Jack *does* know something,' she muttered as she reached for her seat belt. 'Somehow or other I've got to make him talk.'

Fifteen

Sukey's first assignment on Thursday morning was to a market town some thirty miles north-east of Gloucester where a walk-in theft of a valuable clock from an antiques shop had been reported shortly after the close of business the previous evening.

'Apparently the woman was nearly hysterical when she called in,' George Barnes commented when handing Sukey the printout. 'Mike in central control says she sounded scared out of her wits and kept saying, "Can't you come right away?" and "Mr Bryant will be furious when he finds out." She's been on the blower again this morning demanding to know why no one's shown up.'

'Is Mr Bryant the proprietor?'

'Presumably. The name of the business is Joseph Bryant and Son, but whether it's father or son she's scared of I've no idea. Anyway, that's her problem. Mike did his best to calm her down and advised her not to open the shop until our people get there. With any luck someone from uniformed should have shown up by the time you arrive.'

'They'll most likely have been and gone; I doubt if I'll do it in less than an hour,' said Sukey. It would, she reflected, be touch and go whether she would be able to get back in time to catch Jack at midday, even supposing he would be there. *Big Issue* vendors could never be relied on to be at the same place at the same time. And time was slipping past; Trevor Blackton was still on the run and, she was convinced, set on tracking Matt down before the police got to him.

Joseph Bryant and Son occupied a double-fronted shop in a prime position on the market square with the name picked out in gilded letters on the facade. It was after half-past nine by the time she arrived, but a sign hanging on the inside of the glass door remained at 'Closed' despite the fact that a smaller notice to one side announced the hours of business as nine until five on weekdays and nine until one on Saturday. One window was entirely occupied by a display of clocks, the other by jewellery, porcelain and silverware, all obviously of the highest quality. A discreetly positioned announcement in a silver frame offered the best prices for gold and antiques and a professional valuation service.

Unable to find a bell, Sukey tapped on the door. A pale, nervous-looking young woman appeared on the other side and gesticulated at the 'Closed' notice. Sukey held up her ID and after a few moments' hesitation the woman unlocked the door and held it open just wide enough for her to step through before closing and locking it behind her.

'I thought a policeman in uniform would be coming,' she said.

'You mean, no one's been yet?'

'No. Mr Bryant is furious. They promised to send someone first thing – I've been here since eight o'clock, waiting.'

'They're terribly overstretched, I'm afraid,' Sukey explained.

'It's very worrying if we can't rely on their help when we need it,' the woman complained in a querulous voice.

'Perhaps you'd like to tell me what happened,' Sukey suggested. 'I'm not really supposed to start work until the police have checked the crime scene.'

'But I thought you were the police.'

Sukey was about to explain the difference between her function and that of the police force when to her relief a uniformed officer rapped on the door and the assistant scuttled over to admit him. Left to herself, Sukey put down her bag and began to wander round the showroom, which was more extensive than appeared from a cursory glance through the window. She was admiring a series of water-colours depicting Cotswold scenes when she became aware of a man's voice coming from a half-open door behind her.

'Scud? Joseph Bryant here. What? Oh, it's you. Put me on to him, will you? Well, tell him to call the minute he comes in! Say there's a problem with today's shipment and there'll be only one package instead of two. What? For Christ's sake, can't you get anything right? Good God, I don't believe this! Hold on!' The door was flung wide open and a tall, spare man with chiselled, clean-shaven features and an abundance of grey hair strode into the showroom and roared, 'Mrs Bateson! Come here!'

'Yes, Mr Bryant.' The young woman came and stood nervously in front of him. He gazed down at her with cold, grey eyes.

'The clock that Express were to pick up this morning – where is it?'

'B . . . but it's been stolen, Mr Bryant. That's why I—'

'Not that one, you fool! The other one.'

'Oh, that one.' She gave a faint, placatory smile. 'That was collected yesterday.'

Mrs Bateson's relief at being able to give a reply that she evidently thought would please her irascible employer was quickly dispelled when Bryant said through his teeth, 'It was supposed to be picked up this afternoon.'

'Yes, I know, but the driver happened to be passing on his way back to the depot so he called in on the off chance. I told him he'd have to call back today to pick up the other one and he said it was no problem. Isn't that why you're calling Express, to tell them—'

Bryant's face turned almost purple; without waiting for her to finish he swung on his heel and marched back into the office. He elbowed the door to behind him, but it failed to catch and swung partly open in time for the two women to hear him say, 'It looks like Blackie's boys have pulled another fast one. Tell Scud to call me the minute he comes in.'

He emerged a few moments later and fixed Sukey with a suspicious stare. Plainly he had not noticed her before; it was equally obvious that he considered her unlikely to be a customer. 'What do you want?' he barked.

Her explanation for her presence, and the ID which she offered for his inspection, were received with a derisive curl of his lip. 'I can't imagine you'll be of much use,' he said dismissively. 'And if you have to scatter your disgusting grey powder all over the place, have the goodness to clear it up when you've finished.'

Sukey opened her mouth to ask him whether there had been

101

previous thefts from his shop, but before she could utter a word he had marched through the showroom to where Mrs Bateson had resumed talking to the police officer and was going over the circumstances of the theft. She was by turns pointing, gesticulating and saying, 'Oh, if only I'd . . .' in a distracted manner while the uniformed constable nodded in sympathy, made notes and asked the occasional question.

'Complete waste of time,' said Joseph Bryant, breaking unceremoniously into the conversation. 'The clock's probably out of the country by now. If you layabouts had got off your backsides and responded more promptly there might have been a chance of catching the thieves.'

'I'm sorry, Mr Bryant, but we do have a great many calls on our time,' said the constable patiently. 'We have to assess everything in order of urgency these days.'

'I suppose the loss of a ten-thousand-pound clock isn't as urgent as a crowd of young hooligans smashing a few windows,' said Bryant with a sneer. 'I shall write to the Chief Constable and lodge a strong complaint.'

'That's your privilege, sir. Meanwhile, your assistant has given me a good description of the suspects. And do I understand you have a problem with a missing package? If you'd like to give me a few details—'

'No, thanks, I'll sort that one out for myself.'

'Right, sir. Now, unless there's anything further you wish to tell me, I'll go and make sure this information is circulated without delay. This lady,' he nodded in Sukey's direction, 'will examine the premises for any evidence the thieves may have left behind.'

'Huh!' Bryant sniffed. 'Very unlikely. I'll have my coffee now,' he barked at Mrs Bateson. 'And you,' he rounded on Sukey, 'will be as quick as you can so I can open the shop. It's bad enough to lose a valuable piece without losing business as well.' He turned and marched back to his office, slamming the door behind him. His assistant scuttled to the rear of the showroom and vanished.

'I'm afraid he's got a point,' the constable admitted. 'About there not being much chance of finding any useful evidence, I mean. We've heard from West Mercia of a lot of this kind

102

of crime during the past few weeks and it's obvious there's a professional gang at work. They use a similar distraction technique, working in pairs but entering the target premises as if they're nothing to do with each other. One asks to see something in the window or a showcase, the other lifts a valuable piece while the assistant's attention is elsewhere and slips out unnoticed. It looks as if they've moved into our patch now.'

'I take it no one's been nicked so far.'

'Not that I've heard of. Like I said, they're pros.'

Sukey was kept busy for the rest of the morning and by the time she was able to make her way to Jack's pitch in Eastgate it was almost one o'clock. He had evidently been on the lookout for her; as soon as she appeared he thrust his bundle of unsold magazines into his holdall along with the scrap of blanket that served as a bed for Jordan.

'Thought you weren't coming,' he grumbled as he hoisted the holdall over his shoulder. 'I'm starving.'

'That makes two of us,' Sukey said a little tartly, and then told herself that a conciliatory rather than an impatient approach was more likely to yield results. 'We'll have to look for another place to eat after yesterday's little episode. That cost me a fiver, by the way, so I'd be grateful if you didn't repeat it.'

'There's a hot-dog place just inside the covered market,' said Jack and strode purposefully in the direction of the entrance.

'Don't apologize,' she muttered under her breath. She bought coffee and hot dogs for them both from a kiosk smelling strongly of onions and – in response to a broad hint from Jack – an extra sausage for Jordan. They perched on stools at the end of the greasy counter. Sukey waited patiently while Jack wolfed his food and took noisy swigs of coffee. He belched, passed the back of his hand across his mouth and rubbed his stomach appreciatively.

'That was good,' he said. 'Not really enough of it to keep a man going for long, though,' he added meaningfully.

'Nice try,' said Sukey. 'If you've got something useful to tell me, maybe I'll get you another.'

'So what are you after?'

'You know very well what I'm after. I want to talk to Matt and you know where he is, don't you?'

'Might do.'

'So where can I find him?'

'He don't want anyone to know where he is.'

'So you've spoken to him?'

'Might have.'

With an effort, Sukey controlled her impatience. 'Did you tell him what I told you yesterday?' Jack nodded and fiddled with the plastic holder of his polystyrene coffee cup. 'What did he say?

'He said he'd meet you.'

'That's great. Where?'

'Down by the river.'

'You live near the river, don't you? Is he sharing your place?'

'He's got his own place.'

'So where exactly do I meet him, and when?'

Jack fumbled in his pocket and produced a grimy scrap of paper on which was drawn a crude map of an area on the outskirts of the city. A dotted line led across a rectangle marked 'field' with an arrow pointing to a cluster of circles on stalks labelled 'wood'. A double line snaking past the wood was labelled 'river'.

'There's a burned-out car in the bushes you can use as a landmark,' he explained. 'What time d'you finish work?'

'Four o'clock, but I don't always get away on time.'

'No matter. I'll tell him you'll be there one evening around half four and he'll find you. So long as you're on your own, that is. Better take a torch; there's no street lighting.'

'I'd rather meet him in daylight,' she objected.

'No way. There's a footpath along the river bank and he don't want to be seen.'

'All right, but I'm hoping to persuade him to accept police protection. Did you tell him that?'

'Yeah, but I don't think he trusts them to do a proper job. He's had threats, you see.'

Sukey's heart missed a beat. 'Who from?'

'He wouldn't say.'

'That makes it even more urgent that I speak to him.' Sukey folded the map and put it in her pocket. 'Well, thanks, Jack. I must be going now.'

'What about that other hot dog you promised?'

She gave the order, paid for it and slid off her stool. 'Tell Matt I'll be in touch as soon as possible. Oh, one other thing. Do you know Tommy Tucker?'

'Yeah, I know him. What about it?'

'He got nicked yesterday for bashing a woman over the head with a poker after burgling her flat.'

'The stupid git!' snorted Jack through a mouthful of bread and sausage. 'He's no friend of ours, he's a crackhead.'

Sukey found the response encouraging. These young drifters might be homeless and living a hand-to-mouth existence, but it was clear they had certain standards and tried to live up to them.

On returning to the SOCOs' office Sukey found DI Castle in conversation with Sergeant George Barnes. When he saw her, he said, 'Ah, Sukey, this will interest you. We've found out a bit more about your Mr Dalsey.' He referred to the file he was holding. 'His full name is Samuel Cuthbert Dalsey, known to his friends as Scud, and he owns a transport and shipping outfit called Express Deliveries based in Tewkesbury. He's also part owner of a sports club and leisure centre on the ring road and a shareholder in a fancy golf club out near Malvern. A very rich man, by all accounts. We're making the usual enquiries of all his business associates, including his right-hand man at Express, a chap called Dowding. Andy Radcliffe says he gets the impression that Dalsey wasn't exactly popular and didn't suffer fools gladly, but no one could actually suggest a motive for killing him. According to the secretary of his golf club he was well enough liked by the committee and the members, but didn't appear to have any close friends or associates.'

Sukey barely heard the details of Dalsey's business interests; her brain had clicked on the nickname Scud and the moment Castle finished speaking she said excitedly, 'This may be a coincidence, sir, but the owner of an antiques shop I've been to this morning was on the telephone while I was there, asking to speak to someone called Scud. He left a message asking for Scud to call him "as soon as he comes in".'

'That's too unusual a nickname to be a coincidence,' said Castle. 'I want to know more about this. Come with me, Sukey.'

He led the way along the corridor to his office and closed the door. 'Right, tell me exactly what you overheard and anything else you remember that might be of interest.'

As accurately as she could, Sukey repeated Joseph Bryant's end of the telephone conversation. Castle made notes as he listened without interruption until she mentioned Bryant's anger at a package having been picked up a day early and his remark about Blackie's boys having 'pulled another fast one'.

'People don't usually get upset because some service has been carried out early,' he commented.

'That's what I thought, sir. I think the officer who'd come round in response to the report of the theft thought so too, because he offered to take details if there was a further problem. Bryant brushed it aside and said it was something he could sort out himself. And another thing; his assistant referred to an outfit called "Express", who I gathered was the carrier.'

'Which would indicate it was Dalsey at Express Deliveries he was trying to contact, not knowing he was dead.' Castle thought for a moment, tapping his teeth with his pen. 'Unless, of course, he knew, but wouldn't let on. What sort of person is this Joseph Bryant?'

'Quite intimidating, something of a bully. He treats his assistant like a skivvy and wasn't exactly cordial toward me. He didn't appear to have much of an opinion of whoever answered the telephone either.'

'Not exactly a lovable character,' Castle observed. 'OK, let's recap. The reference to a shipment, plus the nickname "Scud", makes it a reasonable guess that he was talking to someone at Express Deliveries. Nothing untoward in that, but if by an outside chance "Blackie" turns out to be our old friend Trevor Blackton, then we're into something very interesting indeed.' He sat down, made a few more notes, read them over and then, for the first time since the interview began, gave a half smile. 'Thanks, Sook, you've been a great help,' he said.

Sukey stood up. 'All in the day's work, sir,' she replied, returning the smile.

Sixteen

'I don't like it,' said Fergus.

'What's the problem?' said his mother. 'I thought you were dead keen for me to track down Matt and persuade him to agree to police protection.'

'That was before Jack told you he'd been threatened. Supposing Blackton's on to him already?'

'I can only find that out if I can talk to Matt.'

'I still don't like it. At least let me come with you.'

'If he sees me with someone else he'll take fright and not appear.'

'You could get Jack to give him a message and explain who I am.'

'He might think it's a trick. No, I'll have to play along with him. Don't forget I did a course in self-defence not so long ago, so if anyone jumps out of the bushes and grabs me I'll know what to do to make him wish he hadn't.'

Sukey kept her tone light, but inwardly she shared her son's reservations. For a moment, she considered telling Jim that she had succeeded in locating Matt, but dismissed the thought immediately; he would certainly use his authority to scotch the plan for the riverside meeting.

She inspected the contents of the oven and adjusted the heat. 'Come on,' she said, 'stop fussing and lay the table for me – dinner's nearly ready.'

They ate in silence for a few minutes. Then Fergus said, 'Any joy from fingerprints?'

'Not so far. I'll chase them up in the morning.'

'There's bad news and there's good news,' said a young man with spiky hair in response to Sukey's enquiry. 'Which will you have first?'

'I think I can guess what the bad news is. You haven't found a match between prints left at Belstone House and any of the ones from Glevum Passage.'

'Correct.'

'Oh, well, it was a long shot anyway. Now tell me the good news.'

'We did find a match with a young villain called Tucker who was picked up only a couple of weeks ago. See?' He mounted two transparencies side by side on a viewer and pointed out the common features. 'It looks like he paid a visit to Belstone House.'

'Would that be the one they call "Tommy" Tucker, by any chance?'

'That's him. You know him?'

'I was at the scene when he got nicked yesterday for aggravated burglary.'

'Well, there you are, then. He's been arrested more than once for various offences including possession and suspected supply. The usual story – cautioned and released without charge through lack of hard evidence. He was probably trying to collect a debt from the guy who did a runner from the hotel.'

Sukey sighed. 'Yes, we half suspected something like that at the time, but I thought there might be an outside chance of a link with the Glevum Passage killing.'

'Can't win 'em all, can you?' said the young man cheerfully.

'No, I suppose not. Speaking of Glevum Passage, what about the prints on the earring that had been torn out of Evie Stanton's ears?'

He shook his head. 'Too badly smudged for identification, I'm afraid.'

It was a disappointing start to the day, and more was to come. As she was about to set off on her first assignment of the morning, she received a call on her mobile from a delighted Mrs Milroy. 'I've just heard from David's uncle,' she said, a little breathlessly. 'The dear boy' – Sukey cringed inwardly at the expression – 'has been in touch with him and explained why he ran away. It seems he got mixed up with some undesirable people a little while ago and his uncle has been helping him to make a fresh start. He was afraid his old associates were trying to find him, but uncle's hoping to persuade him that now they believe he's gone away it will be safe for him to return to Belstone House.'

'Well, that is good news.' Sukey did her best to sound enthusiastic in spite of having had another of her theories blown out of the water. 'Incidentally, Mrs Milroy,' she went on, you'll be interested to know that the man who broke into David's room has been arrested in connection with another incident.'

'Oh, that *is* good news,' Mrs Milroy cooed.

You wouldn't be so delighted if you knew what kind of undesirables your blue-eyed boy was mixing with, Sukey thought with a certain malicious glee. She thanked Mrs Milroy for the call and was about to switch off when another thought occurred to her. It had been difficult in the past to get enough firm evidence to charge Tucker, and Somers might have information that would help strengthen the case against him.

'If David does return to your hotel,' she said, 'will you let us know, please?'

'Oh, of *course*! I still have that nice young detective's number and I'll be in touch with him *immediately*.'

'You and Evie Stanton would have made a great pair,' Sukey said aloud as she switched off the phone and put her key in the ignition. 'A couple of nymphos together.'

After dealing with the morning's assignments she called the office for further instructions.

'Got any plans for this evening?' asked George Barnes.

'I'm supposed to be meeting a friend after work,' she replied cautiously.

'Tell him you can't make it. I need you to do three hours' overtime.'

Sukey's heart sank. 'What's this in aid of?' she asked.

'Nigel Warren's called in sick. I want you to cover him until seven o'clock. Mandy's already agreed to do his seven to ten stint.'

'Could we possibly swap? Mandy do the early part and—'

'Sorry. She has to go and look after her mother first. Is there a problem?'

'No, I suppose not. OK, Sarge, I'll do it.'

That makes disappointment number three, Sukey thought disconsolately as she switched off. The meeting with Matt would just have to wait until Monday. She hoped that her non-appearance would not be taken as a lack of interest.

Trevor Blackton sat on his bed with his feet up, an open six-pack and a supply of crisps on a table at his elbow, a half-empty can in one hand and the remote control of the TV in the other.

'Bleedin' load of rubbish!' he muttered as he flicked through a score of channels. He lingered briefly on a pornographic film, the kind he and Evie would have enjoyed together, but switched off after a couple of minutes, overcome with emotion at the recollection of his last sight of her. 'I loved that chick!' he sobbed. 'Why'd she have to do that to me after all I done for her?'

He gave himself up to self-pity for several minutes before emptying the can and cracking open another. He undid a packet of crisps, consumed the contents in a few mouthfuls and tossed the wrapper on the floor, where it joined the accumulated debris of a succession of interminable days.

For almost two weeks now he'd been cooped up in this house, not daring to show his face outside the door yet resisting the advice of friends who offered to help him skip the country while he had the chance. 'Not till I've laid my hands on the bleeder who stole my Evie!' he declared every time the subject was raised. 'If you useless wankers would get off your arses and find him for me, I'd be on the plane the minute I'd dealt with him.' They pointed out that the police were looking for the aforesaid 'bleeder' as well, considering him to be a valuable witness who could help them with their enquiries into Evie's murder, but he refused to listen. At first, that is. After almost a fortnight of skull-cracking boredom in an abandoned, boarded-up house that had been left derelict for years, he found himself dreaming of some sunny resort in Spain teeming with sexy, dark-eyed crumpet that would help him forget Evie. His boys had done their best to make him comfortable; somehow they'd laid on electricity and water and sneaked in after dark from time to time with essential supplies, but the place was still a pigsty, only made tolerable by a limitless supply of booze. Maybe it was time to cut his losses and get out.

The quantity of lager he had consumed that morning was having an effect. Muttering to himself, he swung his feet to the floor and staggered to the bathroom. He was already half drunk and still hungover from the previous night; it was several seconds before he realized that the pounding he could hear above the sound of the cistern flushing was not inside his head, but coming from downstairs. From the front door, to be precise, accompanied by shouts of 'Police! Open up!'

This was the nightmare scenario he had been dreading. He lurched into the bedroom and peered out through a crack in the tattered curtains. Yes, there they were, the bastards. Dozens of them, swarming round the house like a plague of locusts. He ran to the back bedroom; there were more of them in what passed for a garden, clambering over the litter of broken, vermin-infested furniture and rusting kitchen appliances. He looked round wildly for some way of escape, knowing there was none. He cursed the so-called friends who had brought him here, saying it would be safe, that the police would never think of looking for him in this rat-hole, that with his money and influence they'd expect him to have found somewhere luxurious to hide away if he was still in the country. Someone must have grassed him up. If ever he found out who it was, he'd make them wish they'd never been born. There'd be no escape from the Blackton organization. He would still have influence, even from inside.

The pounding and the shouting continued, but he stayed where he was. Let the bastards come and get him. He wasn't going to make it easy for them.

'Well, Trevor, you've led us quite a dance.'

Seated in the interview room with his solicitor, Hamish Grayson, at his side, Blackton scowled at the man with the greenish eyes and hawklike features who sat opposite him and whose name, he had been courteously informed, was Detective Inspector Castle. Beside him was another plain-clothes detective, called Sergeant Radcliffe, a man of similar age and build with a less forbidding countenance but the same steady, intimidating gaze.

112

Blackton fingered the bruise on his right cheek, sustained while resisting arrest. That was just another charge they were going to bring against him, along with murder and – sooner or later, because now they'd got something on him at last, they had an excuse to take him and his business apart – a whole string of other offences.

Receiving no response to his opening remark, Castle said, 'I'd have thought you could have found somewhere a little more comfortable to wait for us to call on you, Trev. With all your money and influence—'

Stung by the underlying sarcasm in the smooth voice, Blackton forgot Grayling's advice and shouted, 'Who grassed me up? I'll wring the bastard's neck when I get my hands on him!'

'Or beat him to death like you did Evie Stanton?' suggested Castle, without varying either his tone or his bland expression.

Blackton leapt to his feet, planted his hands on the table and brought his face to within inches of Castle's. 'It's a lie!' he screamed. 'I never killed her, I only—'

'Mr Blackton, please!' Grayling took him by the arm and pulled him back into his chair. 'Just confine yourself to answering the Inspector's questions.' He turned to Castle. 'I must ask you to bear in mind, Inspector, that my client is naturally overwrought and greatly afflicted by Ms Stanton's violent death, but he categorically denies attacking her.'

'Oh, quite.' This time there was a harsh edge to Castle's voice. It was his turn to lean forward and fix Blackton with a laserlike stare from his greenish eyes. 'So if you didn't kill her, what did you "only" do?'

Blackton and Grayling exchanged glances and the latter shook his head. 'No comment,' said the prisoner defiantly.

Seventeen

'Congratulations, you've hit the murder jackpot again!' George Barnes sounded positively jovial, despite the gruesome nature of his message.

Sukey's stomach gave a familiar lurch. 'What is it this time?' she asked uneasily.

'Someone's spotted a body in the river at Tewkesbury. Frogmen and the police surgeon are on the way, Doc Hillbourne's been notified and the usual mob's securing the scene. Report to Charlie C when you get there.' This was an irreverent reference to Detective Chief Inspector Philip Lord, whose small stature and Chaplinesque moustache had earned him the nickname by which he was known throughout the division.

'Not DI Castle?' said Sukey in surprise.

'They have to share out the interesting jobs. In any case, Castle and Radcliffe are interviewing Trevor Blackton.'

'Blackton? When did they pull him in?'

'A couple of hours ago, I believe.'

'No one tells me anything.'

'Never mind, I've given you a consolation prize in the form of a nice new body. Your first drowning, as well – what more do you want?'

'You're too kind.' The banter and the black humour acted as an antidote to the nausea that always afflicted her at the prospect of dealing with death. 'They say accidents always happen in threes,' she added, 'but I don't remember hearing it applied to murders.'

'We don't know for certain this is murder. We'll call it an accident for the moment if it makes you any happier.' He gave her detailed directions and rang off.

The corpse had been spotted from the garden of a riverside pub. When Sukey reached the scene she found the place littered with police cars and swarming with uniformed officers. The familiar blue and white tape was stretched across the entrance to the car park with a young constable on guard. He lifted the tape for her to drive in; when she had changed into her protective overall she hurried towards the spot where two police frogmen were carefully depositing a pale, dripping form on the grass a few yards from the water's edge. She suppressed a shudder at the sight.

News of the tragedy had already spread and a small crowd had gathered, craning their necks to see what was going on while reluctantly retreating along the footpath to make way for a squad of officers who were sealing the area with more blue and white tape. DCI Lord and a young woman with short dark hair and oriental features moved forward as the frogmen laid down their burden. They conferred for a few minutes while looking down at the body, pointing, nodding and exchanging remarks. When Lord caught sight of Sukey he beckoned and said, 'Come and meet DS Chen, who's just joined us. Dalia, this is Sukey Reynolds, one of our team of SOCOs. She'll be taking the mugshots and pointing out any clues that we mere detectives happen to miss.'

Dalia Chen smiled and held out a small, dainty hand. 'Nice to meet you, Sukey,' she said in a soft, musical voice.

'Sukey's going to join us in CID one day, isn't that right?' said Lord.

'I'd like to think so, sir.' As she returned the smile and the greeting, Sukey wished Jim Castle could have been there to hear.

'Sad case, this.' Lord jerked his head in the direction of the corpse. 'Young woman, not more than twenty at a guess. Not a pretty sight, either . . . been knocked about quite badly, but it's too soon to tell how she sustained the injuries. Her face hasn't suffered too much damage so she's still recognizable. We're waiting for the police surgeon . . . no, hang on a minute, that's him turning into the car park now.'

Lord's final remark was lost on Sukey. Swallowing hard and taking a deep breath to combat the threatened nausea, she had taken a few steps towards the body while he was speaking. The dead girl was lying on her back, her wide-open eyes staring blankly at the sky. There was extensive bruising to the naked flesh, but Sukey barely noticed the injuries. She was transfixed at the sight of the colourless face, wreathed in wet strands of weed-flecked hair and adorned with a familiar pattern of metal rings and studs. 'It's Lucy!' she whispered in horror.

'You recognize her?' said Lord sharply. She put a hand over her mouth and nodded. 'Who is she?'

She swallowed again before answering. 'I don't know much about her, except that I've bought the *Big Issue* off her a couple of times.'

'The magazine sold by homeless youngsters?'

'They don't have fixed addresses, but they usually have some kind of shelter, even if it's only a makeshift tent. Lucy told me she lived in a van.'

'Any idea where she kept it?' Sukey shook her head. 'D'you know her other name?'

'No.'

'So how long have you known her?'

'Only since last week. She took over Matt's pitch after he went missing.'

'Who's Matt?'

'He's a *Big Issue* seller as well. I used to buy my copy from him regularly, and then all of a sudden he disappeared. I haven't seen Lucy since Monday and Jack – he's another *Big Issue* seller – hasn't seen her either.'

'You keep some interesting company,' commented Lord. His mouth twitched under the bushy moustache and his dark eyes held the hint of a twinkle. 'Ah, good morning, Dr Blake,' he added, turning to greet the slight, balding figure of the police surgeon. 'We'll leave you to make your examination. Dalia, I believe there are witnesses waiting in the bar who are anxious to get back to their jobs. Go and get their names and addresses and then tell them they can go.'

'Yes, Guv.'

'Smart young woman, that,' commented Lord as, with evident approval, he watched the slim figure in the black trouser suit striding purposefully towards the entrance to the pub. 'Quite a tough cookie, too, according to her record. She'll be a real asset to the division.'

Sukey made no reply. She felt a pricking behind her eyes

and a lump rising in her throat as she watched Dr Blake mechanically going through the prescribed procedure for establishing death, applying his stethoscope to various points on the undernourished, battered body from which all traces of life must long since have slipped away. She found herself wondering about the girl's background, where she came from, whether her family knew or cared where she was and what had driven her to leave home and eke out a precarious living selling magazines on the streets.

Dr Blake straightened up, peeled off his latex gloves and put away his stethoscope.

'Any idea how long she's been in the water?' asked Lord.

'I'd say at least twelve hours, but not more than twenty-four,' the doctor replied. 'That's only a guesstimate, mind you. Doc Hillbourne will be able to give you a better idea. Incidentally, my opinion, for what it's worth, is that I'm pretty sure she didn't drown.'

Lord nodded. 'Thanks, Doctor. Ah, here comes Doc Hillbourne now.'

The two medics exchanged a few words before Dr Blake went back to his car and the pathologist dumped his case on the ground and squatted down to look at the body. 'Poor kid,' he muttered. 'She took a pounding, didn't she? There's not a lot I can do until I get her back to the morgue, so you'd better let your SOCO take her pics and we'll get the undertakers to collect her. I'll let you have a detailed report after I've done the post-mortem. You'd better bring your camera along to the morgue later on, Sukey. There'll almost certainly be injuries other than those immediately visible that will need recording.'

'Thanks, Doc.' Lord turned to Sukey. 'After you've done with the body, get the frogmen to show you the exact spot where they pulled her out and do some more shots there.' He went to the water's edge and stood for a moment studying the river. 'The current's pretty strong; she could have gone in some distance upstream,' he observed, half to himself. 'This van you mentioned,' he went on, turning back to Sukey, 'have you any idea what type of vehicle it is?'

'I'm afraid not, sir. I don't even know if it's a motor or an old trailer she was dossing in.'

117

'What about your other *Big Issue* friend – Jack, I think you said. Would he know?'

'He might.'

'I'll send a man along to speak to him. Where can we find him?'

'His pitch is in Eastgate, sir, but if you don't mind my saying so, I doubt if he'll be very willing to talk to the police.'

'Oh? Why not? He talks to you.'

'He didn't know what my job was at first, and he nearly blew a gasket when he found out.'

'How did that come about?'

'I was trying to get him to help me locate Matt and he got suspicious and thought I was trying to get him grass on one of his mates,' she explained, conscious of the colour rising in her cheeks. She had no choice now but to admit that she had been doing some unauthorized investigation of her own and DCI Lord would almost certainly tell Jim Castle what she had been up to.

'And why this interest in locating Matt?' asked Lord.

'I think he might be in danger and in need of police protection.'

Lord gave her a long, hard look. 'We'd better have a talk about this,' he said. 'Do the necessary here and let me know when you've finished. I'll be in the bar.

'Right, sir.'

It was difficult to bring to the grim task of photographing the corpse the detached professionalism that normally came to her aid at times like this. It was one of the least attractive aspects of the job, one she would never be able to approach without a degree of revulsion. Today, the emotion that she felt most keenly was not revulsion, but pity and an overwhelming sadness. Lucy could have been no more than two or at the most three years older than Fergus; she found herself wondering how she would cope if it was her child that had left home and come to such a tragic end. Would it be possible to trace the parents and if so, how would they feel when they learned of their daughter's fate? She recalled their first meeting; it was only when she had bent to caress Scruffy, Lucy's little brown mongrel, that the girl's wooden expression had softened. 'Keeps me warm at night,' she had said fondly. What would happen to Scruffy now? Where was he? Locked in the van, waiting in vain for his mistress to return? Or wandering the streets, another pitiful stray? Sukey found herself blinking away the tears.

She finished photographing the body and covered it with a sheet that had been left on the ground in readiness. One of the frogmen was still standing by to show her the exact point where he and his colleague had dragged Lucy from the water; she took several more shots before packing her camera away. 'I guess it's all right for the undertakers to collect her now,' she said and the frogman went to relay the message.

Sukey took her bag back to the van and stripped off her overall before going to seek out DCI Lord. It was going to be an uncomfortable interview.

Eighteen

When Sukey entered the saloon bar of the Brown Dog she found DCI Lord and DS Chen sitting at a table by the window. A handful of customers were hunched on stools at the bar. One or two were exchanging remarks in low voices with a shirt-sleeved barman; the rest sat silently contemplating their drinks. An atmosphere of shocked disbelief hung in the air like stale cigarette smoke.

Dalia Chen was sipping orange juice. Lord had his nose buried in a tankard of ale, but when he saw Sukey he took out a handkerchief to wipe froth from his moustache and stood up, motioning to Dalia to do the same. 'We'll talk in the snug,' he said with a jerk of his round, dark head. 'The landlord's kindly reserved it for us. What are you drinking, Sukey?'

She longed to ask for a gin and tonic, but apart from the fact that she had to drive she felt it would be an inappropriate request to make to a chief inspector so she asked for lemonade. Lord fetched it from the bar and led the way to a small area enclosed by a high wooden screen and containing a carved oak settle and half a dozen upright chairs grouped round an oblong table. A log fire crackled in an open iron grate.

'Right,' said Lord, fixing Sukey with a steady gaze from his bright, almost black eyes. 'What's your interest in this fellow Matt?'

Haltingly at first, then with growing confidence, Sukey explained how the possibility had occurred to her of a connection between Matt's disappearance and the murder of Evie Stanton. 'Evie had a reputation of being in the business as much for pleasure as for money,' she began. 'She particularly enjoyed having good-looking, virile young men as clients and by all accounts Blackton was no great performer in bed. We know from one of her former associates that it was Blackton who set her up in the house in Glevum Passage and according to the neighbours a man answering Blackton's description was a regular visitor.'

Lord nodded. 'His secret love nest,' he observed as Sukey broke off to take a mouthful of her drink. 'Outwardly he lives the life of Riley in a big house by the river, somewhere near Ross. A pillar of the local community, so I hear.' Lord was evidently familiar with the background to the case. 'You probably know we've been trying to track down the man Evie was dallying with in the hope of picking up a clue to Blackton's whereabouts,' he went on. 'We also thought he might be the target of a possible revenge attack by Blackton, but of course, that worry has been eliminated – Blackton was nicked this morning.'

'Yes, so Sergeant Barnes told me.'

'We'll have to see what Castle can get out of him. Let's get back to your friend Matt. Do I understand you think he may have been one of Evie's toy boys?'

'It seems to me a strong possibility, sir. He disappeared from his regular patch under rather peculiar circumstances a short time before the Evie Stanton killing, and neither of the other *Big Issue* sellers I've spoken to has seen him since.' She described Jack's account of the mugging and the 'posh gentleman' who had come to the rescue, and how she had developed the theory that there might be a connection.

Lord sat pulling at his moustache for a few moments before saying, 'Are you suggesting that this so-called "posh gentleman" had some ulterior motive in coming to Matt's rescue? To use him to settle a private score with Blackton, for example?'

'It did cross my mind,' Sukey admitted, wondering what his reaction would be if he knew of her conversation with Trudy Marshall. 'If Evie had been cheating on Blackton, surely she'd have made sure she entertained her toy boy when she knew he'd be safely out of the way – so how did he find out what she'd been up to? If he'd turned up unexpectedly and found her in bed with a rival there would probably have been two corpses for us to deal with instead of only one.'

'You think someone might have tipped him off?' She

nodded. 'Have you run your theory past DI Castle, by any chance?'

'As a matter of fact, I have. I also offered to compile an E-FIT of Matt for circulation.'

'And?'

Sukey thought she detected the hint of a twinkle in the glittering eyes fixed on her face. She flushed slightly and said, 'He wasn't very receptive to the idea.'

'And told you to stick to finding evidence and leaving the detectives to do the detecting?'

'More or less.'

'I suppose you can hardly blame him for being concerned for your safety.'

This time, the twinkle was unmistakable. There had been an occasion in the past when Lord had overruled Jim Castle and given his blessing to Sukey's offer to snoop around some suspect premises, and Lord had quickly divined that Jim's interest in her welfare was more than professional.

'Wouldn't you agree your fears for your friend Matt are no longer necessary?' Lord went on. 'Blackton's not in a position to go after him while he's in custody.'

'Not entirely, sir. If police suspicions are correct, and Blackton does have some sort of scam going that he's managed to conceal so far, he's probably got an organization to go with it. He has form for GBH and is known to have a violent temper. If he's out for revenge and wants to get even with whoever was messing with Evie, he could easily detail someone to do his dirty work for him. In any event, if there isn't enough evidence to charge him, he could be out on police bail within two or three days.'

'True.' Lord put down his empty tankard and stroked his moustache. 'Well, if Matt is in a position to provide us with some evidence against Blackton, it would be useful to have a chat to him. Have you any leads, apart from this fellow Jack?'

'No, sir.'

'Could you persuade him to talk to us?'

Sukey hesitated. She knew that it was her duty to tell Lord everything she knew, but that would mean that the plan for the riverside meeting would have to be discarded. It was equally certain that Jack would refuse to speak to the police and would probably warn Matt. Knowing Matt's nervous temperament, she thought it likely that he might panic and find another hideout, and the process of tracking him down would have to start all over again.

'Well?' Lord's eyes were boring into hers.

'I'm pretty sure he wouldn't agree, sir,' she said, 'but I might manage to persuade him to get a message from you to Matt.'

'Do that. Tell him we'll give Matt protection if that's what he's worried about. And your idea of compiling an E-FIT wouldn't do any harm. Get that organized right away, Dalia.'

'Yes, Guv.'

Lord stood up. 'I'll let you get back to work now, Sukey.' He did not add that he would be telling Jim about their conversation, but she had no doubt that he would.

She went back to her van and called George Barnes. 'I've finished here for the time being, Sarge,' she said. 'Is there anything else for me?'

'Not at the moment, but stay in touch. By the way, something rather peculiar has happened. A member of the public phoned to report what she thought was a broken-down white van with a dog in it parked in a lay-by on the A417. She said the dog appeared very distressed and what should she do? Trudy Marshall was on patrol duty and she went to investigate; the van wasn't locked and when she opened it this scruffy little mongrel tried to make a dash for it. She managed to collar it and contacted the RSPCA, who've taken it to the animal shelter.'

'So what's peculiar about that? People are always leaving animals in unattended vehicles.'

'This one has evidently been used as living quarters. Trudy says she saw a sleeping bag and a blanket, some old clothes and a few provisions, a quantity of dog food and,' Barnes paused as if for effect, 'some copies of the *Big Issue* magazine in a plastic wrapper. She asked me to let you know, seemed to think you'd be interested.'

'Too darn right I'm interested. Get an urgent message to CID, will you Sarge? Say I'm pretty sure it's Lucy's van.'

'Who's Lucy?'

'The girl whose body was fished out of the river this morning.'

'You recognized her?'

'She was one of the *Big Issue* sellers in the city centre. I chatted to her once or twice before she disappeared. She had a brown mongrel and she told me she was living in a van.'

Barnes whistled. 'I've noticed you with the magazine. Do you suspect it to be a cover-up for some kind of mini-Mafia?'

'Of course not, Sarge, it's a perfectly reputable publication with some quite interesting features. I buy it because it helps the homeless.'

'Quite the little social worker, aren't we?'

Sukey let the jibe pass. 'If that's all, I'll find a quiet corner to eat my lunch. I have to report to Doc Hillbourne at the morgue some time this afternoon to take more shots of Lucy's body.'

'There's something for you to look forward to,' said Barnes cheerfully.

'It's not my idea of fun. I'll get it out of the way and then check in again. And you will remember to let CID know about the van, won't you, Sarge?'

'Will do. I'm sure they'll be very grateful.'

Sukey ended the call, uncertain whether the final remark carried a hint of sarcasm. It would be interesting to hear DI Castle's reaction.

'Ah, Sukey. Come over here, will you?' Hillbourne put down a clipboard on which he had been making notes and led the way to an examination table. Once more Sukey found herself looking down at Lucy's battered body. 'There are a few more marks I want recorded,' the pathologist went on. He beckoned to an attendant and instructed him to turn Lucy onto her stomach, revealing more ugly contusions. He stood by while Sukey, steeling herself against the familiar feelings of revulsion, recorded each one under the pathologist's direction.

'Right, put her away,' said Hillbourne to the attendant when he had all the shots he needed. 'Thanks, Sukey, that's the lot.'

Sukey was not normally in the habit of questioning the

pathologist, but having a personal interest in the victim made her ask, almost without thinking, 'Professor Hillbourne, do you think she sustained those injuries before or after she went into the water?'

'Oh, before. There was no water in the lungs, only blood. One of them had been pierced by a broken rib. And by the way, she had sex not long before she died. Not your department, of course.' He gave a dismissive nod and returned to his clipboard.

Sukey packed away her camera, went back to the van and called the office.

'New report just come in,' Barnes told her. 'Nothing sensational, I'm afraid.'

'And there was I hoping for another murder. Never mind, I'll try and contain my disappointment.'

'There's a brave girl. It's a break-in at a private house near the cattle market. Uniformed already in attendance.' He gave the address and rang off.

When she reached the small house in a quiet street off the ring road, Trudy Marshall answered her knock. 'The victim's a widow,' she said. 'She's very distressed because most of the stuff that's missing was jewellery given her by her husband.'

'Poor soul,' said Sukey. 'Does she have any photographs of the missing items?'

'I haven't got around to asking her yet, she's in too much of a state.'

'How did the intruder get in?'

'Through the back door.' Trudy pointed upwards. 'It's the room on the right at the top of the stairs. She's beginning to calm down now so I'll give her some tea and see if I can get a few details out of her.'

'I'd rather you stayed out of the kitchen until I've had a look round in there.'

Having satisfied herself that making a pot of tea would not involve contaminating the probable route taken by the intruder, Sukey gave it the all-clear before setting to work. Meanwhile, Trudy plied the victim with tea and sympathy while extracting from her a description of some of the missing items and also of a possible suspect she claimed to have seen 'hanging around' earlier in the day.

They left at the same time; Sukey said, 'Bye, Trudy,' and made for her van, but the young policewoman put a hand on her arm.

'Got five minutes?' she asked.

'Sure. Why?'

'There have been some developments over the Bishop's Heights killing. Want to hear them?'

Nineteen

'It came out during the house-to-house,' Trudy began. 'One of the residents stated she had just put her car away on the evening before Dalsey's body was discovered when she noticed a car with Mrs Pomeroy in the passenger seat drive into the car park. The witness didn't think anything of it as she knew Mrs P. by sight and had actually spoken to her once or twice, but it rang a bell with us right away as it didn't tie in with what the old biddy had said in her statement.'

'Which was?'

'She was quite definite she always left as soon as she'd served Dalsey's evening meal at seven and never went back until the following morning.'

'So what time was this?'

'About half-past eight, the witness thinks. When Mrs P. was questioned about it she got very flustered and said the woman must have made a mistake, but it was obvious she was lying. Eventually she owned up and admitted that she did go there occasionally – for reasons that had nothing to do with her housekeeping duties.' The prurient gleam in Trudy's eye on the final words left no doubt as to her meaning.

'Don't tell me she was having a steamy affair with her boss!' said Sukey incredulously.

'Oh, no, not him. Her devotion to him is pure and unsullied, but she had to find an outlet for her other needs.' The humour of the story she was about to tell caused the young constable to succumb to a fit of the giggles. 'It's like something out of Mills and Boon,' she hooted. 'Passion behind the bike sheds – or rather, in the tool shed!'

'What on earth are you talking about?'

'Mrs Pompom and Mr Granger, the caretaker at Bishop's Heights. He's been taking care of her all right.'

'You're kidding!'

'It's true. The boys in CID have been killing themselves over it.'

'I remember you said you thought she was sweet on him,' said Sukey. 'He wouldn't be my choice, but I suppose there's no accounting for taste.'

'Well, we know about your taste in men, don't we?' said Trudy slyly. Sukey pretended not to hear; after a moment Trudy went on, 'Anyway, the thing is, when he could make an excuse to get out in the evening by telling his wife there was some kind of emergency at the flats, he'd pick up his fancy lady and bring her to the spare garage he uses as a workshop for a quick bit of leg-over. He's got a bed in there, and an electric kettle for brewing up tea and even a chemical toilet, the kind you take camping. Very cosy.'

'Fascinating stuff, if you're looking for material for a bonkbuster,' said Sukey, joining in the laughter, 'but I don't see what bearing it can have on the killing.'

'It doesn't, not directly, except that a few minutes later the same witness who spotted Mrs P. happened to see a man coming out of the private lift to Dalsey's penthouse. And when the great lovers were questioned further it turned out that as they were sneaking into the love nest that same evening they saw a man walk across the car park, get into his car and drive away. They didn't recognize him and couldn't say which apartment he'd been visiting, but their description matches that given by the other witness so they reckon it was probably the same man. Unfortunately, they couldn't give a description of the car except that it was large and dark coloured.'

'Is that all?'

'For the time being. Must go now, but I simply had to tell you. I'll keep my ear to the ground and let you know if I pick up any more titbits. It'll take a lot to beat this one, though!' She got into her car and drove off, still chortling.

Sukey got into her van and sat for a few minutes deep in thought. Her mind went back to the scene in Scud Dalsey's apartment and the strange sensation she had experienced, almost an intuition, that there was a common factor between

128

this death and that of Evie Stanton. Could the man the witnesses had seen on the evening of the attack on Dalsey be that link? Might he even be the killer? She recalled turning back when on the point of leaving the room, despite her revulsion, and forcing herself to take a long, hard look at the body. Well dressed and obviously well to do, a typical 'posh gent' in the eyes of the homeless.

She thought about the connection between Dalsey and the antiques dealer, Joseph Bryant, in which DI Castle had expressed such interest, and recalled Bryant's fury on learning that a package had been collected early. He had stormed back into his office and said something to the person he had been speaking to on the telephone about 'Blackie' having 'pulled a fast one'. Supposing one of Blackton's operatives had hijacked an Express van and taken something of value awaiting shipment? Were there two gangs at work here, one led by Dalsey and the other by Trevor Blackton – possibly dealing in stolen antiques? Certainly Bryant had shown no interest in accepting police help in tracing the missing package. That in itself might mean nothing, but Castle had mentioned the possibility that Bryant might have only pretended not to know Dalsey was dead. In that case, whose side was he on? But supposing it was the man on the other end, who had not so far been identified, who knew but was concealing the fact. Could he be the man seen leaving Dalsey's apartment on the fatal night? The more she thought about it, the more complex the situation appeared.

She longed for an opportunity to discuss the case in detail with Jim, but dared not risk it. He would be furious if he knew about her arrangement with Trudy.

'All quiet at the moment,' said George Barnes when Sukey checked in at six o'clock.

'DCI Lord wants me to put together an E-FIT of one of the *Big Issue* sellers who hasn't been seen around lately,' she said. 'It's possible he might know something about Lucy that could help trace her killer,' she added, anticipating his question. 'Maybe this would be a good time to come in and do it.'

'Why not?'

129

It was an uncanny sensation, seeing Matt's face take shape on the computer screen. 'Yes, that's him,' she said at last. 'As near as I remember, that's how he looked last time I saw him. He might have shaved off his beard and moustache, though.'

The technician moved the mouse and the face became clean-shaven. 'How about that?'

Sukey frowned. 'It's difficult to say. I think I'd better have both versions.'

'No problem.' As the copies emerged from the printer he slid them into an acetate folder and handed them to her. 'There you go. Let me know if you want more.'

'Thanks. I'll take these to Mr Lord right away.'

She had a hand raised to knock on the door of DCI Lord's office when it opened and DI Castle emerged. His expression as he recognized her was far from friendly.

'Just the person I want to see. Report to me immediately you've finished in here,' he said curtly and marched off down the passage towards his own office without giving her time to reply.

If Lord noticed the acrimonious nature of the command, he gave no sign. He glanced briefly at the two images Sukey handed to him, thanked her politely and dismissed her with a gesture. On her way to Castle's office she put her head round the door of the SOCOs' room to let George Barnes know where she was going. The sergeant pursed his lips and gave her a shrewd glance.

'He told me he'd asked to see you and he didn't look best pleased,' he remarked. 'Have you blotted your copybook?'

'He probably thinks so,' Sukey sighed. 'Well, I'd better get it over with.'

When she entered Castle's office he looked up and fixed her with an angry look in his greenish eyes. 'Just what's the idea of going behind my back and running to DCI Lord with your half-baked theories?'

'I didn't go running to anybody, as you call it, and I don't remember offering any half-baked theories,' she retorted hotly. 'Mr Lord naturally wanted to know how I was able to identify the body of the woman they found in the river—'

'That's not what I mean. I'm talking about the way you've

130

been chasing after this fellow Matt without saying anything to me. I thought I told you—'

'You told me you thought my suggestion that Matt could be the young man seen at Evie Stanton's house was a no-no,' she broke in. 'You didn't say I wasn't to enquire after Matt for any other reason.'

'What other reason could there be?'

'I'm worried about him personally. Even if it's got nothing to do with Evie, I believe he has problems and needs help.'

'You're a Scenes of Crime Examiner, not a social worker.'

'If I show a little concern for someone who's down on his luck, that's my business,' she said defiantly. 'And anyway, when I mentioned my hunch to DCI Lord, he didn't dismiss it out of hand. That's why he told me to compile the E-FIT you turned down.'

Castle opened his mouth as if to make an angry retort, closed it again, got up and began pacing the short distance between his desk and the window. He took a bunch of keys from his pocket, tossing them up in the air and catching them again as he moved restlessly to and fro. It was several minutes before he sat down again, threw the keys on the desk and ran his fingers through his thick brown hair. 'All right, maybe I did lose my cool,' he said, 'but I worry about you, Sook. I'm constantly afraid you'll go blundering into a dangerous situation one day and come to grief. It wouldn't be the first time, would it?'

'No, sir.'

'Oh, forget the "sir",' he said impatiently.

'I thought, as we're both on duty—'

'You're right. Perhaps we'd better continue this discussion later. What time do you finish?'

'Not until seven.'

He glanced at his watch. 'It's nearly that now. OK if I come to your place later on?'

'Sure. Come for supper.'

'Where's Fergus?' asked Jim as he followed Sukey into the kitchen.

'Gone swimming with some of his mates,' she said over her shoulder.

He grabbed her, swung her round to face him and drew her

close. She yielded happily to the embrace, twining her arms round his neck and pressing her body against his.

'Does that mean we have the evening to ourselves?' he murmured.

'I'm afraid not,' she said softly, but she was in no hurry to push him away. Presently, she said, 'I guess I'd better start thinking about food. Gus will be starving when he gets in. What about you?'

'I suppose food is better than nothing,' he sighed. 'What have you got?'

'I picked up some fish and chips on the way home. I'd better get it into the oven or it'll be cold. Help yourself to a beer.'

'I thought we'd have some of this.' He indicated the bottle of Chardonnay that he had placed on the table when he came in.

'Super.' She reached into a drawer and handed him the corkscrew. While he opened the bottle and filled two glasses, she transferred the food from its wrappings onto dishes and put them in the oven. They clinked glasses and drank.

'Not mad at me any more?' she said.

'No – at least, only a little!' He put an arm round her shoulders. 'Come and relax for a few minutes. I want to talk to you.'

'Oh dear, that sounds ominous.'

They settled on the couch in the sitting room. It was already fairly warm from the central heating, but Sukey switched on the coal-effect electric fire, which produced a cheerful glow. 'I know it's a bit naff, but I couldn't be bothered with the real thing,' she said.

'It's not naff at all and it's been there for ages. You're just making conversation.'

'I suppose I am. It's just that I've got a feeling that "a talk" is another word for a telling-off.'

'On the contrary. If anything, I'm the one who got the telling-off.'

'Who from?'

'DCI Lord. He understands my concern for you, but he told me he thinks very highly of you and says I should take your ideas a bit more seriously.'

'Well, bully for Charlie C! I hope you've taken the message to heart.'

'I have indeed, and to prove it I'm going to fill you in on progress so far on the Dalsey case. Interested?'

'Try me!'

Twenty

'According to Prof Hillbourne,' Jim began, 'the man died around two hours after he ate his last meal, which the housekeeper states she served at seven o'clock. We may have narrowed it down still further, because we have two witnesses who saw a man at Bishop's Heights at about half-past eight. One of the other residents actually saw him leaving the private lift to Dalsey's apartment, and Dalsey's housekeeper and the caretaker saw him a few minutes later when he came into the car park and drove away.'

'Can you be sure it was the same man?' said Sukey.

'Not a hundred per cent, but it seems pretty likely. The descriptions match and the times tally. Unfortunately we didn't get a description of the car except that it was large – maybe a BMW or a Jag – and dark coloured.'

'I suppose that's a start. What were the housekeeper and the caretaker doing there at that time, I wonder?' she added artlessly.

'Believe it or not, they're lovers.'

'Really?' she exclaimed with feigned astonishment. 'But neither of them lives at Bishop's Heights, surely?'

'No, they used his workshop.' Without so much as a flicker of a smile, Jim proceeded to give a bowdlerized version of the story she had heard earlier from Trudy. 'It turns out,' he went on, 'the housekeeper discovered she'd left her glasses behind in Dalsey's kitchen and she used the house phone to ask him if it was all right to go up and fetch them. There was no reply so she assumed he'd gone out, went up to the apartment, let herself in with her key, collected the glasses and came away, not realizing he was there all the time.'

'Lying dead on the floor of his sitting room. Gosh, she must feel awful about that,' said Sukey with genuine compassion.

'Dead or dying. We'll never be sure which.'

'And what a fearful shock when she came to work the next day and realized what had happened.'

'It must have been devastating for the poor woman,' he agreed soberly. 'It accounts for the hysterical way she carried on after she found his body. She's tormenting herself with the thought that she might have saved him and at the same time she's scared stiff because she's convinced she came face to face with the man who attacked him.'

'I can understand that. Do you reckon it's true?'

Jim sat twiddling the stem of his glass for several moments before replying. 'The chap they all saw – assuming it was the same man – is obviously in the frame,' he said at length. 'We need to find him, even if it's only to eliminate him from our enquiries.'

'Jim, I have a feeling you're not telling me everything.'

'We don't know everything yet.'

'That's no answer. When did you find this out?'

'Only a couple of days ago. The witness who gave us the information has been away, so she was missed during the first round of enquiries. She expressed surprise that we hadn't heard about it from Mrs Pomeroy – that's the housekeeper – because she spotted her in the car park at the same time and assumed she must have seen the man as well.' This time Jim allowed himself a dry chuckle. 'As you can imagine, that caused a good deal of consternation when we questioned Mrs Pomeroy again. Up till then, she'd stuck to her story that she left Dalsey's apartment just after seven o'clock that evening as usual and didn't come back until her regular time the following morning. When we spoke to Granger – the caretaker – he tried to bluff it out by saying the only reason he took her there that evening was so she could pick up her glasses, but she'd already dropped him in it by owning up to what had been going on.'

'I take it he's a married man?'

'Oh, yes. We invited him to come down to the station to answer a few questions and he was practically in tears, begging us "not to tell the missus". We assured him it wouldn't be necessary.'

'Just like a man to think of his own skin first,' said Sukey scornfully.

135

'Not all men,' he protested, affecting to appear hurt.

'With one or two notable exceptions,' she conceded. 'Anyway, tell me more about the stranger – the man they all spotted. Do you have any leads at all?'

'I suppose there's no harm in your knowing that.' He drained his glass and stood up. 'How's your drink? Can I get you a refill?'

'No, thanks, I'm fine at the moment, but I'm starving. Let's go and eat – Gus will be in any minute.' As she spoke they heard the sound of a key in the front door. 'That's him now. Is it all right to let him know what we've been talking about?'

'I guess so. He'll probably ask anyway.'

Fergus burst into the house in his usual exuberant fashion and gave his mother a hug. 'Hi, Mum, hi, Jim! What's for supper?'

'Nothing for you until you put your gear in the washing machine and get that out of the way before one of us trips over it,' Sukey scolded, pointing to the holdall he had thrown casually on the kitchen floor.

'Oh, right.' He extracted an assortment of crumpled garments, a damp towel and a pair of swimming trunks and stuffed them into the machine. He slammed the door, kicked the holdall into a corner and reached into the refrigerator. 'Can I have a beer?'

'Looks like you've got one.'

'Swimming's thirsty work.'

The three of them sat down at the table and tackled the food Sukey had brought from the oven. After a minute or two Sukey said, 'Jim's been telling me about a man who was spotted at Bishop's Heights the night Mr Dalsey was attacked. The police have got him down as number one suspect, isn't that right, Jim?'

'I didn't say that.' He forked a piece of fish into his mouth, picked up a chip and dipped it into the heap of salt on the edge of his plate. 'All I can say categorically at the moment is that he may be able to help us with our enquiries.'

'You're being very cagey,' said Sukey. 'You said a moment ago there was no harm in my knowing if you've got a lead on him.'

'Yes, well . . .' Jim glanced at Fergus, who read the signs immediately.

'You don't have to worry about me shooting my mouth off,' he said eagerly. 'I won't say a word to anyone, honest.'

'All right, I can tell you a bit more,' said Jim. 'I don't know how much your mother has told you about the case?' he added and Sukey mentally crossed her fingers that her son wouldn't go blurting out any of their private speculations.

She was impressed by his talent for diplomacy as he replied, 'Not very much, except that having to photograph the corpse was pretty unpleasant, and that the victim's name's Dalsey, his friends call him Scud and he belongs to a golf club. Have you found out any more?'

'Quite a lot. He's an exceptionally wealthy man with a lot of business interests – all perfectly legitimate, as far as we know at present – but apparently very few intimate friends. We've begun enquiries among the staff at a company Scud owned called Express Deliveries. Andy Radcliffe has spoken to a man called Joshua Dowding, who seems to have been his right-hand man. In fact it was Andy who broke the news of his boss's death. He appeared very shocked; said they were close friends as well as business partners and he'd been having a drink with him in his penthouse just a couple of nights before. Only –' Jim paused to help himself to more chips – 'we have reason to believe he may have been there on the actual night.' Without revealing any of the prurient details, he repeated the information he had given Sukey earlier.

'Did Dowding answer to the description the witnesses gave?' asked Fergus.

'He seemed about the right age and build, Radcliffe said, but it was a cold night and the man they saw was wearing a hat and overcoat, so it's hardly conclusive.'

'What sort of car does Dowding drive?'

'A dark-blue top-of-the-range Lexus.'

'Express Deliveries must be doing well,' Sukey remarked.

'So it would appear.'

Fergus digested all the information for a few moments and then said, 'It seems to me Dowding is quite a smart guy.'

'Why do you say that?' asked Jim.

'He volunteered the information he was a regular visitor because he'd know he'd been seen there from time to time, and at the same time he planted the idea his last visit was the evening *before* the one Scud was killed.'

Jim raised an eyebrow. 'That's a tortuous bit of reasoning, Gus,' he said. 'Are you doing criminal psychology for A-levels by any chance?'

'It just seemed obvious,' said Fergus, evidently well pleased with the implied compliment. 'What did he say when you confronted him with the new evidence?'

'Hang on a minute. I've just pointed out there's no proof that it was him the witnesses saw. His car answers to the very vague description, but so do countless others. We asked him, naturally, if he'd called on Dalsey that evening and he was quite emphatic that he hadn't and he couldn't off the top of his head think who the man might have been.'

'In any case,' Sukey pointed out, 'the mystery man was seen leaving at about eight thirty. Given the pathologist's estimate of the time of death, the attack could have taken place up to half an hour later, so there was time for another caller to come and do the deed.'

'Exactly. We've issued a press release asking for further witnesses but no one's come forward so far. We've also taken Dowding's prints to compare with any found in Dalsey's apartment, but even if we find a match it won't tell us much as he's admitted to having been a fairly regular visitor.'

'Have they been compared with the prints on the remains of the decanter?' Sukey asked. 'It would have been tricky to take them on the spot so Mandy bagged up the bits and passed them to the people in the lab.'

Jim shook his head. 'Oh, yes, that's been done, with negative results. There were traces of Dalsey's own prints on some of the fragments and the stopper, but the neck had been wiped clean.'

'And whoever used it as a weapon must have grasped it by the neck,' said Fergus.

'That's right.'

'What about a motive?' said Sukey.

'Obviously, that's something we'll have to look into. As I mentioned earlier, Dalsey seems to have been a man with few intimates, and the general feeling seems to be that his employees respected him but didn't particularly like him. Equally, we haven't come across a reason why anyone should particularly *dis*like him.'

'What about the housekeeper and her boyfriend?' said Fergus.

'She claims to have thought the world of her boss and would see his killer boiled in oil if she had her way. We made a routine check on Granger's background; he's ex-army with an exemplary character, a clean employment record since his discharge and according to the agents does a good job and gets on well with the tenants.'

'But you haven't eliminated him?'

'We haven't eliminated anybody. Our enquiries have only just begun.'

'By the way, Jim,' said Sukey as she began clearing the table, 'has anyone interviewed that antiques dealer whose clock was stolen?'

'You mean the man you overheard asking for someone called Scud?'

'That's the one.'

'I sent a man to check with him and there was no mystery about it. Express Deliveries were supposed to ship the clock to a customer in the States and he was calling to let Scud know it had been nicked.'

'Why couldn't he have told whoever answered the phone?'

'He said he couldn't trust an underling to deal with the matter, and anyway he wanted to speak to Dalsey about something else.'

'What about the reference to Blackie?'

'Look, is that there to eat or is it just for decoration?' Jim pointed with his dessert spoon at the apple pie and the jug of custard Sukey had just put on the table.

'Oh, sorry.' She cut slices from the pie and passed them round. 'Well?'

'Well what?' said Jim as he helped himself to custard.

'Blackie?' she prompted impatiently.

'Oh, that. Nothing significant there, I'm afraid.'

'But—'

'Look, love,' he said a little wearily, 'could we give crime a rest for now? It's been a long day and I've answered a load of questions already.'

'He's holding something back,' said Fergus as Sukey returned to the sitting room after saying goodnight to Jim at the front door.

'You're right. He closed up like an oyster as soon as I asked about Blackie. He knows I thought it might be a reference to Trevor Blackton, and if there was a different explanation – I mean, if Bryant was referring to some petty crook he and Scud knew about from previous experience, for example – why didn't he say so?'

'Maybe there's something big in the offing and he's not letting on.'

'Could well be. I know they've been interested in Blackton for a long time, and now he's in custody—'

'Gosh, when did they nick him? You didn't tell me.'

'I haven't had a chance – it only happened this morning.'

'By the way, did Jim tell you any more about the Evie Stanton case before I got home?'

'He didn't even mention it. And come to think of it, I wonder why he decided to be so communicative about the Dalsey case? He's got no reason to think I'd be particularly interested.'

'The conversation you overheard in the antiques shop?' Fergus suggested.

'Maybe, although that didn't come up until right at the end, and I was the one who raised it.'

'And that was when he changed the subject,' said Fergus thoughtfully. 'Mum, you said you thought Dalsey might be the "posh guy" who came to Matt's rescue, didn't you?'

'I said it crossed my mind, and as you know I ran it past Jim, but he didn't bite.'

'I take it you haven't seen Matt.'

'I was hoping to see him today, but having to do overtime put the mockers on it. It'll have to wait till Monday now.'

As Sukey went round switching off lights and checking that all doors and windows were secure she asked herself whether the evening's 'revelations' were nothing more than a smokescreen to give the impression that he was following Lord's advice to take her more seriously. It seemed more important than ever to talk to Matt. Come hell or high water, she resolved, she'd find a way of seeing him on Monday.

Twenty-One

'Good morning, Trevor. I hope you slept well.'
    'Get stuffed.' He was buggered if he was going to play along with that sort of crap, least of all with this green-eyed, beaky-nosed son of a bitch.

'Have it your way.' DI Castle appeared unperturbed by the hostile response to his greeting. 'Do you recognize this?' He put a transparent envelope on the table that separated the police officers from Trevor Blackton and his solicitor, Hamish Grayson, who sat at his client's side, wooden-featured but with sharp, watchful eyes fixed on the inspector.

Blackton picked up the envelope and turned it this way and that, studying the contents with exaggerated care. After a while he put it down and said, 'Correct me if I'm wrong, but at first sight it looks like a mobile phone.' He saw Castle's jaw tighten and gave a smirk of triumph. The involuntary movement told him he'd hit on a way to get under the bastard's skin. He decided to have another dig. 'Course, I may be mistaken, I'm only a simple chap, not clever like a detective inspector.'

Castle ignored the taunt. 'No, you're quite right, it is a mobile phone,' he said.

'Glad we've got that sorted. Next question?'

'Is a repeat of the first. I didn't ask you to explain what it is, I asked if you *recognized* it.'

'Sorry, my mistake.' Blackton picked up the phone again, gave it a brief glance and put it down. 'Looks much the same as any other.'

'True. However, there's something different about this one.'

'Oh, yeah?'

'It was in your pocket when you were arrested and it has your fingerprints on it.'

'Well I never. I wonder how it got there. You're not

suggesting I nicked it, I hope?' Grayson coughed and gave his client a warning glance. 'What's up with you, Hamish? Got a frog in your throat?'

'I think you are being tactfully advised by your brief not to waste police time,' said Castle. 'Isn't that right, Mr Grayson?'

'I think it would be in your interests, Mr Blackton, to answer the Inspector's questions directly, to the best of your ability,' said the solicitor in his dry, slightly high-pitched voice.

'OK, if you say it was in my pocket, I guess it's mine,' said Blackton. 'I came by it honestly and the account's paid regular, so you can't charge me with possession or anything like that.'

'That wasn't what I had in mind and I'm not interested in your accounting arrangements. In fact, we have your latest bill here and it shows quite clearly that it's been settled.' Castle produced a second envelope containing a single sheet of paper and put it on the table beside the phone.

Blackton glared at it. 'Bleedin' cheek! Ain't nothing sacred?'

'Not when a man's being questioned on suspicion of murder.'

'Look, I told you—'

'Yes, we know what you told us and we don't buy it,' said Castle, 'but we'll leave that for the time being. What we're interested in at the moment is this account.'

'What about it?'

As if at a prearranged signal, Detective Sergeant Radcliffe took over the interrogation. He leaned forward and pointed to a series of ticks made against a constantly recurring number on the account. 'All these calls were made to another mobile number listed in your directory as belonging to a lady called Celia,' he said. 'Would that be your wife, by any chance?'

'Me married? Are you kidding?'

'Another girlfriend, perhaps?'

Blackton's features puckered and he covered his eyes. 'I'd never have cheated on Evie,' he muttered through his hands.

'If Evie had found out you were married or were seeing another woman, she wouldn't have been best pleased, would she? And if she'd started shooting her mouth off about it, that might have made you lose your temper and lash out at her, mightn't it?'

'Stop pissing me about!' Now he was getting angry; Grayson put a warning hand on his arm, but he shook it off and snarled, 'She ain't me wife and she ain't a girlfriend. If you must know, she's the sister of an old mate what's inside and I speak to her regular. So bleedin' what?'

'Thank you, that didn't hurt, did it?' said Radcliffe smoothly.

It was Castle's turn to take up the questioning again. 'You must be very fond of Celia to call her so often.'

'I like to make sure she's all right.'

'Where does she live?'

'Find out.'

'Oh, we will, only it would save time if you'd tell us.' Blackton glowered, but kept silent. He wasn't going to do the bastard's legwork for him. 'Has she got a job?' Castle went on.

'Yeah, I think so.'

'What sort of job?'

'How would I know?'

'Does she work for you?'

'No, she bloody don't. She ain't the type for a club hostess. And since you've raised the matter, I own three clubs, they're well run and I've never been in no trouble.'

'Oh, yes, your reputation as a businessman is impeccable. Or it has been up to now. Tell me, Trevor, where did you disappear to after you killed Evie?'

'Inspector, I must object to this line of questioning,' said Grayson. 'If you have evidence linking my client with the unfortunate lady's death, then kindly produce it.'

'All right, I'll put the question another way. You went to the house in Glevum Passage the day Evie was murdered. Neighbours reported hearing you accuse her of being unfaithful to you, and noises that suggested you were beating her up.'

'I didn't beat her up.' Blackton thumped the table. 'I keep telling you—'

'But you admit hitting her?'

'All right, I gave her a slap or two now and again to teach her a lesson, but not on that day. And I did once warn her what

I'd do if I caught her messin' around with other men but she swore she never.'

'On the day Evie's body was found, a neighbour overheard sounds of a fight coming from Evie's house. She said a man was shouting at her, using expressions like "whore" and "faithless bitch", and she was screaming at him to stop. She's quite sure you were the man because she saw you leave the house and drive away shortly afterwards.'

'Look, I'm pissed off to the eyeballs with hearing this garbage. I didn't row with Evie on that day and I didn't kill her. The old bat's got it all wrong.'

'You still maintain that when you left the house Evie was alive and in good health?'

'That's what I keep telling you.'

'According to an earlier statement, you were driving to Worcester to keep a business appointment when you heard about the killing on your car radio.'

'That's right.'

'So you cancelled your appointment. Now, most men, on hearing that their lady friend had been murdered, would have rushed to the scene in great distress.'

'They never said it was Evie, did they? It could have been anyone.'

'But you didn't bother to find out, you did a disappearing act. If Evie was all right when you left her, why didn't you immediately call the police and offer to help with the enquiries?'

Blackton thumped the table in exasperation. 'How many times do I have to tell you? They didn't say it was her and I was scared, if it was, you'd think I killed her because she was my bird and I was round there all the time. I decided to lie low until I knew for certain who it was who'd been topped.' He felt his voice beginning to crack; the air in the interview room was stale and oppressive, but he took in great gulps of it in an effort to steady himself. 'Can I have a drink?' he croaked.

Castle signalled to Radcliffe. The sergeant filled a plastic cup with water and handed it to Blackton, who emptied it in a single draught and held it out for more.

'You were afraid we'd think you killed her, naturally, but that wasn't the only reason, was it?' Castle persisted. 'You

145

didn't just suspect Evie, you *knew* she'd been unfaithful and you wanted to get your hands on your rival, didn't you? First you killed her, and then—'

The thought of another man's hands caressing that smooth, white body sent a tide of rage boiling through Blackton's veins. He clenched his fists; the temptation to wipe the smile off his tormentor's mocking countenance was almost overwhelming, but he felt a warning hand on his arm, heard Grayson make yet another intervention on his behalf and with a superhuman effort managed to resist it. He drew a deep breath and said, 'No comment,' in a voice that was still not quite steady.

'All right,' said Castle. 'We'll leave that for the moment. Where did you go after you cancelled your appointment?'

'I told you – where you found me.'

'You went straight there? Are you telling me the place was already habitable and linked up to electricity and water supplies, just in case you needed a bolt hole? Incidentally,' Castle added casually, 'there's likely to be an additional charge of fraudulently obtaining those services.'

Blackton shrugged. 'So what? If there's a fine, I can afford to pay it.'

'I'm glad to hear it. Now, will you please answer my question, or am I to assume that you had the place ready because you were actually *planning* to commit murder and knew you'd have to go to ground in a hurry?'

This time the anger boiled over and Blackton thumped the table again. 'No, I bloody well wasn't and I bloody well didn't!' he shouted

'Inspector, may I remind you—' Grayson intervened yet again and Castle made a conciliatory gesture.

'All right, let's go back to my earlier question. Did you go straight there?'

There was a long silence before Blackton uttered a reluctant, 'No.'

'So you went and hid somewhere else while your friends found a safe house and fixed it up for you?'

'Maybe.'

'Where did you go?'

'No comment.'

'To your friend Celia's place, perhaps?'

'Don't you go dragging her into this, it's got nothing to do with her.'

'Well, we'll just have to go and check with her, won't we?'

'Get stuffed.'

'Which is where we came in,' Castle remarked. He pushed back his chair and stood up. 'Thank you, Trevor. We'll talk again later, after we've had a chat with Celia.'

Blackton clenched his fists and swore. Radcliffe spoke into the tape recorder. 'Interview terminated at ten a.m.,' he said and switched off the machine.

'What did you make of that?' said Castle.

'I hate to say this,' said Radcliffe, 'but he could be telling the truth – up to a point, anyway.' He took an A4 sheet from the file on the case and handed it to Castle. 'I've been rereading Mrs Pewsey's statement. If you remember, she was the only witness who actually overheard the fight going on in Evie's house. Here's what she said when I interviewed her on the day of the murder: "It went on for a few minutes, perhaps, and then it all went quiet and I thought, perhaps they've made it up. And then I heard the car start up and drive away so I thought no more about it for a while." And then she goes on about talking it over with her neighbour and deciding to report it, much as in the original statement.'

'Right. Go on.'

Radcliffe took out another sheet. 'This is the detailed statement she made the following day down at the station. This time she remembered looking out of the window when she heard the car start up and was quite sure it was the same one she'd noticed parked outside Evie's house on a number of occasions, but here's the weakness in our case, such as it is. She didn't see the car arrive – we already know that – so we can't be sure how long it was there. The trouble is, she was vague about how much time elapsed between the fight ending and the car driving away.'

'You're suggesting that someone else might have come to the house, had a fight with Evie, killed her and made off *before* Blackton turned up? We've already considered that

147

as a theoretical possibility and more or less discounted it in view of the evidence.'

'Perhaps we ought to think again, Guv,' Radcliffe suggested. 'The way Blackton's sticking to his denial and we haven't been able to shake him . . . suppose that part of his statement is true? We could still be right about him wanting to catch up with Evie's killer.'

'You're suggesting that he went to the house, found her body and made up the story about cancelling the appointment in Worcester so he could go to ground and plot revenge?'

'No, Guv, we checked that and it's true. However, what no one spotted at the time is that the call was made *before* the news flash on the radio reporting a body being found at a house in Glevum Passage.'

'It'll be interesting to hear what Blackton has to say about that,' said Castle. He began prowling round the office, doing his usual throwing and catching routine with his keys. 'What we need is a witness who saw him arrive at the house *and* saw him leave. That way we'd have an idea how long he was there.'

'We've already drawn a blank on that one. What we need to know is exactly how much time elapsed between things going quiet after the fight that Mrs Pewsey overheard and her seeing Blackton drive away. All she could say at the time was, "not long after".'

'Then you'd better go and see her again; try and jog her memory.'

'Oh dear,' said Mrs Pewsey. 'I've been over it all so many times in my head since that terrible day. When I think of what that monster did to that poor woman—'

'I'm very sorry to have to bring it all back for you,' said Radcliffe. 'We have a man in custody and he insists Ms Stanton was all right when he left the house. What I'm asking you to remember is this: how long was it after things went quiet that you saw the man drive off in the red car?'

Mrs Pewsey sat for several minutes fiddling with her rose-patterned teacup.

'I told you before, it wasn't very long—' she began.

'Will you try to remember what you were doing when the fight started?'

'Oh, that's easy. I told you at the time, I was watching the telly.'

'And the programme you were watching was called *Homes and Gardens*, I think?'

'That's right, it's one of my favourites.'

'How long had it been on when the fight began?'

'It had only just started.'

'You said the fight went on for several minutes. Did you stop watching when you heard it start?'

'Yes, I think I must have done.'

'And when it ended?'

'I . . . I just thought to myself, "Thank goodness that row's over," and carried on watching. Oh dear—' Mrs Pewsey's eyes began to fill, 'if only I'd known.'

'Mrs Pewsey, please think carefully. Just how much of the programme was left *after* the fight ended?'

'Well, I don't know exactly.'

'It's on one of the commercial channels, I believe, and it lasts half an hour with a break for advertisements?'

'That's right. Yes, I remember now, the commercials came on not long after the rowing stopped.'

'And you carried on watching until the programme ended?'

'Yes.'

'And it was then you heard the car start up and went to the window?'

'A couple of minutes later, perhaps. There were more adverts and then the next programme started. I wasn't interested in that, so I switched off.'

'Thank you, Mrs Pewsey, that's very helpful.'

Helpful in shooting holes in the already circumstantial evidence against Blackton, Radcliffe thought ruefully as he headed back to the police station to report to DI Castle.

Twenty-Two

O n Monday morning, Sukey and Mandy were greeted with the news that Nigel Warren had still not recovered and would be off for at least two more days.

'Sorry about that, ladies,' said George Barnes. 'Same arrangement as before?' The two women nodded resignedly. 'Right, here are your assignments for this morning. By the way, Sukey, DI Castle wants a word with you before you leave.'

'What have you been up to now?' asked Mandy as they set off along the corridor.

'Nothing, so far as I know. Mandy, is there any chance you can take the four-to-seven stint and I'll do seven till ten?'

'Sorry, I have to pick Mum up from the day centre by half-past four. Is there a problem?'

'There's someone I was hoping to meet this afternoon. Seven o'clock's a bit late.'

'Can't you call your friend and explain?'

'I suppose I'll have to.' *Not easy when you don't know where he is*, Sukey thought. *He's probably wondering why I didn't make it on Friday. I just hope Jack will be able to get a message to him . . . I hope he doesn't cry off.*

Mandy was staring at her with a quizzical expression on her pale, freckled face. 'Have you found a new boyfriend?' she asked.

'Nothing like that.' For a moment, Sukey was tempted to tell her about Matt and the plan to meet him down by the river, but decided against. Normally the soul of discretion, Mandy would almost certainly spot the danger in the proposed enterprise and might even be tempted in the circumstances to alert CID out of concern for her safety. 'It's all right, forget it,' she said.

DI Castle was at his desk, studying an open file. Without preamble, he said, 'We've run into a problem with the Evie

150

Stanton killing. Blackton's admitted calling on Evie on the day of the murder but insists she was alive and well when he left and flatly denies having had a row with her.'

'But the next-door neighbour—'

'I know, I know. She heard the fight, things went quiet, she heard a car start up, went to the window and saw Blackton's car drive away. So far, so good, but it now transpires that the interval between the row ending and Blackton's car leaving was longer than we – or she – realized.' He quickly recapitulated Radcliffe's findings. 'That leaves us with two possibilities: either Blackton killed her but didn't leave immediately, perhaps because he took time to clean some of the blood off himself, or someone else killed Evie and made off before Blackton arrived.'

'If we take the second option,' said Sukey, 'it would mean he must have found her body, so either way he's lying when he says she was alive when he left the house.'

'Right. We believe he went to ground not just because he knew he'd be a suspect – whether or not he killed her himself – but also because he wanted to get his hands on the man she'd been two-timing him with. He admits to the first, but denies the second.'

'He would, wouldn't he?'

Sukey's brain was racing. Not being privy to the progress of the enquiries, she had no idea whether it had been possible to establish any kind of pattern to Blackton's visits to the house, but presumably Evie would have known when it was safe to receive her other lovers. Supposing Matt had had an assignation with Evie that day, found her dead and fled in a panic? Her previous knowledge of him, plus what she had gleaned from talking to Jack, seemed to make this more likely. If there was a possibility of Blackton being released for lack of sufficient evidence to charge him, then for Matt's own safety it was more important than ever to make contact with him.

Castle's voice brought her back to reality. 'I want to go over a few points with you. Your report states that you found no traces of blood in the bath or the washbasin, and this was confirmed by subsequent checks of the water in the U-bends, so it looks as if the killer legged it without stopping to clean up. No one actually saw Blackton emerge from the house and get into his car, so we've no idea whether there was blood on his clothing when he left. We've traced this woman he calls Celia and she admits he went to her house but denies seeing stains on any of the clothes he gave her to wash.'

'What about Blackton's car?'

'We found that in Celia's garage. The upholstery's light coloured and appears in pristine condition, but we've sent the mats to the lab for checking in case he had blood on his shoes. Forensics are checking the trainers he was wearing when he was arrested and some other clothing we found in the house, but . . .' From the unfinished sentence and the resigned shake of his head, Sukey deduced that Castle had no great hopes of a lead in that quarter.

'Right,' he said after a moment's reflection, 'let's get back to your report. You've noted and photographed bloodstained shoeprints descending the stairs and heading for the front door, growing steadily fainter. By the time they reach the door the traces of blood have almost disappeared and there were none on the pavement outside.'

'Right.'

'What about the route to the back door?'

'We checked, naturally, but found nothing to indicate anyone had entered or left the house that way.'

'And when you checked the exit through the back yard a few days later, you found no traces of blood?'

'No, but I wasn't actually looking for them. I was there because someone had been seen using that way into the house. I picked up some fibres, but nothing much else.'

'Ah, yes, the fibres from the holly bush; they're a wool and acrylic mix and they match the ones you found on the chair in Evie's bedroom – but of course, there's nothing to indicate how long they'd been there. Anyway, DCI Lord and I think it would be a good idea for you to go and have another look. We haven't had any rain to speak of since the killing so you might get lucky.' Castle sat back and ran his fingers through his hair. 'I'd dearly love to pin this on Blackton, but he's got us over a barrel at the moment. I've been granted permission to detain him for another twenty-four hours, but if we can't come up with something to justify a charge we'll have to release him. See what you can turn up, Sukey.'

'May I make a suggestion, sir?'

'Go ahead.'

'I understand there's evidence that Evie had sex not long before she died.'

'Right.'

'Could it have been with Blackton?'

'I thought of that, but why would he shout abuse at her and beat her to death immediately after they had sex?'

'Maybe in the heat of the moment she called him by one of the toy boys' names by mistake.'

'That's a thought. It'd be hard to prove, but it so happens I've sent the cup he drank from during the interview to the lab for a DNA test. Anything else?'

'If he was naked when he killed her, he wouldn't have got blood on his clothes, except on his boots if he'd trodden in some of it after getting dressed, but his hands and body would have been covered in it.' Carried away with enthusiasm for her theory, picturing the scene, Sukey unconsciously slipped into the present tense. 'His one thought is to get away as soon as possible,' she went on, 'so he doesn't wait to wash away the blood on his body, but he does take the precaution of wiping his face and hands on something, his underpants perhaps before putting them on, then throws on the rest of his clothes and scarpers. There are still traces of blood on his hands, though, maybe enough for a minute amount to be transferred to the latch on the front door when he opens it and perhaps to the steering wheel of his car as well.'

'Good thinking!' Castle made a note. 'I'll make sure the check on the car includes the steering wheel and you attend to the front door.'

'I already have, sir; it's in my report. And on my second visit I made the same check on the back door. I've not heard whether fingerprints found a match, but the sticky tape I used on both doors could have picked up traces of blood that weren't spotted at the time.'

Castle referred to another report from the file. 'There's certainly no mention here of blood on the door and the prints on the latches were too smudged for any positive ID, although there was a match with Blackton's on the front door. Again, that's no help because he freely admits to having been a regular visitor to the house. The man owns the place, after all.' He threw the report back into the file. 'I'll get them to have another look at your samples and at the same time arrange for the complete locks to go to the lab for a thorough examination.'

'Do you want me to do a further check on the rear entrance?'

'Of course. We have to keep our options open; there could still be an outside chance that Blackton has been at least partly telling the truth.' He unlocked a drawer in his desk and took out a small bunch of keys. 'You'll need these to get into the house. Report to me or Sergeant Radcliffe when you get back.'

Sukey left his office feeling distinctly pleased with herself. For the second time in less than a week he had paid her a compliment.

There was an uncanny stillness inside 18 Glevum Passage and Sukey found herself closing the front door behind her as quietly as if afraid of disturbing a sleeper. She went straight through to the kitchen and began re-examining the floor, which was covered in heavy-duty carpeting. She went over it systematically by the light of a powerful torch, paying particular attention to the probable path anyone would use from the bottom of the stairs to the back door. There was no stain of any description visible to the naked eye, which merely reinforced her earlier impression that little or no cookery had been done there.

She went to the window and stood for several minutes staring out at the untidy, weed-infested back yard and trying to visualize Evie preparing to receive a lover. She would either have given him a key or, more likely, been at the back door to admit him, having first unfastened the bolts on the gate. Or maybe she didn't bother to keep them fastened . . . but that seemed unlikely. Someone – probably Blackton – had gone to the expense of protecting the property with new razor wire and would doubtless have impressed on her the importance of taking every possible security measure. But Sukey recalled that when she checked the bolts on her previous visit, they were unfastened. It wasn't conclusive, of course; there could be several reasons why Evie hadn't closed them right away. She might have been busy removing traces of her lover's presence before Blackton's next call. Maybe he had arrived sooner than expected, found something that aroused his suspicions, accused her of being unfaithful and beat her to death in a jealous rage. That would account for the shouts of abuse overheard by Mrs Pewsey. And if the lover was Matt, it would make his evidence even more crucial.

She went outside and took another, closer look at the door into the alley. Again, she could detect no visible mark that might be blood, and the surface of the wood was too rough to yield any fingerprints. It would be up to Castle or DCI Lord to decide whether it was worth having the door removed bodily to the laboratory for examination. There was nothing further she could do, so she went back to the office and wrote out her report. Both Castle and Radcliffe were out so she left it on Castle's desk. It was still only eleven o'clock. She slipped out of the building and went in search of Jack. She found him in his usual spot opposite where first Matt and then Evie used to stand.

'Matt said you didn't show,' he said. 'He wants to know if you changed your mind or what.'

'I didn't change my mind, I had to work overtime,' said Sukey. 'And the way things are, I won't be able to make it until Wednesday. Will you tell him that?'

'If I see him.'

'I thought you knew where to find him.'

'He moves about. I move about.'

Sukey gave an exasperated sigh. 'Jack, you aren't being very helpful.'

'It's probably 'cos I'm hungry. I can't think properly when I'm empty.' He assumed a mournful expression and rubbed one grimy hand over his stomach.

'Oh, all right, I get the message.' She took a five-pound note from her purse and gave it to him. 'I'll take the magazine and you can keep the change. Will that help you to think?'

'Might do.' He put the note in his pocket, handed over the magazine and rubbed his nose with the back of his hand. 'He says he wouldn't mind talking to you,' he said after a moment, 'but he wants no truck with the police.'

'But I told you, the police will give him protection if he's willing to answer a few questions.'

'Forget it. He's says he's had enough hassle from them in the past and he can take care of himself.'

'All right, if that's the way he feels, I'll have to accept it. Just tell him I'll do my best to be there on Wednesday, OK?'

There was no reply. Jack had already gathered up his few possessions and with Jordan at his heels was heading for the hot-dog stand.

Twenty-Three

S ukey's last assignment for the morning was in Cheltenham. Having completed it she parked in a quiet street in Pittville, ate her sandwiches and then called George Barnes.

'Anything else for me, Sarge?'

'House off the Evesham Road. Garage broken into and food stolen from a freezer.'

'That's only just up the road from here. Right, I'm on my way.'

She found the house and parked on the drive. As she got out of the van she saw DS Dalia Chen emerging from a small private hotel on the opposite side of the street. She was carrying a small suitcase; as she went to unlock her car she glanced across, spotted Sukey and beckoned. 'Guess what's in here,' she said.

'Proceeds of a bank robbery?' suggested Sukey.

'Hardly. Could be more interesting for you, though. Remember the E-FIT you did for DCI Lord?'

'What about it?'

'It appeared in the early edition of today's *Gazette*,' she said. 'The owner of that hotel, a Mr Vaughan, called straight away to say he thought it might be a young man who'd been staying there until a couple of weeks or so ago and then disappeared, leaving quite a lot of stuff and this suitcase behind him. It looks as if it might be your friend.'

'That's brilliant. Did Mr Vaughan say when he disappeared?'

'He seemed a bit vague; he said his wife would know, but she's out. I've left a message asking her to call the station and have a word with me. Meanwhile I'll be handing this lot over to forensics.'

'Will you let me know what happens?'

The young detective looked at her curiously. 'You seem very interested in this chap. What name did you know him by?'

'Just Matt; I never knew his surname.'

'He registered at the hotel as Matthew Braine.'

'I suppose that could be his real name. I used to buy the *Big Issue* from him – but you know about that, you were there when I told DCI Lord.'

'Yes. I remember he asked you to try and get a message to him. Have you had any luck there?'

'Not so far, I'm afraid.'

'Well, keep trying.'

'Will do.'

'According to Mr Vaughan, this chap Braine was quite clean and well dressed.'

'I doubt if they'd have given him a room if he turned up in his usual clothes. They were pretty scruffy.'

'You're probably right. It'd be interesting to know how he came to be there.'

Sukey had her own ideas about that, but for the moment she kept them to herself. DS Chen got into her car and drove away while Sukey returned to her task.

Having completed her examination of the garage and the freezer and given the householder the usual assurances that everything possible would be done to trace the culprit, she returned to the van. She was about to get in when she saw a car approaching from the main road. It slowed down and turned into the drive of the hotel where Matt had been staying. The driver was a woman; without stopping to think, Sukey relocked the van and crossed the road. By the time she reached the hotel the car had vanished, but a few moments later the woman reappeared and made for the front door.

Sukey stepped forward and said, 'Excuse me, are you Mrs Vaughan?'

'That's right.'

'I wonder if you could spare a minute?' Sukey held up her ID. 'I'm a Scenes of Crime Officer – I work for the police.'

'Oh?' The woman raised her eyebrows as she glanced briefly at the badge. She was about forty, smartly dressed, with short, beautifully styled hair. 'What is it about? We haven't reported a crime.'

'I understand you recognized the young man whose picture appeared in the *Gazette* this morning?'

'That's right. My husband called police headquarters as soon as this morning's *Gazette* arrived. He – Mr Braine – left unexpectedly and we found some clothes and things in his room. We were expecting him to come back for them, but he didn't. Is he in trouble?'

'Not that we know of. The police think he might be able to help them with some enquiries, that's all.'

'I see.' A pair of intelligent hazel eyes scrutinized Sukey. 'So why have they sent you and not a police officer?'

'A detective sergeant has already called and spoken to your husband, and I believe she wants to have a word with you. I'm interested because Matt Braine is a friend of mine and I've been very concerned about him since he disappeared. Could you tell me if he ever seemed at all anxious or frightened about anything?'

Mrs Vaughan thought for a moment and then shook her head. 'I don't think so – at least, not until he saw that report in the *Gazette.*'

'What report was that?'

'It was about that woman being murdered in Gloucester.'

So I was right, Sukey thought, *Matt did know Evie.* Aloud, she said, 'When he came to your hotel, was anyone with him?'

'Yes, a middle-aged gentleman who seemed to be sort of looking after him. I remember noticing that Matt had a bruise on his cheek, as if he'd been in an accident, but it soon faded.'

'How long was he with you before he disappeared?'

'A couple of weeks, perhaps. I'd have to check our records for the exact date. He was very quiet, went out quite a lot, but settled his bill at the end of every week – except for the week he disappeared.'

'And after he left, did anyone come asking for him?'

'Yes, his friend called round to see him.'

'The friend who was with him the day he arrived?'

'That's right. I said we hadn't seen him for a few days, but we expected him to come back because he'd left most of his things. His friend seemed quite upset. And I remember

159

something else,' Mrs Vaughan added as if a thought had suddenly struck her. 'He didn't seem to have any visitors while he was here, but after he left, a rather strange-looking man appeared and asked for him. When we told him Mr Braine had left suddenly he seemed rather put out and asked to see his room. Naturally, we refused.'

'What do you mean by "strange-looking"?'

'Well, a bit common, if you know what I mean, with cropped hair and studs on his face. Not a bit like Mr Braine, who was quite well spoken and gentlemanly.'

'Yes, that's how I always found him. Did this man come asking for Matt before or after his friend came looking for him?'

'Oh, before.'

'I don't suppose you can remember the day when Matt disappeared?'

'As it happens, I can. It was the day that report appeared, the one I told you about. I was in reception when the paper came, and he was just going out and saw it lying on the counter. He picked it up and read it and said something like, "Oh, my God!" I had the impression he might have known the victim. He looked really upset.'

'And he disappeared soon after that?'

'He was just going out when he read the report. Now I come to think of it, I don't believe he ever came back.'

It all fits, Sukey said to herself as, having thanked Mrs Vaughan for her help, she made her way back to the van. For some reason, Matt had been set up by this middle-aged stranger who, she was sure, was the 'posh gent' Jack had described. He had somehow engineered a meeting between Matt and Evie Stanton. Evie, as was intended, had found Matt more attractive than her wealthy protector, who had found her out, lost his temper and killed her. He had then gone into hiding, having sent one of his sidekicks to locate Matt so that he could mete out his own form of punishment. But Matt had seen the press report, which she remembered had contained a reference to Blackton, whom he probably knew by reputation, and was not taking any chances. That was why he disappeared, but it still didn't explain how Blackton's agent, the 'strange-looking man' referred to by Mrs Vaughan, knew where to find him. Unless the 'posh gent' had tipped him off. Could that have been Scud Dalsey? If so, why would he do that? An awful possibility crept into Sukey's mind: had Matt realized how he had been used, gone to Scud's flat to confront him and in a fit of rage taken that fatal swipe with the crystal decanter? She was reluctant to believe it; whatever weaknesses he might have, she believed he was fundamentally a gentle soul, not given to violence.

The rest of the day slipped past, punctuated by a series of run-of-the-mill incidents. At five o'clock it began to rain, a steady, persistent drizzle. Sukey found herself thinking about all the homeless youngsters huddled in their makeshift shelters. Some of them she knew had more fortunate friends who allowed them to sleep on the floor of their bed-sits for the odd night or two, but she doubted whether Matt was among them.

At half-past six she returned to the office. George Barnes was on the point of leaving and he pointed to a sheaf of printouts on Mandy's desk. 'Nothing desperately urgent,' he commented as he pulled on his overcoat. 'See you tomorrow, Sukey.'

'Goodnight, Sarge.'

She settled down to write her report. She was just putting it with her samples into her out-tray for collection when DS Chen popped her head round the door. 'I hoped I'd catch you,' she said. 'Mrs Vaughan phoned a couple of hours ago. You might remember I asked her to.'

'Yes,' said Sukey, 'and you're going to tell me she mentioned I'd spoken to her.'

'You realize that was out of order, don't you?'

'Yes.'

'So why did you do it?'

'Because I have a particular interest in the case and in the past I've not had much encouragement to take a proactive role in any enquiry.'

'You mean, any enquiry DI Castle's in charge of?'

'Well, yes. I've always found DCI Lord a bit more encouraging, but—'

'I get the picture.' Dalia's pretty, oriental features relaxed in an enigmatic smile. 'You realize, of course, that I have to include your conversation with Mrs Vaughan in my report to Mr Lord?'

'I suppose so.'

'But if I were to mention that I'd given you a ticking off for stepping out of line and that you hoped it wouldn't go any further—?'

'Sarge, you're a pal.'

Twenty-Four

'Gentlemen, this is simply not good enough!' Superintendent Wells, newly appointed following the retirement of his predecessor, glared across his desk at the two senior detectives seated opposite. 'Three murders in less than a fortnight, no leads and no arrests. The press are hounding us and the public are demanding to know how it is we can afford the manpower to launch operation this, that and the other against speeding motorists and yobs mugging kids for their mobile phones while three killers have the run of the county.'

'With respect, sir, we have made an arrest in the Glevum Passage murder case,' DCI Lord reminded him.

'And had to let the bugger go from lack of evidence,' Wells reminded him. 'What the hell are your people playing at?' He jabbed a lean forefinger at the open file in front of him. 'The villain leaves his prints scattered like confetti all over the murder scene . . . and you still maintain you haven't enough to charge him!' He drank deeply from his mug of lukewarm coffee before adding, 'On top of that, it took you for ever to find him.'

'Excuse me, sir,' said DI Castle, 'it isn't quite that straight-forward. Trevor Blackton has only one previous conviction—'

'For GBH,' Wells interrupted.

'Yes, sir, but it was some years ago and we haven't been able to pin anything on him since. His prints were at the scene,' the DI continued, ignoring a contemptuous sniff from Wells, 'because he owns the house where the body was found and he was the dead woman's lover. He freely admits to having been there around the critical time, but insists she was alive and well when he left her.'

'So he rushes out, cancels an appointment on the pretext of

a news flash that hasn't happened yet, and disappears. Just the sort of thing any innocent citizen would do, of course.'

'That was the one discrepancy in his story,' Castle admitted, keeping his voice level with some difficulty. 'When we challenged him he was stumped, but only for a moment.'

'You've got to hand it to the guy; he's good at thinking on his feet,' said Lord. 'He said it must have been the call to this Celia woman that he made after hearing the radio news flash, and that checks – he didn't contact her until mid-afternoon because she has a part-time job and works in the morning. He claims he got muddled about times because of the shock, but he's sticking to his story that the reason he went to ground as soon as he heard the news of the killing on the radio was that if it was Evie who'd been topped he'd be number-one suspect.'

Wells raised an eyebrow, tilted his head to one side and tapped the file again. 'I can read, you know,' he said. 'What I can't understand is how you can allow yourselves to be conned by such a load of cobblers.'

'But we aren't conned by it, sir,' Lord insisted. 'We're as certain as you are that he's our man, but we haven't been able to get him to change his story and we haven't found any evidence strong enough to refute it. We simply had no alternative but to let him go for the time being.'

'We've been over the house where we found him with a tooth comb and examined every stitch of clothing we've been able to lay our hands on for traces of blood,' Castle added. 'He fell over himself to be obliging, maintains he's as anxious as we are to bring the killer to justice. Incidentally, he remembered exactly what he was wearing the day he went to the house and found the body – claims it's imprinted indelibly on his memory, haunts his dreams and all that jazz.'

'My heart bleeds for him,' said Wells.

'And made no bones about handing his kit over,' Castle continued patiently.

'Also, sir,' said Lord, 'you'll see from the report that we've spoken to Blackton's friend Celia Bateson. She's backed him up; she even confirmed what clothes he was wearing when he turned up on her doorstep after calling her at work on his mobile, "all shook up and in a dreadful state", as she described it.'

'She would, wouldn't she? There's been plenty of time for Blackton to rehearse her story with her, and with a brother in the nick she's hardly the most reliable of witnesses. If that's the best you can do . . . '

The interview continued in this vein for several more minutes, with the superintendent raising point after point and his subordinates taking turns to deal with them, only to have their comments brushed aside. At last Wells pushed the file away and reached for another. 'Now, what about the Dalsey case? Any progress there?'

'We think so, sir,' said Castle. 'We found a computer in the dead man's apartment and we've got a man working on it. One set of files is simply a back-up system for the records at Express Deliveries, but then our man stumbled on another set that indicate Dalsey was running a separate business from home – something of an entirely different nature. We've interviewed his second in command, a man called Dowding, but he claims to know nothing about it and we've no reason to disbelieve him.'

'What kind of business is it?'

'That's the odd thing about it, sir. There's an extensive list of what would seem to be transactions or deals of some sort, but no details of how much money was involved, what he was dealing in or who with. Each one has a code against it, but clicking on the code didn't get anywhere. Hodgson – our IT whiz-kid – suspects there's a master folder that's protected in some way, which would suggest that whatever the business was, it wasn't entirely legit. He's confident he can find it, given time.'

Wells grunted. 'Tell him to get his finger out, then.'

He sat frowning for a moment. Taking advantage of his momentary silence, Lord said, 'On a point of interest, sir, if you'd just turn to page two of the report on the Glevum Passage case you'll find a reference to one of the *Big Issue* vendors in the city who we think may be able to help us with our enquiries.'

'I have read the report, Lord. It would be nice,' Wells pronounced the word with unmistakable irony, 'if I had also read of progress towards making contact with the individual concerned. In any event, I was under the impression that we're discussing the Dalsey case and I fail to see any connection.'

'There may not be one, sir, but I was informed just before this meeting that there has been a development. We've traced the man's movements up to a point when he disappeared in rather odd circumstances from a local hotel, after being identified by the proprietor following publication of an E-FIT supplied by one of our SOCOs.'

'And?'

'The same SOCO has offered to try and get a message to the man, telling him we want to talk to him. She also stated,' Lord hurried on as Wells opened his mouth, apparently about to utter another dismissive comment, 'that what she has learned from other *Big Issue* vendors leads her to suspect that there might be a link with the Dalsey case.'

'For God's sake, man, are you saying you have to rely on SOCOs to do your job for you?'

'No, sir, but they have been known to come up with useful observations in the course of their examination of a crime scene. Mrs Reynolds makes very helpful contributions from time to time.'

'I'm glad somebody does.' Wells reached for the third file. 'All right, we'll leave that for the moment. Now, what about this tom they fished out of the river?'

'With respect, sir, there's no evidence that she was a tom,' said Lord. 'Incidentally, it was Sukey – Mrs Reynolds – who identified her as another of the *Big Issue* vendors.'

'I take it you've got a more accurate ID than that?'

'Yes, sir, we've traced her mother, who's come down from Derby and made the formal identification.'

'Right, get on with that one as well. Get your pet SOCO on the case if you can't handle it yourselves.' He swept the files into an untidy heap, pushed them across the desk with a dismissive gesture and pressed a key on his intercom. 'Get me some more coffee, this lot's stone cold,' he barked into the microphone.

Lord and Castle read the signals, gathered up the files and took their leave. Outside the superintendent's office, they exchanged glances. 'I reckon *we* need a coffee as well, don't you?' said Castle.

'Personally I could use something stronger, but I suppose coffee will have to do,' said Lord. 'Come along to my office, Jim. I wonder,' he added with a sigh as the door closed behind them, 'what we've done to deserve that sarcastic bugger for a Super.'

'He sees himself as the new broom, I suppose,' said Castle.

'Yes, and I'd like to tell him where to put his broom handle,' said Lord.

'Jim rang about half an hour ago,' said Fergus as Sukey sank wearily into a chair in the kitchen and reached for the mug of tea he had just put on the table for her. 'He'll be round about eight o'clock unless you call him on his mobile to say don't.'

She glanced at the clock and said, 'Gosh, he'll be here in a quarter of an hour and I haven't even peeled the potatoes. Why couldn't he have said so earlier? I almost bumped into him coming out of DCI Lord's office at lunchtime and he didn't say a word. Come to think of it, he was looking pretty miffed about something.' She drank her tea in silence for a few minutes. 'Is that all he said – just that he'd be round about eight?'

'That's all. He sounded in a bit of a hurry.'

'Oh, well, if he wants feeding he'll have to take pot-luck. What sort of a day have you had? How are the mocks going?' Fergus was preparing for A-levels the following year and hoping to read law at university.

'Today's English paper wasn't too bad. How about your day?'

'Interesting. My E-FIT of Matt has had results.' She recounted her conversation with Mrs Vaughan.

'That's brilliant, Mum. It looks as if you were right after all.'

'Up to a point. There's still nothing to connect him with Dalsey. If it was him with Matt, you'd think Mrs Vaughan would have recognized him from the picture that appeared in the *Gazette* the day after the murder.'

'Maybe she didn't happen to spot it.'

'She spotted the E-FIT.'

'Have you still got the edition with the photo?'

'Sure. I keep cuttings of all my cases.'

'Well, why don't you trot along to Mrs Vaughan's hotel and show it to her?'

'I suppose I could. I don't suppose anyone from CID will make the connection.' There was a ring at the doorbell and Sukey hastily finished her tea and stood up. 'Heavens, there he is already! Will you let him in, Gus, and whatever you do, don't say a word about any of this. I've already had a rap on the knuckles from our new DS for poking my nose in.'

'God, what a day!' Jim slumped wearily into a chair and accepted the cup of tea Sukey put in front of him with a grateful smile. 'I'm shattered. You must be as well, Sook, doing extra hours.'

'A bit, but I'll survive. I understand you and Mr Lord had an interview with the new Super. What's he like?'

'Don't ask!' Jim groaned. 'He made us feel like a pair of rookies. He's from the Met and I'll bet they were glad to get shot of him.'

'So what's he doing in our neck of the woods?'

'Something to do with wanting to be near an aged mother, so I'm told. Let's not talk about him.'

'OK. Any new developments?'

'Yes, your E-FIT struck oil.'

'So I heard.' Sukey was careful to keep her voice casual as she added, 'I'm still hoping to get a message to Matt on Wednesday.'

'And we've made some progress in the Dalsey case, but our chap still hasn't cracked the computer – at least, not entirely. We're pretty sure there's something there that could help us find a motive for the attack on him.'

'What about Blackton?'

'Hadn't you heard? We had to let him go. On police bail, of course.'

Still hell-bent on revenge, no doubt, Sukey thought. A cold shiver ran down her spine. Could she get to Matt in time and persuade him to accept police protection? Aloud she said, keeping her voice casual, 'Where's he gone?'

'Back to his Herefordshire pad, I suppose, after picking up his car from Mrs Bateson's place.'

'Mrs Bateson? Is she a friend of Blackton?'

'Do you know her?'

'There's a Mrs Bateson working for Joseph Bryant.'

'The antiques dealer who reported a theft from his shop one day last week? Uses Express Deliveries?'

'That's right. I'm sure he addressed his assistant as Mrs Bateson. I wonder if it's the same person?'

'Of course it is! It has to be!' Jim put his empty mug on the table with a thump, jumped to his feet and gave her an exuberant hug. 'Sook, you're a genius! I do believe you've given us a breakthrough!'

Twenty-Five

'You realize what this means, don't you?' Jim Castle jabbed buttons on his mobile phone as he spoke, then sat impatiently tapping the table with his left forefinger. 'Oh, come on, answer will you!' he muttered through compressed lips. After a few moments he said, 'Jim Castle here, Philip. I think we're on to something. Please call back urgently.' He made tutting noises as he put the phone back in his pocket. 'Would you believe it, his bloody mobile's switched off!' he grumbled.

'Maybe he's at the theatre or something,' Sukey suggested. 'While you're waiting to hear from him, maybe you could explain what I've done that's so clever?'

'But it's obvious, Mum,' said Fergus, his eyes shining with excitement. 'Blackton has a spy in Joseph Bryant's camp.'

'You mean Mrs Bateson?'

'Of course.'

'She knew about the valuable package that Express Deliveries were supposed to pick up the day you went to Bryant's shop about the distraction theft of a clock. Didn't you overhear Bryant say something about Blackie's boys pulling another fast one?'

'Ye . . . es.' Sukey put the chicken casserole she had been stirring back in the oven, went to the freezer and took out a packet of frozen vegetables. 'But I assumed it was the distraction theft he was talking about.'

'Maybe he was, but don't you see, the driver who picked up the package a day early wasn't an Express driver at all, he was working for Blackton. That was probably an even more valuable item. I reckon Mrs Bateson told him about it and one of his boys nicked an Express vehicle to do the job.'

'Or used a hired van on the pretext that one of their own

was off the road,' Castle said. 'I reckon Gus could well be right, Sukey.'

'So what made Bryant suspect Blackton, I wonder?' she said.

'Good question.'

'And why the insistence on speaking to Dalsey personally if it was so urgent? You said he had a right-hand man who's been running things since Dalsey's death.'

'That's right, Joshua Dowding. Presumably he wasn't in the office when Bryant called. I'll have a word with him.' Jim pulled out his notebook and scribbled in it. 'The thing is,' he went on, 'our IT expert has been checking Dalsey's PC. He's come across some files that seem to refer to some sort of sideline, but there's key information missing and he hasn't been able to reach it.'

'Perhaps it's on a separate CD that Dalsey kept hidden away,' suggested Fergus.

Castle pursed his lips and shook his head. 'The apartment has been pretty thoroughly searched.'

'But were your people looking for any kind of secret hiding place? A concealed drawer in the desk, for example?'

'Probably not,' Castle admitted. 'Maybe we should have another search.'

After dinner they watched television for a while, but with Jim fidgeting and checking the time every few minutes the atmosphere was anything but relaxed. At ten o'clock there had still been no word from DCI Lord; Fergus had gone to his room to work on his computer and Sukey was making no effort to stifle her yawns.

'Jim,' she said, 'you might as well go home and let me get to bed. I've got another long day to look forward to.'

'Warren still not recovered, then?'

'He's much better and hopes to be signed off tomorrow afternoon and back on Wednesday. It can't come soon enough for me.'

'I'm sorry, love; you must be shattered and I've been rotten company this evening. Thanks for a lovely meal; I'll see you tomorrow.' He had just put on his overcoat and was taking his time over saying goodnight when his mobile rang. 'Sod's law!' he said with a sigh as he released her to answer.

'Well?' she said when the brief conversation had finished.

'He said to tell you, "Well done, Sukey", and to order another search of the Dalsey apartment first thing in the morning.'

'It should really be, "Well done, Gus".'

'That's a point. I'll make sure he gets a mention.'

As he reached out to open the door, Sukey said, 'I've just thought of something else. When Bryant was talking on the phone, he referred to there being only one package instead of two. Presumably he was referring to the item that had been nicked.'

'What of it?'

'Whatever the person the other end said, it made Bryant very angry and he said, "Can't your lot get anything right?" As if—'

'But we know all that,' Jim interrupted impatiently. 'What's the problem?'

'Could it mean that the person the other end was only expecting one package anyway, because he – or she – knew that it had already been collected: but if the driver who picked it up was working for Blackton, possibly driving a hired van, he wouldn't have had access to Express Deliveries' work schedule—'

A gleam appeared in Jim's greenish eyes. 'I see what you're getting at, Sook. And since Bryant wasn't at all keen on giving details to the officer who offered to have it looked into, it rather suggests that not all his dealings are above-board. I think I'd better find out who took that phone call.'

'So that's where the big money has been coming from!' exclaimed DI Castle as Hodgson scrolled through the contents of a folder named 'Transactions' on the computer screen. 'Just look at them! Only a handful of deals but they add up to a small fortune – and look who's had a cut from every one. None other than Dalsey's sidekick, Joshua Dowding. He swore blind he knew nothing about his boss's other business interests, and all the time he was up to his neck in a very profitable scam.'

'How d'you suppose they got their hands on all this stuff?' said Radcliffe.

'That's something we have to look into, but I'd be willing to bet that Joseph Bryant has something to do with it.'

'Sukey mentioned that he does insurance valuations. You reckon the owners get him to insure their property for them and he passes the information on to Dalsey, who arranges for it to be nicked?'

'I haven't figured out how they worked it,' said Castle. 'It's obvious Dalsey got the information from somewhere, but Bryant wouldn't want his name associated with a string of claims on insurance that he'd arranged, even if it was with different companies.' He thought for a moment. 'Suppose you inherit an antique vase from your Auntie Flo, or pick up something off a junk stall that looks as if it might be valuable. You want to know what it's worth, so what do you do?'

'Take it to a reputable dealer and get him to value it, I suppose.'

'And if he tells you it's worth a lot of money, what do you do next?'

'Flog it!' said Radcliffe with a grin. 'Unless it's a family heirloom, of course. I suppose I might hang on to it if it had a sentimental value.'

'In which case, you'd probably insure it.'

'I suppose so.'

'Which is no doubt what the valuer would recommend, but not necessarily offer to arrange.'

'OK, I say, "Thank you very much, I'll take your advice," and arrange the insurance myself.'

'Not so fast.' Now Castle was thinking on his feet. 'Let's suppose the shop owner needs a day or two to do the valuation. Or maybe he suggests getting a second opinion from someone specializing in your particular kind of treasure. Either way, you have to leave the item with him. He gives you a receipt and says he'll phone you when the valuation's complete, so you give him your number. And when you go back to collect the item and the valuation certificate, you have to pay his fee and ten to one you write him a cheque. Maybe he asks you to put your address on the back, which makes things even easier for him, but in any case he's got enough information to find out where you live and where the valuable piece is probably going to be kept.'

Radcliffe whistled. 'And passes it on to Dalsey, who sets the machinery in motion for nicking it.'

'Dalsey will have to find a customer for it first. He won't want to keep it at home.'

'Maybe he's got a go-between who knows exactly where to place it.'

'Good point, Andy. There must be plenty of unscrupulous collectors happy to lay their hands on art treasures without being too fussy about where they came from.' Castle turned to Hodgson, who was sitting beside him with his finger hovering above the mouse. 'What else is on this disk, Larry?'

'Quite a lot, sir.' He clicked the mouse and brought up a list of folders.

Castle ran an eye down the names. 'Try "Targets",' he said. Hodgson obeyed and a series of names and addresses, each with a code number, some with red ticks against them, flashed onto the screen.

'Right, now we're getting somewhere,' said Castle. 'Hodgson, I want you to check every item on this list that's been ticked against the code numbers of the items you found on the hard disk.'

'No problem, sir.'

'How long will it take?'

'Only a few minutes. Shall I do a printout?'

'Yes, why not? And when you've done that, see if you can find a name that sounds as if it might be the go-between we're after. Meanwhile,' he turned back to Radcliffe, 'I'd like you to go and have a word with Mr Dowding.' With a lean forefinger, Castle indicated the most recent name on the list of targets to carry a tick. 'See what he's got to say about that one for starters. And run off a copy of this list for me, Hodgson. I'm going to have a chat to DCI Lord. Some of these "targets" are in neighbouring counties. I have a feeling the Regional Crime Squad might be interested.'

'I'm obliged to you for sparing the time to see me, Mr Dowding.' Radcliffe sat back in a chair in Josh's office and sipped the coffee served by the receptionist at Express Deliveries. 'I'm sure you're as anxious as we are to establish the exact circumstances of Mr Dalsey's death.'

'Naturally.' Josh did his best to appear at ease, but his mouth felt dry and there was an uneasy feeling in the pit of his stomach.

'I'd like to begin by asking you to cast your mind back to our conversation the day after Mr Dalsey's death,' Radcliffe went on. He consulted his notebook. 'I understand that at around nine o'clock on the day his body was found, a Mr Bryant, an antiques dealer, called this office and asked to speak to Mr Dalsey. Can you remember who took the call?'

Josh licked his lips. 'I did,' he said. 'I told Mr Bryant that Mr Dalsey wasn't in yet and asked if I could help.'

'But Mr Bryant declined to tell you the reason for his call and asked for Mr Dalsey to call him the minute he arrived.'

'Yes.'

'But of course, he never did arrive because he was dead.'

'That's right.' Josh's hand trembled so violently as he put down his coffee cup that it clattered against the saucer.

'You couldn't have known that, of course, because the last time you visited him in his apartment was the evening before he was attacked.'

'That's right.' Josh repeated. He felt his pulse begin to race. Where the hell was this leading?

'Right, we'll leave that for the moment. At a subsequent interview, I raised the matter of some information we found on Mr Dalsey's computer, which appeared to refer to another business enterprise other than those we already knew about. You disclaimed all knowledge of such an enterprise.'

'Mr Dalsey didn't tell me everything,' Josh said.

'Are you saying he didn't trust you?'

'I didn't mean that.'

'What you were trying to say was that you had no knowledge of the very profitable sideline in stolen art treasures that Mr Dalsey was running in collaboration with Mr Bryant?'

'Stolen art treasures?' Josh had difficulty getting the words out. 'No, of course not.'

'Then how can you account for the fact that your name appears on this schedule?' Radcliffe unfolded the printout Hodgson had given him and passed it across the desk.

Josh felt his jaw drop. He tried to speak, but his throat seemed to close up and for a moment he found difficulty

175

in breathing. When at last he got his voice back, it was so weak that Radcliffe had to lean across the desk to hear his reply. 'I'd like to consult my solicitor before I answer any more questions,' he said.

'Very wise,' said the detective smoothly. 'You can call him from the police station. I'm arresting you on suspicion of involvement in the theft of a number of valuable works of art.'

Twenty-Six

Tuesday morning was grey and cold, with an icy wind. 'Not much fun for the homeless,' remarked Mandy as she and Sukey went down to the yard to collect their vans. 'Any sign of your friend Matt yet?'

'I'm hoping to . . . make contact with him tomorrow.' Just in time, Sukey checked herself from saying 'hoping to see him', which would have aroused immediate suspicion. As it was, she caught Mandy's raised eyebrow; evidently she had noticed the slight hesitation, but she made no comment.

By a stroke of luck, Sukey's first job was in Cheltenham, so she was able to call in at the hotel where Matt Braine had been staying. Mrs Vaughan was at the reception desk, arranging bronze and golden chrysanthemums in a copper jug.

'Aren't they lovely!' Sukey exclaimed. 'Are they from your garden?'

'If only!' said Mrs Vaughan. 'I'm a hopeless gardener. My husband cuts the grass and keeps the shrubbery under some sort of control, but I got these from the local florist. Our guests do appreciate fresh flowers.' She placed the jug beside a brass bell at the side of the desk and wiped her hands with a tea towel. 'What can I do for you, Mrs Reynolds? Have you found Matthew Braine?'

'Not yet, I'm afraid.' Sukey took from her pocket the cutting from the *Gloucester Gazette* containing the report of the death of Samuel Cuthbert Dalsey, Managing Director of Express Deliveries Ltd. A colour photograph appeared alongside the text. 'This is rather a long shot, I know,' she said, 'but did you see this?'

Mrs Vaughan glanced at the cutting, frowned for a moment and then nodded. 'Oh, yes, I remember seeing that. A very sad case. I understand the poor man was attacked in his flat and died as the result of his injuries. As a matter of fact, Mr Dalsey belonged to the same golf club as my husband. Raymond didn't know him very well, but he remembered seeing him at the club from time to time. Why do you ask?'

'You don't by any chance recognize him as the gentleman who brought Matt to your hotel?'

'Good gracious, no! I'm sure if it had been him my husband would have contacted the police straight away. Whatever made you think—?'

'Several things, but it's too complicated to explain,' said Sukey. 'I've obviously been putting two and two together and making five.' She put the cutting back in her pocket. 'I apologize for having bothered you; I'm always being told to stick to my job of finding evidence and stop playing at being a detective,' she added ruefully.

'I'm sure you'd make a very good detective,' said Mrs Vaughan.

'It's kind of you to say so. I hope you didn't mind my asking.'

'Of course not. I'm sorry I can't help you and I do hope you find Matthew soon.'

'Thank you.' Sukey hesitated for a moment before saying, 'I don't suppose the police will pay you another visit, but if they do, I'd be grateful if you didn't mention that I've been to see you.'

Mrs Vaughan gave a knowing wink. 'Not a word – Guide's honour!' she said.

Sukey drove to her next assignment feeling somewhat deflated, her self-confidence shaken. A little unreasonably, she felt a stab of irritation towards Fergus.

After dealing with a job in Prestbury, which concerned the theft of tools and garden machinery from a garage, she drove on to her next assignment, a break-in at a sports and social club belonging to a large company with headquarters on an industrial estate close to the motorway. On a notice board at the entrance was a plan showing the location of the various companies on the estate; among them, she noticed with interest, was Express Deliveries Ltd. 'Well, there's a coincidence!' she said aloud as she pulled up to check the directions to her destination. She almost stalled her engine in surprise as, driving slowly forward to take the first turning to the left, she caught sight of DS Radcliffe's car approaching from her right. He did not appear to see her, but she watched in her rear-view mirror as he turned into the main road and drove off in the direction of the city centre. A man whom she did not recognize was sitting in the back of the car. A short distance along the road from which it had emerged she saw a low building with several white vans parked outside it with 'Express Deliveries' painted in blue on their sides.

The main damage to the club premises was to the bar, which was protected by a metal grille. Having failed to gain access to the stock of drinks by attacking the grille, the intruders had smashed their way through the wooden counter. The club steward, a youngish man with a swarthy complexion and heavily tattooed, muscular arms, estimated that a considerable quantity of liquor and cigarettes had been stolen.

'Can't say exactly how much the buggers nicked until I can do a proper count,' he explained. 'The copper who answered my call said not to touch anything till your people had checked it all over.'

'That's right. It's easy to destroy evidence.'

'You reckon on catching them?'

'You never know your luck.'

By the time Sukey had finished her examination and given the steward the all-clear to begin the task of assessing the damage, it was a little after midday. Her way out of the building led past the entrance to the canteen, from which drifted an appetizing smell of food. She remembered a pub advertising lunches a quarter of a mile or so down the road from the entrance to the estate. A bowl of hot soup in a cosy bar seemed more attractive than a cheese-and-pickle sandwich in the van. She called the office, took details of a couple more assignments and then headed for the Five Bells.

She bought a glass of orange juice, gave her order for homemade leek and potato broth with crusty bread, and settled at a corner table. It was still early and there were few people in the bar, but after a few minutes two young women entered, greeted the barman as Reg and demanded 'the usual'.

'Only two of you today?' he asked as he drew their half-pints of lager. 'Where's Georgie?'

'She'll be along in a minute,' said one of the newcomers, a voluptuous girl with pouting lips and bleached hair whom the barman addressed as Blondie.

'She's got something exciting to tell us and we can't wait to hear what it is,' said her companion, a mousy-haired girl with strikingly white skin whom Reg called Paleface. 'Ah, here she is now!'

The third member of the group came in and barely had time to pay for her drink, which Reg poured without waiting for her to order, before being hustled to a table by her friends. 'Come on, Georgie, spill it!' they exclaimed simultaneously as they sat down.

Georgie was evidently determined to keep them in suspense as long as possible. 'You'll never guess!' she said, her heavily made-up eyes round with excitement. 'I can hardly believe it myself,' she added and took a long swig from her glass. 'I mean, he's such a nerd, you can't imagine him getting up to anything criminal.'

At the word 'criminal' her two companions uttered squeaks of anticipation. Paleface clapped her hand over her mouth and Blondie said in a voice made shrill with a mixture of shock and disbelief, 'You can't mean—?'

'Yeah, that's right. Our late boss's pet whipping boy.'

'What's happened to him?'

'He's been arrested.'

'Arrested!' chorused the enthralled listeners, making no attempt to keep their voices down despite the fact that the bar was beginning to fill. In her corner, Sukey, who up to this moment had been only half listening, began to give the revelations her full attention. Were they talking about the passenger in DS Radcliffe's car?

A stream of questions followed. 'Was there a struggle?' 'Was he in handcuffs?' and finally, 'What's he done?'

'Stole the cheese from someone's mousetrap?' Blondie suggested scornfully. It was evident that the subject of their speculation was not held in particularly high regard.

'Perhaps it was him who bumped off the boss,' giggled Paleface. 'Wouldn't have blamed him, either, the way the old sod pushed him around.'

'He wouldn't have had the guts,' said Georgie. 'Why d'you think everyone calls him "Dalsey's doormat"?'

'I've called him worse things than that,' said Blondie. 'He could be a real bastard at times – not just to me, everyone.'

'Yeah, anyone lower down the line than he was. He's a bully all right, but old man Dalsey was a bigger bully still.'

'So maybe the worm turned at last.'

Sukey, tucking into her soup, sat there spellbound. It seemed almost certain that it was Dalsey's deputy, Joshua Dowding, who was the subject of the discussion, in which case he had to be the passenger in Radcliffe's car. She lingered for several minutes after finishing her lunch in the hope of hearing more, but by now the three women appeared to have exhausted the topic and had begun exchanging intimate details of their love lives. Fascinating as this was, there were more important matters to deal with. She hurried back to the van, made a hasty record of what she had overheard, called the station and asked for DS Radcliffe.

'Hold on a minute.' There was a pause. 'Sorry, he's with DI Castle. They're questioning a suspect. Do you want to leave a message or can anyone else help?'

'Do you happen to know if the suspect has anything to do with the Dalsey case?

'I've no idea.'

'Do you think you could find out? It might be important.'

'Hold on.' There was another pause, during which Sukey heard sounds of conferring in the background. 'It's a chap called Joshua Dowding,' the detective said. 'And yes, we think it's to do with the Dalsey case.'

'I thought it might be. Listen, could you possibly get a message to either DI Castle or DS Radcliffe? I have some information about Dowding that they might find interesting.'

'Right, Mr Dowding, let's recapitulate, shall we?' DI Castle sat back, crossed his legs and clasped his thin fingers round one knee. 'Do you still maintain that you have no idea why

181

your name should appear on the list of transactions we found on Mr Dalsey's computer?'

'No comment.'

'That hardly constitutes a denial, does it? According to this list, considerable sums in respect of the sale of certain valuable antiques and works of art – all of which have been reported stolen – were either paid to you or possibly credited to you in some other way. Which was it?'

'No comment.'

'You're asking us to believe that commission on the sale of, for example, an early Monet or a bracket clock by Thomas Thompion, with your name alongside it on this list, means nothing to you?'

'No comment.'

'All right, we'll leave that for the time being. Let's return to your late employer, Mr Dalsey. According to your original statement to DS Radcliffe, Mr Dalsey was "an old friend of long standing. We had an excellent working relationship and everyone liked him. I can't think why anyone would want to harm him". Do you agree that those were your very words?'

'If you say so.'

'And he treated you at all times with the respect and consideration due to your position as his second-in-command?'

'Of course.'

'That's very interesting.' Castle picked up a note handed to him a few minutes previously. 'It has just come to my notice that certain members of your staff see the relationship between you and the late Mr Dalsey in a rather different light.'

Dowding stiffened and his face turned a dull red. 'I don't know what you're talking about,' he said. 'Scud and I . . . we had our differences now and then, of course . . . one does in business . . . but we were good friends and good colleagues.'

'Then why was a young woman employee overheard referring to you as "Dalsey's doormat"?'

'I'd like to know who said that. She'll be looking for another job if I find out.'

'So you consider it to be a totally unjustified remark?'

'Of course I do. I told you—'

'Yes, I know what you told me. Another employee was heard to say something to the effect that –' here Castle read aloud from the paper in his hand – 'if you had "bumped the old sod off, she wouldn't have blamed you after the way he pushed you around".'

'Really, Inspector, I must object.' It was the first time that Dowding's solicitor, who had been sitting at his side throughout the interview, had spoken. 'I consider this a most improper way to conduct an interview. What you have just quoted is pure hearsay.'

Castle ignored the interruption. He leaned across the table, bringing his face to within a few inches of Dowding's. 'May I remind you that as well as investigating what appears to be a very lucrative trade in stolen art treasures, we are also carrying out a murder enquiry. Perhaps the two are not unconnected?'

Dowding's jaw dropped at the word 'murder', but he stared back defiantly at Castle. 'Who said the things were stolen?'

'You're claiming that they were purchased legitimately from their owners? By a Mr Joseph Bryant, for example?'

Dowding drew a sharp breath on hearing the name. His heavy features, flushed red a few minutes ago, had turned a pasty yellow. 'I don't know anything about that,' he muttered.

'But you are no doubt acquainted with Mr Bryant?'

'I've heard of him.'

'This doesn't surprise me,' said Castle drily, picking up yet another sheet of paper. 'A routine check carried out by one of my officers reveals that Bryant's wife was a Miss Laura Dowding before her marriage.'

Dowding's brief show of defiance crumbled; he gave a strangled gasp, covered his face with his hands and began to weep. His solicitor put a hand on his arm and said, 'Inspector, I must ask you to suspend this interview. As you can see, my client is in a state of considerable distress and I wish to confer with him.'

'Very well.' At a signal from Castle, DS Radcliffe switched off the tape. The inspector glanced at his watch. 'This might be a good time to break for some lunch,' he said. 'We'll resume this interview at two o'clock.'

An hour later, Dowding's solicitor informed DI Castle that his client had agreed to make a full statement.

Twenty-Seven

W hen the interview resumed, Dowding found himself
faced with two senior detectives instead of an inspector
and a sergeant. On learning of the latest development, DCI
Lord had decided to take part.

'Right, Mr Dowding,' Lord began quietly, 'we're waiting
to hear what you have to tell us. Just take your time – there's
no hurry.'

The prisoner's shoulders, already bowed, appeared to sag
even further as the implication of the inspector's words sank
in. 'It won't take long,' he said miserably.

'All right. We're listening.'

'It was Joe Bryant's idea,' Dowding began. 'It all started
when this friend of his, a dealer – I don't know his name –
was telling him he'd been approached by a man who was
on the lookout for work by a particular nineteenth-century
landscape artist. He was pretty annoyed because he thought
he'd missed out on a bargain.'

'What artist is this?'

'Some Frenchman, I can't remember his name. I'd never
heard of him, but it seems he's beginning to be recognized and
his work has started increasing in value. One of his canvases
turned up at a charity auction about four years go, but obviously
the person who donated it had no idea of its value and it seems
there was no one at the sale, including the auctioneer, who
recognized it. Someone just took a fancy to the picture and got
it for a couple of hundred pounds. He paid cash and walked
away with it under his arm without even leaving his name.
The dealer was kicking himself for missing out on it.'

'How did the dealer come to hear about it?'

'The chap who bought it took it along to the pub to show his
mates what he called "the new addition to his art collection".

185

One of them suggested, more or less as a joke, that he should get it valued. He took the suggestion seriously, and by coincidence he went to Joe and asked him what he thought. Joe's no art expert – his speciality's clocks – but he told the chap he thought it might be worth a bit more than he'd paid for it and offered to get another opinion. It was Saturday morning and Joe closes at one; the chap indicated there was no hurry, so Joe took his address and phone number, put the picture in his safe and promised to deal with it the following Monday.' Dowding broke off to take a drink from the plastic cup of water on the table in front of him.

'Yes?' prompted Castle, who was enjoying a moment of satisfaction at having his earlier guesswork at least partially confirmed.

'It so happens Joe and this dealer belong to the same golf club—'

'Would that be the one Scud Dalsey belongs to?' interrupted Lord.

'That's right. Anyway, Joe saw his friend that afternoon. When he mentioned the picture his friend was dead keen to look at it and lo and behold, it was by this artist he'd been talking about. He said his client would have been prepared to pay many times the auction price and asked Joe to sound out the new owner about selling it on for a substantial profit.'

'And what happened?'

'It seems the chap was tickled pink when he realized he'd bought such a bargain and flatly refused to part with it, even when a figure of two thousand pounds was dangled in front of him.'

'Would two grand have been a fair price?'

Dowding shrugged. 'Knowing the way that pair work, it was probably worth a lot more. Anyway, the owner said he'd keep it as an investment for a rainy day, paid Joe's valuation fee and left. Joe passed the message on to his friend and so far as he was concerned that was the end of the matter.'

'Only?' prompted Lord as Dowding hesitated again and gulped more water.

'The dealer friend came back asking for the owner's name and address, "so that he could make a direct approach to him on his client's behalf", he said. Joe gave him the information,

186

but thought no more about it – or so he said. Then, a month later, it was reported stolen.'

'How very surprising,' said Lord drily.

'It was a surprise to me,' Dowding retorted with an unexpected flash of spirit.

'But was it a surprise to Joe Bryant, I wonder?' There was no reply. 'I take it the police were informed?' Lord continued.

'Of course.'

'Was Bryant questioned?'

'Only to confirm the story about the valuation. It was never suggested that Joe had anything to do with the theft.'

'What about Joe's dealer friend?' said Castle. 'Did the police question him?' Dowding fidgeted with the plastic cup and appeared reluctant to answer the question. 'Well, did they?'

There was a further pause before Dowding muttered, 'Not that I know of.'

'You mean Joe didn't bother to mention the dealer's interest in the missing picture?'

'Why should he?'

'I would have thought that any honest citizen would have been anxious to help the police recover stolen property – but of course we're not talking about honest citizens, are we?'

'Joe had no reason to suspect that Gl— his friend, I mean, had anything to do with it.'

Lord pounced. 'So you do know his name, but you and Joe withheld it from the police. Is that because you'd been given a cut from the proceeds of the theft?'

The solicitor laid a warning hand on Dowding's arm, but he shook himself free. 'What's the point?' he said resignedly. 'It's all going to come out.'

'Very sensible,' said Lord. 'Now perhaps you'd care to answer my question. Were you and Joe given a share of the rake-off?'

'Yes.'

'And the police were left to guess how the thieves knew how much the picture was really worth, and where to find it?'

'It wasn't difficult for them to figure it out. They learned during their enquiry that after the victim had the picture valued he couldn't resist boasting to his friends in the pub how it had turned out to be worth much more than he paid for it. He even named the figure. It was obvious the information had somehow got back to a professional gang who had carried out the job.'

'And that was the start of this very lucrative sideline?'

Dowding sat back in his chair and wiped sweat from his brow. 'That was the start of it,' he repeated wearily. 'If anything Joe thought would be of interest was brought to him for valuation, he would pass on details of the owner and where the piece was kept. There was always someone who'd buy it with no questions asked. Even after the men who carried out the job were paid off, there was still a tidy sum to be shared out.'

'I see.' Lord tore a sheet from his notebook and pushed it, with a pen, across the table. 'Perhaps, before we go any further, you'd care to give me the name of this dealer friend of Joe's.'

Dowding stared at the paper as if it were some loathsome insect. 'I can't do that!' he said in a voice that shook.

'Why not?'

'They'd kill me if I grassed on them.'

'Who are "they"?'

'The heavies who carry out the robberies. They're not above beating up anyone who gets in their way; in fact, I think they enjoy it. I suggested to Scud we get them to deal with Blackton, but . . . Oh, my God, now what have I said?'

'You're beginning to get really interesting,' said Castle. 'Tell us more about Dalsey. When was he brought in?'

'He was in it from the beginning. They needed him to handle the shipping side of the operation.'

'What arrangements were made for the stuff to be stolen?'

Dowding shook his head. 'I told you – Joe's dealer friend and his boys took care of that side of things. I wasn't party to any of the arrangements and I don't think Scud was either. He wouldn't have cared anyway. All he's ever been interested in is money.'

'So where do you come in?'

'Scud and Joe had been friends for years and whenever Joe sold an item to an overseas client and needed it to be shipped, Express Deliveries got the business. That part of it was perfectly legal. That was my department, and of course there had to be special arrangements to handle anything hot.

That was down to me as well. Scud liked to keep his hands clean,' he added bitterly.

'What made him trust you with the job? I mean,' Castle continued mercilessly, 'despite, shall we say, not holding you in very high esteem, he chose you to oversee an essential link in the chain . . . and paid you quite a handsome cut into the bargain.'

Dowding gave a harsh, mirthless laugh. 'I was taken on in the first place as general dogsbody, looking after the admin, because that's basically all I'm good at. Once they embarked on this game, they realized I was bound to find out sooner or later what they were up to so they gave me a cut from every deal to keep me quiet. It was Laura who suggested it,' he added with another touch of bitterness. 'A bit of extra pocket money for me, she called it, as if I were still a kid at school.'

'You're speaking of your sister, Mrs Bryant?'

'That's right.' Dowding's voice became husky and his eyes grew moist. 'She's the only person in the world I really care about, and she uses me like everyone else does.' He fidgeted with his hands, locking and unlocking his fingers. 'And then I got the dirtiest job of all,' he went on.

'Which was?' prompted Castle.

'Setting up a honey trap for Trevor Blackton's woman, and making sure Trev knew about it.'

'So that Trev would get done for GBH or worse.'

'Yes.'

'Which of you dreamed up that charming little scheme?' asked Lord.

'Scud thought of it, but when it went wrong he made out it was my idea and accused me of making a hash of it. He threatened to find a replacement for me.'

'Would it be fair to say that there wasn't much love lost either way?' said Castle. 'He despised you, and you hated him, didn't you?'

The solicitor was quick to intervene. 'You don't have to answer that, Mr Dowding,' he said.

As if the interruption had not taken place, Castle continued, 'You hated him so much that you stunned him with his own whisky decanter and left him to die choking on his own vomit.'

Dowding brought a clenched fist crashing down on the table. 'I wish I had!' he shouted. 'God forgive me, I wish it had been me, but I didn't have the guts.'

'But you were there that night?'

'Yes,' Dowding whispered. His flash of defiance had vanished like a puff of smoke; he bowed his head and covered his face with his hands.

Once again, his solicitor came to his rescue. 'Gentlemen,' he said, 'I ask that this interview be suspended. I need to confer with my client.'

'Agreed,' said Lord briskly and reached for the control button of the tape recorder. 'We'll take a fifteen-minute break. And then' – he turned and addressed Castle, but it was obvious that he was speaking for Dowding's benefit – 'we can get our friend here to tell us exactly what happened the night Dalsey died.'

When Sukey checked in at four o'clock from the last job on her list she was told there was nothing outstanding for the moment so she decided to return to the station and write up her reports. The office was empty and she was able to work without interruption. She was just sealing up her samples ready for collection when DI Castle put his head round the door. 'Any idea where Sergeant Barnes is?' he said.

She shook her head. 'Sorry. He was out when I got back half an hour ago.'

'Never mind, it can wait. By the way, that was a useful tip you picked up about Dalsey. It enabled us to make a lot of progress.' He glanced back over his shoulder to satisfy himself that there was no one within earshot. 'I expect you'd be interested to hear about it.'

'Yes, please!'

He lowered his voice. 'I could bring you up to date this evening if you've no other plans.'

'Are you kidding? I don't finish until seven.'

'All right, I'll see you about eight and I'll bring a take-away, OK?'

'Lovely.'

*   *   *

At about six o'clock, DI Castle was summoned to DCI Lord's office.

'Things are moving,' said Lord as Castle entered. 'Take a look at this DNA report.'

Castle picked up the sheet Lord handed him, scanned it briefly and gave a low whistle. 'Now we know for certain Blackton was lying when he said Evie was alive and well when he left her,' he said.

'That's not all we know for certain.' Lord handed over a second sheet. 'That one shows conclusively that whoever Evie had sex with before she was killed, it wasn't Blackton. And this,' he picked up a third sheet, 'is a report from our own forensic lab. They found a match between the fibres that Sukey picked up at the crime scene and a woolly sweater that Matthew Braine left behind when he did a bunk from his hotel.'

Castle whistled again. 'So Sukey was right after all!'

Lord grinned. 'Looks like it. I think you owe her an apology.'

'Have you pulled Blackton in yet?'

'A couple of the lads are on their way at this moment to do just that. We should be able to get him on two charges now: murder and dealing in stolen art treasures.'

'Which is exactly what the Dalsey–Dowding plot was aiming at. Ironic, isn't it?'

'It sure is.' Lord rubbed his hands together in anticipation. 'I'm really looking forward to a chat with that blighter.'

'You're planning to interview him this evening, sir?'

'Got a date, have you? Well, I'm sure she'll excuse you if you're a bit late. And tell her to pull all the stops out to contact Braine. Until Blackton and his heavies are behind bars, he's in mortal danger.'

Twenty-Eight

'Here's the nosh. I got Indian; I hope that's all right.' Jim handed over a paper carrier and sank wearily into a chair. 'Heavens, what a day it's been!'

'You can tell us about it while you're drinking that.' Sukey put a can of beer and a tall glass on the table and began unpacking the food. 'This smells wonderful. We're starving, aren't we, Gus?'

'Famished,' Fergus agreed, 'and we're dying to hear about the latest developments. Mum said you sounded quite mysterious on the phone.'

'I was merely being discreet. The Super had just stuck his head round the door demanding to be updated, and Philip Lord was doing his best to sound positive and noncommittal at the same time. I think he wants to wrap this case up without giving the new boy an excuse to take charge.'

'Which case are we talking about?' asked Sukey.

'The Evie Stanton and Scud Dalsey killings.'

'Don't you mean "cases"? Or are you saying they're related?'

'In a tortuous kind of way, it looks as though they might be.' Jim opened the can, filled his glass, drank half at a single draught and refilled it. 'Ah, that's better!' he said with feeling.

'Oh, do get on with it!' said Sukey impatiently.

'All right, don't rush me. Well, to begin with, there doesn't seem much doubt that Scud Dalsey was a thoroughly nasty piece of work who was universally detested.'

'You've lost me already. What did Scud Dalsey have to do with Evie Stanton?'

'Quite a lot, if Josh Dowding is to be believed. Josh hated his guts, by the way.'

'Did he say so?'

'His brief managed to shut him up before he admitted it in so many words, but it came across loud and clear while he was being interviewed. He was like a man with a boil that's burst without warning; the poison positively spewed out and he ignored his brief's advice to follow the "No comment" routine. The poor man was practically tearing his hair out.'

'Did Josh kill Dalsey, then?' asked Fergus.

'He swears he didn't, but admits he'd have liked to. Thanks, love,' he added as Sukey put a heated plate in front of him, handed him a serving spoon and told him to help himself from the assortment of dishes set out on the table. 'It's a very complicated story.' He took generous helpings of rice and curry and set to. 'Let's eat this while it's hot and I'll do my best to explain afterwards. You have to take your usual vow of silence, Gus.'

'Of course.'

When they had finished the curry and the table had been cleared, Sukey brought out a bowl of fruit. 'There's ice cream or yoghurt if anyone would like it.'

'Fruit will do fine,' said Jim, reaching for a banana.

'Come on, Jim, spill it!' pleaded Fergus. 'We've been very patient.'

Jim began peeling the banana. 'Like I said, it's so darned complicated, it's not going to be easy to explain, or to understand,' he began. 'We still don't know when the rivalry between Dalsey and Blackton's mob began; we're hoping Blackton will fill us in on that part of the story tomorrow, but for the moment we're concentrating on getting enough evidence together to charge him with Evie's murder.'

'Are you saying you've arrested him again?' said Sukey.

'He was brought in at about seven o'clock this evening. That's what made me late; I'd have been later still, but he refused to be interviewed without his brief and the brief isn't available till the morning so he's spending the night in the cells. Still telling us what fools we're going to look when we have to let him go again.' Jim finished peeling the banana and took a bite from it.

'Does that mean you've found new evidence?'

'Right. There were minute traces of Evie's blood on the

193

steering wheel and in the foot well of his car, so there must have been blood on his trainers before he scrubbed them.'

'I seem to remember mentioning that possibility,' said Sukey smugly.

'All right, clever clogs, that's one to you.'

'So Blackton's claim that she was still alive when he left her is poppycock?' Fergus exclaimed.

'It has to be. And here's something else to give your mother a laugh at my expense, Gus.' Mother and son listened open-mouthed as Jim told them of the match between Matt's jumper and the fibres Sukey had found in Evie's bedroom.

'I said all along I thought Matt might have been one of Evie's playmates, didn't I?' Sukey said gleefully.

'You did, love. That's another Brownie point you've earned – although to be fair, all we have so far is evidence that he had at some time been in Evie's bedroom. We've no means at the moment of checking whether it was on the day she died or if he was the last person to have sex with her. That's another reason why it's so important to interview Matt, if only to eliminate him, so make that your number one priority.'

'What about Dalsey?' said Fergus. 'If Josh didn't kill him, who d'you think did?'

'We're not convinced yet that it wasn't Josh, but we'll have to wait for the results of a DNA test on blood found on fragments of the decanter that was used to fell Dalsey.'

'It might be Dalsey's own blood,' Fergus suggested.

'Unlikely. This was found on the neck, where it broke away from the base, so we think the killer probably cut his hand during the assault. Dowding has a slight injury to his hand that's partially healed, but he said he got it tinkering under the bonnet of his car and he made no bones about giving a DNA sample.'

'If it isn't his blood, what then?' said Sukey.

Jim shrugged. 'Then obviously we'll have to widen the enquiry.'

'You still haven't told us what the connection is between Dalsey and Evie Stanton,' said Fergus.

'This is where it gets more complicated, but we think it probably has something to do with the stolen antiques racket. It seems too much of a coincidence that one of Trev's associates works for Joseph Bryant.'

'You mean Mrs Bateson?'

'Right. She denies passing on any information, of course – in fact, she claims not to have known that Bryant was up to anything dodgy. She insists that the phone calls that passed between her and Blackton were always of a purely personal nature and at the moment we've no means of proving otherwise.'

'So Dalsey suspected Blackton of muscling in on his territory and decided to do something about it?' said Fergus.

'Right. This is where Dalsey's devious mind begins to show. Josh was all for sending in the heavies, but Scud had devised what he thought was a better idea, one that would avoid any chance of an attack being traced back to them or their associates. He was obviously sufficiently well acquainted with Evie to know her weakness for virile young men and he'd spotted Matt flogging his *Big Issue* magazines and thought he'd be ideal for what he had in mind.'

'Dalsey doesn't sound like the kind of man who'd buy the *Big Issue*,' said Sukey.

Jim shrugged. 'He seems to have been the kind of man to whom observing people was second nature. Not for any altruistic purposes – quite the contrary, in fact. It's as if he was constantly compiling a mental dossier of people who might come in useful to him. He knew all about the arrangements Blackton had recently made for Evie and how violently jealous of her he was, and he decided it would be fun to set her up with a rival and then give things a nudge and watch the fur fly. In other words, make sure Blackton knew she was cheating on him, knowing what his reaction would be. He'd already been done for GBH and served several months inside.'

'So if he was banged up again, this time for GBH or possibly murder, he wouldn't be a threat to Dalsey and Bryant's antiques scam,' said Fergus.

'That was the idea.'

'And Dalsey figured Matt was the kind of man who'd appeal to Evie,' said Sukey. 'Once he'd been smartened up, of course, hence the new clothes and the hotel. I suppose,' she went on after a moment's thought, 'the "mugging" was a put-up job to give Josh the chance to intervene and play the fairy godfather?'

195

'Exactly.'

'I feel a bit sorry for Josh,' said Fergus. 'He sounds like a man with very low self-esteem who's been manipulated by a pretty ruthless individual.'

'It was his idea in the first place to "send in the heavies" to deal with Blackton,' Sukey reminded him.

'Your mother's right,' said Jim. 'Save your sympathy for Matt and Evie. Dowding's no put-upon innocent. I believe he enjoyed putting the scheme into operation as much as Dalsey enjoyed hatching it, but when it went pear-shaped, Dalsey threw all responsibility for the idea on to Dowding, blamed him for making a cock-up of it and told him he was going to be replaced because he wasn't up to the job. That really riled Josh. When he was telling us that part of the story the mean streak in his own nature came through with a vengeance.'

'I wonder why it was necessary to go to all that trouble to provide Evie with a toy boy?' said Sukey. 'From what I've been told about her, she was quite capable of making her own arrangements.'

'According to Josh, she stayed faithful to Trevor for a while after he'd installed her in the love nest. Scud seems to have known her weakness – he had eyes everywhere, Josh said. What really rocked the boat, of course, was Blackton managing to hide from us for so long while his heavies tried to track down his rival. They assumed he'd be arrested within twenty-four hours; when it didn't happen, and another of their "treasures" was lifted under their noses, Dalsey ordered Josh to pass on an anonymous tip-off to one of Blackton's known associates, telling him where to find Matt. But of course, by this time Matt had read the press report about Evie's murder, realized whose woman he'd been having it off with and did a runner. Dowding got the blame for that as well.'

'So they were both prepared to have Matt beaten up and possibly killed if it would serve their purpose and land Blackton behind bars?' said Fergus.

'Oh, yes. They're pretty well level-pegging in the nastiness stakes.'

'So where do you go from here?' said Sukey.

'First thing tomorrow we confront Blackton with the evidence that Evie must have been dead, or at least dying, when he left her.'

'What about the trade in stolen art treasures? Have you got any evidence to link him with that?'

'All we have at the moment is Josh Dowding's allegation that he was involved. We'll need something a bit more substantial than that. The important thing is we've got enough to keep him in custody, hopefully for several days.' Jim glanced at the clock and stood up. 'It's getting late; I'd better be going.' At the door, he said, 'Do your best to persuade Matt to contact us, Sook. Make sure he knows Blackton's in custody again and we'll give him all the protection he needs. He could be a very valuable witness.'

'I'll do my best. Jim, have there been any developments in the hunt for Lucy's killer?'

He shook his head. 'I'm afraid not.'

'I don't suppose you know where they took Scruffy?'

'Scruffy?'

'Her little dog. He was found locked in the abandoned van, remember?'

'Ah, yes. Sorry, I've no idea. Trudy Marshall might know.'

'Of course. I'll have a word with her.'

Later, as Fergus was helping with the washing up, he said, 'I take it Jim doesn't know you're planning to actually meet Matt tomorrow?'

'Of course not – he'd insist on sending a posse to grab him. He's got to be handled gently.'

'I'm not happy about you walking alone by the river in the dark.'

'It won't be pitch dark. I'll take a heavy torch with me so I've got something to bash a mugger over the head with, if that'll make you any happier.'

'It won't, at least not much. At least tell me exactly where you're going.'

'So you can follow me? Nice try, but no.'

'I promise not to follow, but I'd like to know where to start looking if you don't come home.'

'What a cheery chap you are! All right.' Sukey took from her handbag the crude map Jack had given her. 'I'm to leave the car here, go across the field towards the river and Matt will meet me in this patch of woodland,' she explained, 'but, please Gus, stay away. If you show up and scare him off, you'll louse up the whole enquiry.'

Twenty-Nine

The DNA report on Lucy Minchin, whose body had been pulled out of the River Avon the previous Friday, landed on DCI Lord's desk at half-past four on Wednesday afternoon. He skimmed through it, picked up the phone and summoned DI Castle to his office.

'Read that,' he ordered as Castle entered, 'and then get on to Sukey right away. Find out where we can contact this fellow Jack – the *Big Issue* seller.'

There was no need for explanations. Having scanned the report, Castle whipped out his mobile and called Sukey's home number. 'Can I have a word with your mother?' he said as Fergus came on the line.

'I'm afraid she's not home yet.'

'Then tell her to call me the minute she comes in. Say it's very urgent, all right?'

Standing in the kitchen with the phone in his hand and his eye on the clock, Fergus wrestled with his conscience. 'She might not be home for a while yet,' he said after a moment.

'What do you mean?'

Something in Castle's tone made Fergus uneasy, but he tried to keep his voice level as he said, 'I think she was going to meet someone. Why don't you try her mobile?'

'All right, I'll do that.'

Two minutes later, Castle was back again. 'Her mobile's switched off,' he said and this time there was no mistaking the urgency in his voice. 'Was it Jack she was going to meet?'

'She made me promise not to tell—' Fergus began, but Castle broke in.

'The hell with promises! She may have information that can help us track down a killer – and she may be in danger herself. So tell me everything you know . . . NOW!'

In a voice that shook, Fergus obeyed.

There was a touch of frost in the air on Wednesday evening as Sukey, following Jack's directions, parked her car in the gated entrance to an area of field and woodland bordering the stretch of dual-carriageway that formed an arc on the northern outskirts of the city. She locked her bag in the boot, first taking out her torch and checking it before attempting to open the gate. Not surprisingly, it was padlocked and she clambered over it, mentally crossing her fingers that no one in any of the vehicles racing along the road would spot her and decide to inform the police. The minute she was over she ducked behind a screen of low bushes before cautiously making her way across an open space towards a patch of woodland some hundred metres away. Here, Jack had told her, she could expect Matt to make contact with her.

The day had been fine and bright, with a clear sky and a surprising amount of warmth in the late November sun, but as the light faded and the western sky changed from limpid blue to fiery orange, the temperature plummeted and the still air grew steadily colder. She shivered, pulled her fleecy cap down over her ears and plunged her gloved hands into the pockets of her jacket. Despite her bold words to Fergus, she felt a twinge of apprehension. In the gathering dusk the distant trees seemed at first to recede rather than become nearer. The hum of traffic grew fainter until she felt herself surrounded by an uncanny, intimidating stillness.

She found a point where the tangle of brambles and nettles at the edge of the field had been trodden down to form a rough pathway into the wood. As she moved forward, the gloom closed around her like the walls of a prison. She had a sudden, nightmarish sensation that a door was about to shut behind her, cutting off her retreat. It was all she could do not to turn and flee across the field, back to the car, to the lights of the city and the safety of home. Then she told herself through gritted teeth not to be such a wimp, and pressed on.

She must be close now to the spot where Jack had indicated Matt would meet her. She shone her torch right and left and picked up a blackened shape. Drawing nearer, she recognized it as the burned-out car she had been told to use as a landmark. Surely, he could not be far away now.

'Matt, are you there?' she called.

There was a movement behind her; a hand gripped her elbow and a man's voice said, 'Turn that off.' She gave a gasp of alarm and instinctively did as she was told, but her hand closed tightly round the heavy metal casing, ready if need be to use it as a defensive weapon. Then the man said quietly, 'Sukey, I thought you weren't coming.'

She turned to face him and said, 'Oh, Matt, I'm so relieved to see you! I'm sorry I'm so late; I got held up at work and then it took me ages to get through the traffic.'

In the remaining dregs of light she could just make out his features. His beard was unkempt and his hair straggled round his collar. In the days when she used to chat to him while buying the *Big Issue* he had always managed to look clean and tidy, despite his shabby clothing. She recalled Mrs Vaughan describing him as 'well spoken and gentlemanly' and was saddened to see the change in him.

'Matt, I've been so worried about you,' she said. 'It's a bad time of year to live rough like this. I know why you ran away from the hotel,' she went on as he made no reply, 'but you've nothing to be afraid of now. The police have arrested the man who killed Evie and all they want with you is to ask a few questions, to get you to help them put their case together.'

'Jack said you were coming days ago.'

'I know; I meant to, but I had to work overtime. Didn't he tell you?'

'Yeah, he told me.' His grasp of her arm tightened a little and she felt herself being drawn deeper into the wood. 'Come this way, it'll be warmer in my tent. We can talk in there.' He led her to a crude shelter made out of what she could only guess were layers of plastic sheeting draped over some kind of rough framework. It was impossible to tell what material he had used to build the walls, but pieces of sacking hung down to form a curtain over the front. He lifted one by the corner and gestured to her to enter, which she did by crouching practically on all fours. He followed, allowing the curtain to fall behind him. The darkness became almost complete.

'You can sit on my bed,' he said with a dry chuckle. Still

bent almost double, she groped on the ground. Her hand encountered something that felt like a woollen blanket and she sat down on it cross-legged. 'We can talk in here,' he repeated.

He squatted down beside her; their shoulders touched and in the confined atmosphere it became even more apparent that he had not washed, cleaned his teeth or changed his clothes for some time. Hoping that she could get the encounter over quickly, she said, 'You know why I'm here, don't you?'

'I think so,' he replied, still with the hint of amusement in his voice.

'I want you to talk to the police about how you came to meet Evie.'

'I thought you said you knew all about it.'

'I know you were set up by a man called Josh, who was working for another man called Scud Dalsey.'

'Dalsey? Never heard of him.'

'Josh was working for him. Scud was the brains behind a plot to get Evie's lover, Trevor Blackton, out of the picture. You were part of the plot.'

'Really? Tell me more.' This time there was an unmistakable touch of irony in Matt's tone.

'I think you know most of it. In fact, you probably know more than I do.'

'I'd like to hear your version.'

'Matt, it would make far more sense for you to tell the police everything you know. It would help them to nail Blackton for Evie's murder, and you'd be safe. In fact, you're safe now because as I told you, they've got him in custody. And you need help; social services would find you a room somewhere and take care of you. They say on the radio that we're in for some really bad weather,' she went on urgently. 'You can't spend the winter here – you'll die of exposure.'

'It's good of you to care so much for my welfare.' That note of irony again. Sukey had a feeling that she was wasting her time. In the darkness, she felt him move closer to her. She shifted sideways and found herself wedged between him and something rigid that formed the side of the shelter. The stuffy atmosphere was becoming unpleasant; she felt an urgent need to breathe fresh air.

'Matt, I have to go home now. Please, think carefully about what I've said.'

She made a move to get up, but a hand on her arm held her back. 'You're not going yet, are you?' he said softly. 'I've been looking forward to this meeting for such a long time.'

'I promised my son not to be too late. He'll be waiting for his supper.'

'Oh, you have a son?' He seemed surprised, as if in some way the information had significance.

'Yes, and I said I'd be home by half-past five at the latest and it must be gone that already. Look,' she made another attempt to get up, but again he held her back. 'I've said what I came to say. I can't force you to talk to the police, but apart from helping them catch Evie's killer—'

'Ah, yes, poor Evie. Such a lot of blood, wasn't there?'

'You saw her? Saw her body?'

'But of course!' He sounded triumphant now, like a child after playing a successful trick on a parent. 'You didn't guess, did you?'

Something cold seemed to fall into the pit of Sukey's stomach like a pebble dropping into a well. It was followed by a wave of sick terror at the realization that she had made a dreadful, possibly fatal miscalculation.

Humour him – it's your only chance, said a voice in her head. 'You've been very clever,' she said in a shaky whisper.

'Yes, haven't I? I knew about Trev, of course, she had to go with him, but she shouldn't have gone with anyone else, only me, me, ME!' The words came pouring out in a frantic babble; in his agitation he released his hold on her and began flailing the air with both arms. In a flash, she dragged the heavy torch from her right-hand pocket and shifted it into her left. To her relief, he was still so carried away by the spasm of jealous fury that he appeared not to notice the movement. *Talk to him, try and calm him down, promise to come back, promise to tell no one where to find him . . . anything.* The desperate thoughts chased one another through her head, but in her heart she knew that she was in the most dangerous situation of her life.

'She was boasting about another conquest who'd given her gold earrings.' He was breathing heavily; now the words came in a harsh, staccato whisper. 'She was wearing them, flaunting them, asking why I didn't give her presents. I tore them out of her ears and there was blood . . . lots of blood.'

He paused, and Sukey made one more frantic effort to calm him. 'Listen, Matt,' she began. 'Please, don't upset yourself . . . listen to me.'

She might as well have saved her breath. 'Lucy, too,' he almost shrieked. 'At least, I thought, she'd stay faithful, but no. She had others. They're all the same, go with one man, go with anyone.' He grabbed Sukey's right arm again, this time so tightly that she gave a gasp of pain. 'You won't do that, will you? You won't go with anyone else?' Using both arms now, he pulled her towards him in a crushing embrace. The stench was almost overpowering.

'Matt, stop it, I can't breathe!' she gasped.

'Sorry – forgive me.' The bear hug relaxed. 'Got carried away, didn't I?' He sounded almost sheepish. 'Yes, they both cheated on me, but they didn't matter much anyway. You're the one I really fancied all along.' He took her right hand in both his and began gently fondling it, then raised it to his lips and kissed it.

Sukey felt her gorge rise; she took a deep breath of the foul air and almost puked. 'Matt, I'm really flattered, honestly I am, but I simply have to go. We can talk about this another time—'

'The hell with another time! I want you now!'

The time for talking was over. In one frantic movement she rolled onto all fours and at the same time lashed out blindly with the torch. She had no clear idea of where the blow had landed, but his howl of pain told her it had found a sensitive target. He released her hand; she flung herself backwards through the flimsy curtain of sacking, scrambled to her feet and began to run towards the distant lights of the main road, but he was after her like a flash, grabbing at her jacket, spinning her round again to face him, snatching the torch from her grasp and flinging it away. Once more he pinned her against him, all but driving the breath from her body.

'So, you bitch,' he panted, 'you want to play rough, do you?'

She screamed and made a frantic effort to free herself. She clawed at his face but her gloved hands could do no damage;

204

she kicked him in the shins, but still he held her in a grip of iron. She felt a heavy blow on the side of her head, and then another. Bright lights flashed in front of her eyes; she managed to give one more despairing cry for help before total darkness overwhelmed her.

Thirty

She was flat on her back and her head was hurting. Whatever she was lying on seemed to be moving and she could hear a siren wailing and vague sounds like traffic. Someone, it sounded like a woman, was calling her name and asking if she could hear them, but she couldn't make out where the voice was coming from so she didn't answer. She felt a hand gripping her wrist and screamed in terror; she tried to sit up, but another hand on her chest held her back and the voice became warm and reassuring and said, 'Lie still, Sukey. Everything's all right.'

The panic slowly subsided. Whoever was speaking plainly intended her no harm. 'What's going on? Where are you taking me?'

The voice asking the questions had to be her own, but it sounded as if it was coming from a distance. She opened her eyes and turned her head, trying to locate the speaker, but all she could see was a round, misty shape against a white background. She blinked and tried to bring it into focus by giving her head a shake, but someone began shooting arrows into her brain. She groaned, the voice repeated, 'Lie still, Sukey,' and she was only too glad to obey. She closed her eyes for a few seconds; when she opened them again the mist began to clear and the shape resolved itself into a human face. An unfamiliar but friendly face that smiled down at her.

'Where are we going?' she asked feebly.

'To the hospital,' it said. 'You're in an ambulance.'

'Why? What's happened?'

'You've been hurt. We're going to get a doctor to look at you.'

She gave another faint groan. 'My head aches,' she complained.

'I'm not surprised. You've got rather a nasty head wound.'

'Wound?' She put her free hand to where the pain was worst and found a bandage. 'How did I get that?'

'Don't you remember?'

'No . . . yes . . . I think it must have been—' She closed her eyes again and a series of pictures took shape behind her eyelids. The open field: the dim woodland: the dark, ill-smelling tent: the terrifying, life-and-death struggle. For the second time she tried to sit up and was gently restrained. 'Jim, I have to speak to Jim!' she heard herself saying.

'Who's Jim?'

'He's Detective Inspector Castle of Gloucester CID.' Her vision had cleared completely now and her brain was functioning again, despite the throbbing pain in her head. 'I'm on police business.'

'There's a couple of police cars escorting us,' said the paramedic. 'I'll have a word with one of the drivers. We're arriving at the hospital now.'

The siren had stopped wailing and the sensation of movement ceased. The bed on which she was lying turned into a stretcher that slid smoothly from the back of the ambulance and was borne through doors that parted as they approached. Then she was lying on a proper bed and a nurse was asking questions: 'What's your name, dear? Who's the Prime Minister? Do you know what day of the week it is?'

She answered everything to the nurse's apparent satisfaction and then said impatiently, 'I need to speak to Inspector Castle. Please, can you get a message to him? I've got something very important to tell him.'

'All right, in a moment.' Now the nurse was holding her wrist and consulting her watch. 'That's pretty good in the circumstances,' she said with an approving nod. 'Now, don't you worry. Inspector Castle is here and waiting to see you, but the doctor wants to examine you first.'

'It'll only take a moment. Please, let me see him for two seconds.'

'I'll see what I can do.' The nurse left the cubicle where she was lying and after what seemed an hour Jim was at her side, holding her hand in both of his.

'I just wanted to let you know that Matt as good as confessed to me that he killed Evie and Lucy,' she said before he had a chance to speak.

'We already know that.'

'You do? How?'

'Never mind that now. The important thing is we've got him, but you were very nearly his next victim.'

'Tell me about it – I've got the prince of all headaches to prove it. And please don't say, "Serves you right".'

'As if I would.' He clasped her hand more closely; his mouth went a funny shape and she realized that he was fighting emotion. 'Darling,' he said huskily, 'after all I've told you, what on earth possessed you to go off on your own like that?'

'It never entered my head that he was the killer. I just thought he needed help and that I could . . . Oh, hell, I just got it all wrong. A fine detective I turned out to be.' She turned her head away, fighting tears of pain, weakness and humiliation.

'I'm not going to comment on that. And I'm not going to kiss you either, not while your face is in such a mess,' he went on in a weak attempt at humour. 'Have you got your car key, by the way?'

'I hope so.' With some difficulty, she fumbled in her pocket and found it.

'Give it to me. I'll see someone picks the car up and drives it home for you. Incidentally, there's a nice yellow "Police Aware" sticker on it. Getting that off should keep you out of mischief for a while; they use some pretty powerful glue to make them weatherproof. I'll see you in the morning.' He gave her hand a parting squeeze and disappeared.

Despite Sukey's protests that she was perfectly all right to go home, the doctor insisted that she remain under observation in hospital until the morning. Fergus, who had been despatched to the scene in a patrol car as soon as the alarm was raised and brought to the hospital in one of the escorting vehicles, was sent home to collect toilet things, nightwear and a change of clothes. There had been a touch of grim humour when her fellow SOCO Nigel Warren was given permission to photograph her injuries before they were covered with dressings. 'I'm afraid this isn't going to be your most flattering portrait,

Sukey,' he had said cheerfully before he was hustled away by the nurse.

After her wounds had been stitched and dressed she was given injections and eventually transferred to a ward, given some unidentifiable food that she made a half-hearted effort to eat and promptly threw up again, and finally, under the influence of a strong painkiller, fell asleep.

She was allowed home the following day on condition that she avoided any kind of excitement and did not return to work or drive her car until she had express permission from her doctor. The district nurse would visit daily to dress her wounds and report any rise in temperature or other adverse conditions. For the rest of the week Fergus took time off from college, prepared meals under her direction and watched her like a hawk for any sign of transgression; Jim telephoned her every morning and visited every evening to bring flowers, books and videos and enquire about her progress, but he refused point blank to discuss police business other than to assure her that they were now on course to bring the investigation into the murders of Evie Stanton and Lucy Minchin to a satisfactory conclusion. On Sunday she was allowed out for the first time; after lunch at a local carvery the three of them settled round the fire in her sitting room and she curled up on the sofa with her head on Jim's shoulder while Fergus dispensed cups of some rather weak coffee he had insisted on preparing. As they drank the coffee and dipped into a box of chocolate mints that had been Jim's offering of the day, she at last learned of the final piece of the jigsaw that, by a matter of minutes, had saved her from rape followed by a violent death.

'It was the DNA report on the traces of semen found in Lucy's body that put us on to him,' said Jim. 'It matched the sample taken from Evie so it was obviously the same man in both cases. We'd already eliminated Trevor Blackton as the last person to have sex with her; we knew that Matt had been a visitor to Evie's house and was presumably her lover, but we couldn't be sure she didn't have another, or even several, regular "playmates". However, both the women were battered to death which, taken with the other evidence, suggested they were victims of the same killer. The only obvious link between Evie and Lucy was Matt, so he immediately became

209

number-one suspect. You can imagine how I felt when I realized you'd actually gone to meet him.'

'Sorry,' she whispered. 'Like I told you, it never entered my head that there was any harm in Matt. I still don't know how you managed to figure out where I was meeting him, though. I suspect Fergus, but he goes all cagey every time I try to raise the subject.'

'I suppose I have to own up now.' Far from appearing guilty at being thus caught out at having betrayed his mother's confidence, Fergus wore a self-satisfied smirk. 'Even before Jim phoned to ask if I could get a message to you, I checked the details you gave me on a local map and was pretty sure I could pinpoint the area you were heading for fairly accurately. He sent a car to pick me up and I more or less directed the search,' he finished with an air of triumph.

'He's right, you know,' said Jim. 'If he hadn't memorized those details so precisely, we could have been too late.'

'I know,' she sighed, 'I always knew my son inherited his mother's brilliance. But at least you have to give me credit for doing some useful ground work.'

'Such as?'

'Who was it who kept on insisting that Matt could hold the key to Evie's killer and persuaded DCI Lord that an E-FIT of him might be useful?'

'OK, I'll give you that.'

'Thank you. Do you know how he came to meet Evie?'

'We already know that from Josh. Scud has a mole who's a member of one of Blackton's clubs. He took Matt along one evening and got him signed up as a member, knowing that it wouldn't be long before he caught Evie's eye.'

'Has Matt confirmed this?'

'We haven't been able to interview him. After his arrest we got the FME to check him over and he advised us to call for a psychiatric report. As a result of that, he's been sectioned and there's some doubt whether he'll ever be fit to plead.'

Sukey felt an unexpected wave of compassion. 'Oh, poor Matt,' she said softly.

'I'd save your sympathy for his victims, if I were you,' said Jim drily. 'He may have been responsible for at least one other unsolved killing. Gus, is there any more of that wishy-washy coffee?'

Fergus reached for the cafetière. 'Sure. I'm sorry if it's on the weak side. I thought too much caffeine would be bad for Mum.'

'It probably is, but I'm not sure she deserves so much consideration.'

'Well, thank you very much,' said Sukey indignantly. 'Now I've solved your case for you I think it's an official commendation I deserve.'

'You'll be lucky not to get an official rap over the knuckles.'

'I can see I'll have to look elsewhere for appreciation,' she sighed. 'By the way, what about the Scud Dalsey killing? Has Josh Dowding confessed?'

'On the contrary. His DNA doesn't match the blood we found on the broken glass, so we've had to let him go. Perhaps you can solve that one for us when you come back to work?'

Her eyes met his and they both burst into laughter, in which Fergus joined.

'I'll do my best, Guv,' she promised.

Thirty-One

Sukey's doctor called on Monday and pronounced her fit to attend the outpatients' department every other day to have her wound dressed. On Wednesday she took a taxi to the hospital, reported to the clerk on the reception desk, was given a card and told to wait. She found a seat and had just picked up a magazine when someone spoke her name; Trudy Marshall sat down in the empty seat beside her.

'Gosh, Sukey, it's good to see you,' she said. 'We've all been so worried about you.'

'I'm doing all right, thanks. What are you doing here?'

'Accompanying an assault victim who's here to have her injuries treated. I'm on special duty in the rape support unit.'

'That must be pretty harrowing.'

Trudy raised an eyebrow. 'That's rich, coming from someone who tracked down a psychotic rapist-cum-killer single-handed. We're dying to hear all the gory details.'

'Shh!' Sukey put a finger to her lips. 'I don't think we should discuss it here. What time do you finish?'

'I'm off at four this afternoon.'

'Then come and have tea with me and I'll tell you all about it.' Sukey took out one of her cards and scribbled her home address on the back.

'Fine. I'll look forward to it. Ah, here's my protégée; I'll have to go.' Trudy stood up as a pale young woman with a black eye and one arm in a sling appeared from behind a curtain, accompanied by a nurse. 'I'll see you later,' she said.

'You know, I'm not sure I should be feeling well disposed towards you personally,' said Trudy as she accepted a cup of tea and helped herself to a chocolate biscuit.

'Why not? What have I done?' said Sukey.

'We were supposed to share the sleuthing and the kudos, remember? And now you've gone and wrapped up the case without my help. Your conspiracy theory was proved right, the killer's been arrested thanks to you . . . not much left for me to do, is there? As for keeping my ear open for anything CID let drop, all I seem to hear from them is how wonderful you are.'

'I don't believe a word of it.'

'Just kidding,' Trudy admitted, 'but even before all the excitement, I hadn't picked up anything significant for days.'

'It isn't all wrapped up by a long way. They're still look-ing for the person who attacked Scud Dalsey at Bishop's Heights.'

'I thought someone had been nicked for that.'

'You mean Josh Dowding?'

'Is that his name?'

'He's the man who took Matt – the *Big Issue* seller – off the street and introduced him to Evie Stanton. He was working for Dalsey and he was the prime suspect, but a comparison between his blood and traces found on fragments of the decanter used in the attack has proved negative, so CID are back to square one. Apart from being up to his neck in dealing in stolen antiques and in direct competition with Trevor Blackton's mob, Dalsey seems to have been less than popular with his staff and had no close friends that anyone knows about. He must have quite a few enemies, which isn't going to make the investigation any easier.'

'Blood and negative DNA tests,' said Trudy thoughtfully. She was silent for a few moments and then said, 'Something's just occurred to me.'

'Do tell.'

'I suppose it's a long shot really, but—' She explained her idea and what she proposed to do about it.

'Gosh!' Sukey exclaimed. 'It's an interesting theory, but where's the motive? And don't you think you should mention it to a senior officer rather than go off sleuthing on your own?'

'Hark who's talking! Anyway, I don't want to cause unnecessary upset to the parties concerned. If I'm wrong, they'll be none the wiser. What do you say?'

'I say, go for it. Can I come with you?'

'Are you sure you can stand the excitement?'

'It's hardly likely to end in a punch-up, is it? When do you suggest?'

'I'll have to phone and arrange a convenient time.' Trudy glanced at her watch and stood up. 'Thanks for the tea. I must go now; I've got a date with a new boyfriend this evening. I'll be in touch.'

Sukey was pronounced fit to return to work the following Monday. Before starting on her first assignment, she and WPC Trudy Marshall requested an interview with Detective Chief Inspector Philip Lord. As a result of that interview, Oliver Granger, the caretaker at Bishop's Heights, was arrested some days later and charged with the manslaughter of Samuel Cuthbert Dalsey. At the same time, his lover, Martha Pomeroy, was also arrested and charged with conspiring to pervert the course of justice. The day after the arrests, WPC Marshall and SOCO Sukey Reynolds were summoned to DCI Lord's office.

'I can't deny that your bit of unauthorized detection saved CID a good few man-hours,' he said without preamble, 'but I've no intention of putting your names forward for the commendation you probably think you deserve. Nor am I going to recommend an official reprimand.'

'Thank you, sir,' they replied in chorus.

'I suppose you'd like to know exactly what happened?'

'Yes, please, sir.'

'Well, tough! You'll have to wait for the trial. Now get back to work, the pair of you – and remember to stick to the rules from now on.'

'What gave Trudy the idea that it was Granger who attacked Dalsey?' said Fergus over supper that evening.

'She felt sorry for Mrs Pomeroy because she was so upset at finding Dalsey's body. She lives quite near Trudy, so it was easy for her to pop in now and again on her way home from work. One day not long after Dalsey was killed Mrs Pomeroy mentioned that Granger had a cut on his hand that wasn't healing properly and she was a bit concerned about it. When I mentioned that Dalsey's killer probably suffered a cut on the hand, but that the DNA in the blood on the glass didn't match Dowding's, she told me that Granger's a heavy smoker and there are often cigarette ends in the ashtrays in Mrs Pomeroy's flat. Mrs P. doesn't smoke herself, so—'

'So you decided to go along with her,' Fergus interrupted. 'Wasn't that a bit risky, after all the fuss about you meeting Matt without telling anyone?'

'I suppose so, but you've no idea how bored I was getting sitting at home with nothing to do, and Trudy was anxious not to cause unnecessary upset if Granger and Mrs Pomeroy turned out to be innocent.'

'So what d'you reckon really happened?'

'At a guess, Dalsey found out about Granger's affair with his housekeeper and warned him off,' said Sukey. 'Maybe he even threatened to report him to his employers and get him sacked. There was probably an argument, Granger lost his temper and clocked him with the decanter.' She bit her lip in frustration. 'DCI Lord meant what he said; no one will tell me anything.'

'Not even Jim?'

'Especially not Jim. He says it should be a lesson to me not to play detectives in future.'

'They do have a point, after the narrow escape you had last week.'

'Don't keep reminding me.'

'What about Mrs P? Would Dalsey have sacked her as well?'

'Unlikely. She kept his domestic arrangements running smoothly and she understood his every need. I'd say he was the kind of man who goes to considerable lengths to avoid any upset to his comfortable routine.'

'So why not just leave things as they were?'

'Who knows? Maybe it was Granger who went up to the apartment to retrieve Mrs Pomeroy's glasses and came face to face unexpectedly with Dalsey.'

'I've just had another idea,' said Fergus. 'Suppose Dalsey tried to score with Mrs P. and she told Granger, and he—'

Sukey burst out laughing. 'Oh, Fergus, you are a goose!' she chortled.

But it turned out to be a piece of inspired guesswork on

her son's part. Dalsey had indeed 'tried to score' with his housekeeper and threatened to report her liaison with Granger to his wife if she complained. According to the story that Granger told in court, he had gone to the flat to confront his rival; there had been a fierce argument during which Dalsey, who was drunk, took at swing at Granger with the decanter he was holding. Granger claimed to have wrested it from the other man's hand and then lashed out with it in self-defence, leaving him unconscious on the floor. He had had the presence of mind to go into the kitchen to find a piece of cloth to wipe his fingerprints from the neck of the decanter that he was still holding, and used the same cloth to wrap round a cut on his hand. He admitted to being aware that Dalsey was vomiting and apparently in some distress, but denied deliberately leaving him to die. The story about the spectacles had been concocted in case either of them had been seen at Bishop's Heights on the fatal night, since they were still hoping to keep their relationship a secret.

'I really think you and Trudy should have some credit for bringing Granger to trial,' said Fergus after reading the report of the day's proceedings in court. 'It was the DNA on Granger's fag-ends that you smuggled out of the ashtray in Mrs Pomeroy's flat that proved he was the one who broke the decanter over Dalsey's head.'

'Don't you ever mention that again, Gus, not to a living soul,' said Jim severely. 'It would be a serious embarrassment if ever it got to the ears of the press.'

'And probably put an end to my hopes of a career in CID,' said Sukey. 'From now on, I intend to do everything by the book.'

'Can we have that in writing?' said Jim.

Epilogue

The day after the trial opened, Sukey was sent to the animal shelter in Cheltenham. A valuable pedigree dog had been found wandering the streets with no collar or means of identification. The dog warden caught it and handed it over to the manager of the shelter, who published an appeal in the *Gazette* for information about the owner. The following day a Mrs Broughton-Smythe telephoned to claim the animal, only to be informed that during the previous night thieves had cut through the wire fence surrounding the shelter, broken into the kennels and stolen it.

The shelter was approached by a gravelled track. Sukey parked her van a short distance from the heavy metal gate that barred the entrance. A notice at one side read, 'Please ring for attention'; she pressed the switch and a bell sounded, setting off a cacophony of barking. After a few moments a young woman clad in khaki jodhpurs and a waxed jacket arrived to let her in.

'I'm Cherry Lander, the shelter manager,' she said after checking Sukey's ID. 'I do hope the police catch the thieves,' she went on as she led the way to the kennels. 'I've had the missing dog's owner on the phone every few hours, demanding to know if it's been found and threatening to sue me for negligence. She claims the advertisement was an open invitation to a rival breeder to steal it. She said I should have made private enquiries through the Kennel Club or the breeders' association or whatever – as if I haven't got enough to do.' She bit her lip and ran her fingers through the mop of untidy hair that hung round her face. 'The *Gazette* have always been very helpful in finding homes for our animals so I thought—'

She broke off as a young man in jeans and duffel coat

appeared pushing a trolley laden with sacks of animal food. 'Where d'you want this lot, Cherry?' he said.

'In the main shed, please.'

'Right.' He began to move away, then stopped and turned to stare at Sukey. 'What're you doing here?'

'I'm a Scenes of Crime Officer,' she replied, a little surprised at the question. 'I'm here to investigate the break-in.'

'That's right, you said you worked for the police.'

'Do I know you?'

He grinned. 'You used to, but I looked a bit different in them days.'

She looked at him more closely. It took her a moment to recognize him without his beard and his ragged, stained overcoat. 'Gosh, it's Jack, isn't it? I've been wondering what became of you. None of the other *Big Issue* vendors seem to know.'

His grin widened. 'Yeah, well, I felt I'd let the side down, getting a regular job. By the way, I'm sorry about . . . you know. It never entered my head that Matt, of all people—'

'Nor me. Messed it up good and proper between us, didn't we?'

'So long as you're OK.'

'I'm fine. Anyway, how come you're here?'

'If you don't mind,' Cherry cut in impatiently, 'I've got work to do and so have you and Mrs Reynolds. You can have your chat some other time.'

'OK, boss.' Jack gave a mock salute and winked at Sukey behind Cherry's back. 'Come and find me when you've finished. I'll be around.'

It became obvious as soon as Sukey inspected the point of entry and the way in which the thieves had managed to open the cage where the missing dog had been housed that she was looking at a professional job. She did what she could to gather evidence, but when she reported back to Cherry she had to admit that she had found very little that might be useful.

The young manager shrugged. 'Thanks for trying, anyway,' she said.

'It looks as if whoever took the dog knew exactly what

218

they were doing,' Sukey commented. 'Do you know if it was carrying a microchip?'

'So the owner says. Of course, I should have checked on that right away, but we've had such a rush of admissions this past week and I never thought of it at the time.'

'In that case there's no way the thief could sell it to anyone who knows anything about the world of dog breeding, is there?'

Cherry shook her head. 'No, I suppose not. I wonder if whoever took it will try and get money for its return.'

'That sounds quite likely. If you get a ransom demand, make sure you inform the police right away.'

'Oh, I will. I just hope that whoever's got the dog doesn't hurt it, that's all.'

'I hope not. Now, I wonder if I could have a word with Jack before I leave?'

'Of course.' Cherry glanced at her watch. 'He's probably having his coffee break in what he calls his cubby-hole. It's over there – he shares it with his dogs, so be prepared for a lively reception.'

Jack's cubby-hole was a ramshackle lean-to structure at the end of a row of sheds. Sukey knocked on the door and immediately there came a frantic barking and scrabbling of paws against the other side. When it opened, two brown shapes came bounding out. 'Calm down, you guys,' said Jack, but the dogs took no notice. Recognizing Sukey, they leapt up at her, tails wagging and tongues lolling.

'Hullo, Jordan,' she said, patting his head, 'and . . . gosh, it's Scruffy, isn't it? How on earth—?'

'Lucky bit of guesswork,' said Jack. 'I got worried, wondering what would become of him after Lucy got topped and I thought they might know here so I came to enquire, and there he was. Knew me and Jordan right away, didn't you, Scruff?' He bent to caress the dog, which eagerly licked at his face. 'I wanted to keep him, but they wouldn't let me 'cos I didn't have a proper address or a job. So I asked if I could work here and they needed someone so they said yes, and here I am. I don't have a proper home yet, only a bed-sit, so the dogs stay here at night. I reckon Lucy'd be happy with the arrangement, don't you?'

Sukey's mind went back to her last encounter with Scruffy's late owner and recalled how affection for her pet had softened the hard lines of her young face.

'Yes,' she said. 'I reckon she would.'